The Darkness *is one of the best books I have read this year. I found it to be well written and easy to get lost in. It tells the story of Adam, who is a special child to say the least. It follows his arrival into the lives of many different types of people, two of whom he calls Mother. It is full of suspense and, in some instances, heartbreak. It is very easy to care for the characters involved and the author, Crystal Connor, does a marvelous job developing all the characters. Anyone who reads this book will definitely not regret it.*

- Amazon customer Michelle C.

From the mind of Crystal Connor comes a story set in the not too distant future, where the manipulation of science crashes into the practice of the dark arts. Where light is but a fleeting notion and all paths lead to one conclusion ... that there's only one shade of darkness. -Dave Frizzell, Executive Producer, Necropolis Studio Productions

The Darkness *is a dark tale spinning the reader into its web of sci-fi, fantasy, and reality. From the moment you read, "I used to call you Mommy" you have to know more. You are drawn into a world where science overrides common sense and the pursuit of knowledge walks a thin line right along with insanity. I would place this right along with the works of writers such as Dean Koontz and Ray Bradbury.*

-Amazon customer Tsilvercoin1

The novel starts with a strong prologue. It sets the tone and voice for the novel, while giving enough background to pull the reader in. Had I picked up the novel in a bookstore or library, I would definitely have taken it home with me. The novel itself is action packed, the plot is solid, and the scenes set in exotic countries are rich with description. The ace of the novel picks up as it hurtles towards an unforeseen conclusion. I was totally taken by surprise at the ending. It left me wanting more. I will buy the second novel. Great characters, great storyline, great read!

-Stacey Turner, Writer, editor, and member of She Writes Horror

I was sucked into The Darkness *right off the bat. The opening lines are now some of my favorites! I'm a complete science nerd, so I must say I love all the genetics and science research aspects that come in on Artemisia's side. Then you get the magic side of it all with Inanna. Add in the creepy stalker and horror effects and I'm one happy girl!*
-Amanda Leigh, Paranormal & Urban Fantasy book reviewer

Author Crystal Connor *has created a world that blurs the line between fiction and reality. It's not hard to imagine the events described taking place; in fact, it's rather hard NOT to. The lead character narrates much of the story with glimpses back to prior times from her own memories and draws you right into each scene with such intensity, you won't want to break free. Every page, every line is pulling you closer to a final conclusion that's inevitable and yet hidden from view as your attention is so focused on the current moment. Part sci-fi, part fantasy, and bound together with fictional thread, I'd recommend this book for fans of all three genres in a heartbeat. Though neither long nor short, you'll be amazed how fast the pages fly by as you immerse yourself deeper into the story. Definitely one not to be missed ...*
-Amazon customer Theresa J.

The only problem I have with this brash new writer is her blatant disregard for the established rules of story telling. Connor's The Darkness *does not offer us a tale of good vs. evil, dark vs. light, or the hero vs. the bad guy. In her debut novel Connor presents us with two super villains and shrugs her shoulder as the reader struggles to pick the lesser of two evils.*
-The Anonymous Reviewer

Admittedly, the momentum of the storyline took some time build up, but once at full throttle, the suspense was all-consuming. Just when I thought I could breathe a sigh of relief, something unexpected and startling happened. The novel answered just as many questions as it left unanswered. Fortunately, The Darkness *is the first installment of a planned trilogy.*

This crossover novel is a celebration of genres – it will thrill you, scare you, and make you think twice about the power of science. I find the science fiction and fantasy books I enjoy usually have considerable overlap with other genres. By no means is The Darkness a hard-core fantasy book. Even if you do not consider yourself a reader of fantasy novels, I believe there are enough elements from science fiction, thriller, and horror genres in The Darkness to capture your attention.

-Libby for Author Exposure

Magic, science, mystery, and dark fantasy ... this book left me wanting more!

-Jacqui, for Ins and Outs book reviews

I had the privilege of reading an ARC of The Darkness, *by* Crystal Connor *the other day. I reacted to this book the way I react to some of Dean Koontz's work. If you enjoy sci-fi and horror, there's every chance you'll enjoy this book.*

-Amazon customer Alien Lurker

Crystal Connor's The Darkness *is a very interesting and captivating novel. She created characters that keep the reader interested and makes you care about them in a way that only few authors can. It is full of mystery and magic, love and heartbreak. What more could a reader ask for? I would definitely recommend this book to anyone looking for a great way to spend a weekend.*

-Barnes & Noble customer Gina R.

The Darkness

by Crystal Connor

Cover illustration: Yvette Montoya

Title font: Kelly Ann Gothic by Mike Allard, DeNada Industries. Licensed for use here.

ISBN-13: 978-1466369559
ISBN-10: 1466369558

Colors

I am the color of the red sands of Africa, the land where my roots were first planted.

I am the color of oxidized iron, from shackles that bound my predecessors in the storage hold.

I am the color of green, brown, and white cotton fields, and I am the color red from the blood that ran down the fingers that picked them.

I am the blue of the Civil War Union uniform.

I am the white-hot color of rage, I am the iridescent color of tears, I am every color on the spectrum from orange to red in outrage, and the bottomless color of black, for the betrayal that the Choctaw people felt when being removed from lands they had held since antiquity.

I am the silver-blue color of The Rio Grande that "Los Mojados," the wet ones, risked their lives to cross, in order to make a better life for their heirs.

I am the color of fire that burned bras in the 60s.

I am all the bright colors of the arrogant peacock because I am the color of my ancestors.

This poem and this book are dedicated to my mother, Barbara Jean Thompson-Connor.

Acknowledgements

Wow, where do I begin? The Darkness has been a long time coming. It started almost six years ago as a short story ... and now here I am, but I did not get here by myself.

First I would like to thank Mike Jones, who took one look, or shall I say read, of The Darkness and told me that my writing was more than just a hobby and that I needed to start taking my craft seriously. Mike also told me to stop being lazy and make time to write because there was no way that The Darkness was going to be a short story ... Boy was he right.

My mom, who told me that she has been listening to my stories ever since I learned how to lie. I do not read very well out loud, but night after night she patiently listened to me read the latest chapter of The Darkness. Not only did she cheer me on, she also called me every night to hear the next chapter and make sure I kept pen to paper. Yvette Montoya for the most beautiful book cover art that I have ever seen.

Special Thanks to:
Cynthia Connor LPCC, for her help with human behavior & psychology.

Domestic Security Officer Ulen R. Connor III for the refresher course in weapons & domestic security procedures.

Amani Darby for help with Egyptology, Occult, & Christian Studies (Old Testament), and for being the first set of eyes for The Darkness.

Kathi Vallade, the DNA Witch seen on the book trailer, for child development information, and for allowing me to use her as a test subject for The Darkness.

Star "Sky" Lanton for your support, patience, and excitement, especially when I called you in the middle of night.

Latrice Hill for everything.

The Spectrum Trilogy

Book 1
The Darkness

by Crystal Connor

Second Printing

"Do not participate in the unfruitful deeds of the darkness …"
-Ephesians 5:11

I have removed essential steps and crucial ingredients from the spells and rituals performed in this story. This is not a textbook. The Darkness was written for entertainment purposes only. Do not, under any circumstances, attempt to cast spells or reenact ceremonies performed by these fictional characters.

I hope you have as much fun reading The Darkness as I did writing it.

-Crystal

"People used to go off to war; but modern science can now bring it to your doorstep."

– Anonymous

Prologue

"The cup of life was poisoned forever, and although the sun shone upon me, as upon the happy and gay of heart, I saw around me nothing but a dense and frightful darkness, penetrated by no light but the glimmer of two eyes that glared upon me."

-Victor Frankenstein

 m Alchemist. Yes I am both a creator of and slave to jewelry, but I am no mere blacksmith of gorgeous metals. My very legitimate jewelry business is just a front for something far more sinister than vanity.

I am the owner of Periodic Element Au, and I employ the most elite goldsmiths and jewel artisans on the face of the planet. The embellishments created there are for the very rich and extremely vain.

I am also the owner of Atomic Weight 196. The jewels sold there are for the hard-working, law-abiding, God-fearing citizens who envy the taste of the wealthy but cannot afford the luxury of Periodic.

The jewelers who design for Periodic are world renowned and handsomely paid, but all of them completed their internship at 196 first.

While the most economical pieces of jewelry in Periodic float around the twenty thousand dollar range, nothing in 196 costs over five grand, and all the jewelry created at 196 are custom pieces designed by the best up and coming jewel artists in the industry.

If you think it's difficult working for someone who has to save several months of their earnings for an engagement ring, try working for someone who has a half a million dollars to blow on a bracelet.

If you couldn't work for a union member who counted every dime, there'd be no way for you to work for an heiress who did not know the value of a dollar.

As an Alchemist I prefer, of course, to wear gold. My brown skin holds within it undertones of amber and honey hues that make the prized metal blaze against my skin as if it had just been poured from the crucible.

Well "prefer" is the wrong word. I have to confess I am obsessed, and at times I am absolutely delirious with my obsession. Some days I wear pieces that are so large and so heavy that the jewels could either feed legions of nations or pay for the assassination of kings.

On those days when my vanity gets the best of me I have to be accompanied by armed guards. The men I employ to provide the personal barrier between me the jealous, the desperate, and the foolish are twins from Sudan who, at six foot seven, tower above most other men.

The twins enjoy wearing light colored suits because it so contrasts against their mega dark skin. They also enjoy leaving their suit jackets unbuttoned, to allow those who stare a clear view of the weaponry at their waist.

After opening my seventh Periodic store, in India, I was able to step away from the madness of vanity and practice the truer art of my craft.

I, with a few others, founded The Skyward Group. I bought a building on the corner of Fourth and William, right in the middle of everything. To the naked eye and the greedy patron, it's seventy six thousand square feet of "all that glitters." Every country in the world, along with their valuable export, is represented in my building.

It's as loud and chaotic as the trading floor of the New York Stock Exchange.

The only auditory difference is that every merchant in *my* building tends to conduct business in their native tongue. I doubt the Tower of Babble could have boasted such a cacophony.

My commerce, on a bad day, is in the low millions, so securing armed guards from a clandestine private security agency was no problem – I employ ten. What's not seen is the vast labyrinth of subterranean laboratories and offices beneath the jewelry-trading floor, that we simply call The Facility, or what goes on there.

The core of our research is, among other things, the study and development, and the manipulation and regeneration of, embryonic stem cells using messenger RNA.

And that is the extent to which I will explain things to you. You're not a scientist so I doubt you'd understand if I tried. What you are, however, is the product of Poe, Bradbury, Stevenson, Lovecraft and King, so I invite you to use your imagination.

You can consider The Skyward Group as CERN's narcissistic altar ego – their evil twin if you will. While CERN, the European Organization for Nuclear Research conducts absolutely no military research and is extremely transparent with the findings of their studies, The Skyward Group's projects are largely (80%) military in nature and most of our findings remain secret.

I know the things my team and I are working on will have others questioning my moral compass, but I simply do not care. You must understand that the things that we have done, are doing, *and will continue to do,* are in the name of human advancement. You don't believe me?

Allow me to redirect your attention to some of the experiments conducted by a few of my predecessors working in Germany in the mid 1900s.

Dr. Clauberg helped improve the X-ray. Dr. Helmuth Vetter conducted pharmacological trials for Bayer. Chief SS doctor, Dr. Edward Wirth, and his brother Dr. Helmut Wirth studied the precancerous growths of the cervix.

All their medical accomplishments have been stripped of honor, though they remain in use today, and the men have been made monsters, their names associated only with The Third Reich.

Now, after all that's happened I am not going to sit here and lie to you. I'm not going to tell you that we were working towards ensuring that every child could live without hunger, because the truth of it is I could have cared less.

The only things I truly cared about were my reckless pursuit of excess and the obtainment of forbidden knowledge, of divine knowledge. I wanted to whisper in the ear of God – or maybe I want him to whisper in mine – and for that I shall not apologize.

Human progress has always come with a price. There's no sense in whining about it now.

I

ooking back on it, I think the first time I saw him was at the dog park. The only reason I noticed him was because he was standing in the shadows and didn't have a dog. I really couldn't make him out from where he was standing. The only thing I knew for certain was how unnerved I felt watching his head swivel as he tracked my dog. I have a little Jack Russell that went flying past him in hot pursuit of a ball three times bigger than he was. The man just watched Jack with disdain. Yeah my dog's name is Jack, last name Russell, and he is the very love of my life.

I dragged my eyes away from the man in the shadows at the sound of my dog barking. The sight of Jackie happily struggling to bring the beach ball back up the hill melted my heart.

When my eyes drifted back to the spot, the man was gone, so I didn't think any more about it. We played in the park for another hour or so until Jack started bossing all the big dogs around.

The next time I saw him was about two months later, and I didn't even think it was the same man, but now I have no doubt. Jackie and I were leaving The Facility, and he was standing across the street. He wasn't looking at Jack with hatred this time. He was looking at me. I scooped Jack up and motioned to Dr. Astor who was speaking to the armed guard posted outside our building. By the time I attracted Dr. Astor's attention the man was gone.

"Do you think it's a spy from the The Alpha Omega Foundation?"

At that I had to laugh out loud. If our competition were that smart they'd be the ones with government contracts. Thinking it was the guys from The Foundation, I didn't put two and two together until things became much worse.

I drive my electric blue Aston Martin swiftly through the city streets, capitalizing on its speed and superior agility, disregarding the fact that I could walk to work. But if I wanted to stroll the city streets in shoes that cost five grand I wouldn't have spent $175,000.00 for a car.

Out of the four vehicles I own, the Martin is the one I drive the most. As I was jumping out of my suped-up sports coupé, the valet handed me a letter. He explained he didn't know who it was from because he wasn't on shift when the letter was left. It was just a plain envelope with my name, written in beautiful penmanship. I thought it was from my guy. Who else would know to leave a message for me down here in the garage? I opened it before I got on the elevator. It was a blank piece of paper.

In confusion, standing in front of the elevator door with Jack and my feet whining with impatience, I called the hospital to speak with my boyfriend. I was told the doctor was still in surgery. He's not actually my boyfriend; our relationship is, well let's just say we are two consenting adults.

I stormed back to the guy who had parked my car and asked how someone could just waltz right in to leave notes without somebody finding out who they were or where they were from? "Did you forget about Homeland Security?" I demanded. "Didn't he have to sign the visitor's log?"

I was so pissed off! I didn't have time for childish games that wasted my time. Not to mention the fact I was wearing a pair of Cesare Paciotti boots handmade just for me in Italy, and these boots were *not* made for walking. They weren't even broken in, and I'd been envisioning taking them off since lunch. Now I had to stand here with this young kid who didn't know how to do his job.

I demanded to speak with his supervisor, who had to be called at home. I went upstairs an hour later, satisfied that the valet would no longer be around to pass notes. After dinner, a hot bath, and a visit from the good doctor, I felt much better. After all I'd had an exceptionally beautiful day. Today I'd brought to life The Chasm Project – my new baby. I'd recruited two genetic engineers (one from The Foundation), a biophysicist engineer, and a psychophysicist for Chasm. I'd finalized the contract that only the founding members knew about, along with securing some pretty phenomenal kickbacks.

I like to get a few hours of work done before going to bed, but Jackie was out on the balcony barking at something, someone, or some smell below. I went to bring him down off the ledge and close the doors that would silence the noises from the city below. When I got out on the balcony and picked Jack up, I saw a man standing right under the street light. I couldn't see his face or even the clothes he was wearing. Fourteen floors down he was like a shadow within the light, looking up at us.

I yelled an apology to the guy under the light then closed and locked the French doors. Jack jumped from my arms and went flying into the bedroom, barking all the way. As wound up as Jackie was, I knew I wouldn't be getting any work done.

When I got to my bedroom Jackie was in the window still barking at the city's movements. I went to see what the big deal was. I thought maybe it was another dog owner, and Jack wanted to take a walk. But when I looked out the window I saw that Jackie was barking at a man.

For a scary moment I thought it was the same man, but it couldn't have been unless he was an Olympic track star.

I own the top-floor apartment in a small but beautiful historical building that has been gorgeously restored. The renovations were meant to be exclusive, with all the accommodations expected by those privileged few who demand nothing from life but uncompromising luxury. My bedroom was *literally* on the other block.

I watched him watch me and I was a little relieved to see him walk away. He went into the phone booth, but Jack-O was still barking at him. I was yelling at Jack to shut up … when the phone rang.

For some reason I looked out the window. The man was standing outside the phone booth with the phone to his ear, looking up at my apartment. Jackie added growling and stomping to his barks, as if somehow that made up for his size.

The man hung up the phone. I stood watching as he dialed another number, and then I heard my cell phone ring. For the briefest of moments I wished I had a larger dog.

I felt myself digging through my Prada bag to answer my cell, even though my entire body was screaming in protest. I was slightly aware that Jack had bitten me, barely registering the warm blood dripping down my calf. The voice on the other end of the phone sounded a million light years away, despite the fact he was standing just fourteen floors below my bedroom window – which now felt far too close.

"The darkness. The darkness … *is calling me*. I – I can't control these feelings. It's calling me. *'Primun non nocere,'* remember Doctor? Do you even remember me? I used to call you Mommy." The phone went dead, and my own darkness began to settle in as my mind wrapped itself around what my caller had said in Latin.

"First, Do No Harm."

The automated operator was informing me I had to hang up the phone if I wished to dial another number, before I was focused enough mentally to formulate the possible ramifications of this call. Calling the authorities was out of the question.

Like the Knights Templars, the Freemasons, and the Alpha Omega Foundation, my organization is a secret society of scientists, doctors, and engineers privately funded and bound by nothing other than the laws of science – and we are slowly rewriting even those. I felt like a hypocrite then, asking God for guidance.

Our fame is not that of our big brothers the Templars, but our power is just as great. No one knew we even existed, except those few sworn to secrecy. And they knew that the price of loose lips was not their life, but the lives of their loved ones.

Our facility was hidden in plain sight; a building right downtown that was so secure that a S.W.A.T. team couldn't have gained entry.

With the phone call still dancing in my head I was moving in a daze. One moment I was wiping the blood off of my leg and looking for my dog. The next I was dialing pound eight on my landline to alert my colleagues there had been a problem. The next thing I remember is that I was driving to The Facility, and Jack wasn't with me.

II

The child was only allowed to explore his world as far as he could see through the steel bars of his locked cage.

The child learned long ago that his cries were to go unheeded, so the child simply stopped crying. The child passed the time by studying those who watched him from the other side of his confinement.

The child's development was different than others of his age. At twelve weeks the child was able to stand without the aid of the steel bars, but only for a short duration. Even so, the child could not crawl or walk.

The child knew things that others of his age could not know. For instance, Dr. Howard was 48, Dr. Tarkin was 51, Dr. Hill was 47, Dr. Morgan was 63, Dr Kim was 60, and he knew his name was Subject 06138-AH24 and that he was twelve weeks, three days, and nine hours old – except his numbers kept changing. Although no one knew it, the child could read the uppermost layers of the mind. It was like catching words that floated by.

The child could do things that others of his age could not do. If he wanted the blue ball with orange stars on it, he could make the ball come to him. It would not come through the steel bars of his cage, so the child just made the ball roll back and forth: from the cage to back where it was, to the cage again, with tepid indifference.

There was something else near the ball that held the child's attention, and it was always looking at the child. One day Dr. Kim noticed the child eyeing the bear and asked, "Oh, do you want the teddy?" Dr. Kim held up the bear but did not give it to the child.

And yes, the child wanted the teddy.

Finally the child was able to convince Teddy to come to him. The child liked Teddy and wanted to be friends. The child could not get Teddy to come inside the cage with him. Teddy just kept slamming into the steel bars, backing up and then slamming into the steel bars over and over again.

After awhile the child grew weak and Teddy fell on the floor outside of the child's cage. The child lay on the floor of his cage, on the side nearest to Teddy, reached his arm through the steel bars of the cage, and rested his hand on Teddy's stomach. Teddy felt soft. The child fell asleep holding on to his only friend.

Everyone wore gloves when the child was handled. Sometimes he was put on a cold scale, other times he was given a shot or had blood drawn, other times he was placed in a tub of water. But most of the time he was just left alone and looked at.

This is how the child knew life.

When the child was seventy-six weeks, two days, and seven hours old the child was not well. The child had lain listless in his cage all day. The child did not move nor did the child sleep. The child just lay there gazing at his friend Teddy, who gazed back.

Dr. Kim explained to Dr. Morgan that the child had a fever, and then both doctors left the room. Once alone, the child raised his head and Teddy floated off the shelf and towards the child. The child was standing now and had managed to squeeze his entire arm and shoulder through the steel bars, his tiny hand outstretched to catch Teddy. All the child wanted was to be with his friend.

Dr. Morgan reentered the room, observed the bear in flight, and had no trouble guessing its itinerary.

"No," commanded Dr. Morgan in the same tone one would use when speaking to a dog.

Dr. Morgan cancelled the bear's travel plans and put the bear back on the shelf, where it sat with the other unused toys.

The child became upset and made something happen to Dr. Morgan. When Dr. Morgan was still, the bear resumed his flight with a hopeful prospect of reaching his destination.

When Teddy was lying outside the child's cage, the child was able to clutch his friend from within his imprisonment, and the child slept. For sixteen days no one entered the room where the child's cage rested. For eleven of those sixteen days the child drifted in and out of a fever-induced delirium – but no one entered the room.

"CLEAR!"

"CLEAR!"

"CLEAR!"

Startled, the child woke and did not see Dr. Kim, Dr. Howard, or Dr. Hill. The child saw Dr. Morgan because he was still on the floor, but he didn't see Dr. Tarkin, just these three men who were now in the room.

The first words he caught were "extraction" and "rapid deployment" but he didn't know what they meant. The child studied these newcomers and noticed that where their hair should be it was very smooth and green. Where their mouths should be was also smooth and black. The men wore all black clothes with lots of pockets that had a lot of stuff in them, and big black boots.

They were wearing gloves, so the child knew he was to be handled. These were not like the other gloves, the ones the doctors used that you could see through. These gloves were black. And they all wore gloves over their eyes.

One man (Tactical Leader: Wilson, K. 36) moved the thing from over his mouth, pulled his gloves off his with his teeth, and started speaking to the child, "Hey there squirt, wanna go on an adventure?"

The other man (Point Man: Barrett, J. 29), who had covered up the heap of decaying flesh that once was Dr. Morgan, was now also kneeling at the child's cage. He pulled out something from the pocket that he had been carrying on his back but that was now on the floor in front of him, and he used it to remove the lock from the child's cage.

"Twenty-eight seconds!" called the man (Sniper: Allen, M. 30) at the door.

"OK little buddy, let's ride. Grab your bear and blankey," instructed (Tactical Leader: Wilson, K 36). "We gotta roll." And then he did something no one before him had ever done.

He grabbed the child, the blanket, and Teddy *without his gloved hands* and then held the child close to his body. That was the first time the child has ever been held that way or touched without gloved hands, and with eyes wide with awe and wonder the child's bottom lip poked out and began to quiver.

"Thirty one seconds!"
(Tactical Leader: Wilson, K 36) looked down at his spoils and noticed the child was about to cry so he soothed, "Hey, oh no little guy, I gotcha now. Don't cry, I gotcha." And as they were running through the corridors, racing to the appointed extraction point, the child cried.

Wilson cooed and comforted the entire time, which made the child cry more.

Once airborne, in the helicopter that removed the child from where he had spent the first part of his life, he was given to Allen, M. who held the child in a way that made the child feel comfortable and drowsy. The child turned his head so that he could listen to the soldier's heartbeat and feel the vibrations in his chest that were caused by words he was speaking. The men were discussing a spider that apparently had been washed out by the rain, but there seemed to be a disagreement on the distance that the spider traveled, and an argument ensued.

The child knew nothing of a spider or the rain. He'd seen neither, and didn't care. All the child knew was that he never, ever, ever wanted to be put down or left alone again. The child, holding his friend Teddy close to him, fell into a peaceful sleep, cradled within the mercenary's arms.

III

veryone was in a frenzy until I walked in. Then everyone froze and stared at me in silence ... and I was livid. Usually the subjects we receive are from the fringes of society: transients, drug addicts, prostitutes, runaways, whoever had given up hope and no one would miss. They came to us under the guise of some research study that paid a substantial monetary gain and, after signing their life away, were never seen or heard from again.

But this one was different. We rescued him from The Foundation when he was just a baby. He was only nineteen months, and we had to steal him once we learned of what they had done. The Foundation is out of control and God only knows what those megalomaniacs have unleashed into the world.

When the Skyward Group was first established it was to directly compete and surpass The Foundation. Once we had a true understanding of what they were doing we refocused our efforts to disrupt and dismantle or sabotage their projects, and I started seeing a priest.

By the time we received this subject it was far too late. His capabilities led to frightening conclusions and accusations. All our efforts to reverse his genetic makeup and thought processes had failed. I became unprofessional and emotionally attached to this subject. I never thought I'd ever wanted children, but looking into his large green eyes melted me completely. My team warned me that I was under his influence, but I dismissed them. Once I explained that I was removing him from The Facility and taking him home; a member of my team; without my knowledge decided to have him destroyed. The boy I had come to think of as my child was only four years old. And now to find out that he had been alive all that time! This meant I had been lied to, and he had been out there all on his own.

My simmer of rage exploded, and my tongue unleashed the six realms of hell before the people who sat before me in terror.

"I want every Goddamned case file on Genesis and I want it right fucking now!" Assistants fled, happy to escape my wrath. All the doctors in the room with me had played a hand in the Genesis project, and I knew that they all could be trusted to keep the vilest of secrets because these men and women who sat before me were the founding members of The Skyward Group.

The decision was made to put the Chasm Project on the back burner and return to the Genesis Project—to find out how things had gone with our "Adam." The first level in Damage Control Procedures is to deploy the Situation Team. It was felt that Adam had become a liability, so the Situation Team was to be given orders to "clean up." The general feeling was that we would select another subject and just start over.

But there were some in our ranks who disagreed with the cleanup order, and I was one of them. This of course caused another fight, and the uproar of our bedlam grew in violence until Dr. Ujay spoke.

"How old is our Adam now, about seventeen, eighteen?" Over the current disarray his voice was like a cool breeze, more felt than heard. "Despite any crimes he may have committed or will commit, we have to recognize the possibility that our boy is sexually active. There could be a kid or two of his out there."

Someone whispered "Oh my God" while Dr. Ujay continued speaking. "Just because Adam must be neutralized, and he must be, doesn't mean it's the end. Our efforts did not result in failure." He was slowly looking around at each of us. "The Genesis Project was ultimately a product of The Foundation's ... however any children Adam may have sired will be solely *ours*."

The sun was coming up when I finally made it home, and I was planning to spend the rest of that day sleeping. But those plans changed when I opened my door and Jackie wasn't waiting for me. I was beginning to feel uneasy as I called out to him with no answer.

"Jackson Russell!" Nothing. The fear in the pit of my stomach began to spread through my body like a cancer. I found him in the bathtub. He'd been ripped to pieces. At that moment I felt something in me break. I frantically tried to put my dog back together, and deep within me I knew I'd never be the same again.

I was in such a state of shock that I don't remember picking up the letter, don't even remember really seeing it, but I will never forget the ornate hand in which it was penned, for this was the second time I had seen that beautiful handwritten script. I recognized it from the envelope handed to me just days before down in the garage. I will always remember what it said:

"Do you remember me? I've thought of you often. There's going to be a day when you find yourself wishing you'd done things differently. And as you're gasping the last breath of your life, please understand it's not God, but Me. No matter the face of your tormentor, I will be the drive of motivation behind your anguish. For the rest of my life, I will ensure yours is miserable. I will have vengeance. I am coming for you and not even God can save you now."

I let the letter fall from my hands, and cried as I went to get an array of cleaning supplies and find a shoebox large enough for my dog.

Through my experiments and associations I have a learned a technique that enables one to build a barricade around their mind, to ensure their thoughts aren't intercepted or infiltrated.

This technique resembles Dissociative Identity Disorder or what was once known as split personality disorder. The key and crucial difference being that you are aware and in control of both personalities. This technique, simply called "cloaking," defies the laws of physics by offering one the ultimate form of camouflage in sensorial perception warfare – invisibility.

I employed that technique as I placed my beloved companion into his makeshift coffin. I knew from then on I'd be under constant virtual surveillance. I allowed my thoughts and feelings of sorrow to filter through for anyone who might be "watching," all the while burying deep within me my true intentions.

It's been nearly fifteen years now, since we acquired Genesis. I remember I was in a meeting with a CIA agent and a couple of generals – none of whom I can mention by name.

The biophysicist was in the middle of answering a question when Kenneth Astor burst in. The whirlwind in his wake caused papers to be brushed off my desk.

"We've become aware of a situation that requires your undivided attention – immediately!" Dr. Astor was rushing from my office before he had finished speaking.

The biophysicist and I were quick to follow Dr. Astor into his labyrinth, but not before locking my office door from the outside to keep my visitor's "safely" within. The men had arrived at The Facility under heavy guard and escort, and I wanted to make sure we did not suffer a security breach by allowing our guests free movement to roam about.

Dr. Astor is The Facility's quantum physicist and the director of Skyward's Clandestine Surveillance Division. Out of all present here at Skyward, Dr. Astor is the only scientist who is quite mad.

He even looks the way you would imagine a mad scientist should look: with disheveled hair; a wrinkly lab coat; circular wire-rimmed glasses; wild, distant eyes and skittish movements. The things he talks about make people afraid of him. His methods of research are unethical, even to a group such as ours, but his results are spectacular so we turn a blind eye.

His entire life was held in captivity by facts, data, truths, and discovery. Nine years ago Dr. Astor stumbled on something the rest of us *could not see*, and quite frankly it frightened us. But Dr. Astor was also a founding member, and who were we to judge? Birds of a feather, right?

We were all in the same boat. Each of us had our own projects we were working on, and all of our projects orbited around and eventually collided into one another, fusing several projects into one. When Skyward was first established there were roughly 1,087 ideas, theories, and experiments. At the time of Genesis there were sixty-two.

Dr. Astor's project at the time of the Genesis acquisition was remote intelligence gathering using clairsentience mediums and techniques that fused together psychoacoustics, extrasensory perception, and remote viewing with ritualism folklore, mythology, religion, and necromancy. To maintain complete secrecy Dr. Astor developed a technique that ensured the remote viewer, oracle, or medium he was using at the time kept no recollection of what they foretold. His studies were heavily funded by the military – both ours and those abroad.

You're probably thinking something along the lines of the MK project or a Manchurian candidate, but to compare the crude and brutal experiments that the CIA performs to what Dr. Astor has achieved would be like comparing Otto Lilienthal's paper plane to Gene Roddenberry's Starship Enterprise.

It was something he had discovered through the use of these techniques that summoned us to his lair. What we were about to witness demonstrated the awe-inspiring power of Dr. Astor's work.

When we arrived at Dr. Astor's lab, his assistant, Ernesto was fast-forwarding images on a 46" L.C.D. screen. As the images rushed by, a male nurse was wiping the blood from the nose of a subject and handing him a small cup of juice. When the subject regained enough strength to stand he was helped into a wheelchair, and rolled out of the lab and into the recovery room.

The images on the screen stopped and Dr. Astor began, "This is from Romeo-Victor-Zero-Five-Six," which meant Remote Viewer number fifty-six. I glanced over my shoulder as RV56 was ushered from the room and the door to Dr. Astor's lab was closed. Then I looked back up at the screen.

I was amazed beyond words. From my first encounter with Dr. Astor, though he was just Kenneth at the time, I never for the life of me understood a word he said when he was talking about his work. It seemed, from what I could gather, that Dr. Astor had found a way, through some subspace wave wormhole, to manipulate the time cycle of energy flow – thus allowing the remote viewer to enter the body of a host like a parasite, regardless of where in the world the host was located.

To make contact for the invasion the R.V. simply called the host on their cell phone.

Once the host answered, the R.V. would become a "passenger" of the host; and everything the host did, saw, or said while occupied was recorded.

The footage we were viewing was of a doctor for The

Foundation. We watched as the doctor entered his lab via four checkpoints requiring a photo I.D. badge, a thumbprint, a retina scan, and voice recognition.

The lab was brightly decorated with images of nursery rhyme characters painted on the walls. The ceiling was a midnight blue with twinkling silver stars that were probably small halogen bulbs. The painted moon was ducking beneath a cow.

In the middle of the lab was a baby encased in a reinforced steel cage that looked as if it was erected to withstand several wild beasts.

We watched through the doctor's eyes as a stuffed bear floated through the air towards the tiny outstretched arm of the baby, who had managed to squeeze his arm and shoulder through the steel bars.

We watched as the bear was snatched out of mid air and returned to a shelf lined with other toys and books. We watched the baby's face frown into fury.

I lost my equilibrium as we were hurled – as the doctor was hurled – the distance of the laboratory, and we gasped in pain as the doctor must have gasped as he was slammed repeatedly on the floor until his body was broken and dying.

We watched through the doctor's dying eyes as a stuffed bear floated through the air towards the tiny outstretched arm of the baby, who had managed once again to squeeze his arm and shoulder through the steel bars.

We had just watched a child who had yet to learn to walk, kill a man and retrieve a stuffed teddy bear using telekinesis. "Dear Jesus," I whispered, "what have they done this time?"

"What I don't understand," Dr. Astor contemplated "is

why the subject could not have the toy."

With my actions concealed within the penumbra of my mind, it appeared as if I'd gone to the bank and withdrawn valuables from my safe deposit, and I had. What was hidden was what I had placed inside.

Years ago I broke all contact with my family, or so it seemed. I did not have as much as one photograph or any contact information. I did not wish for my family to pay for my sins.

To ensure total anonymity I shed the name my mother had given me at birth, and am now only known now as Artemisia.

In some parts of the Arab world Artemisia is known as Sheba. I found it more than fitting to be associated with a great queen with whom I share geographical lineage. Though I do not offer spices or exotic woods, I do bring forth gifts of gold and precious stones.

There was also an ancient Persian Queen who was a botanist – but more importantly she like me was a medical researcher, and it is from these two great queens that I adopted my name.

What I put in that safe deposit box was a note for my sister. We devised a plan for communication. I check the box on the 3rd of each month and she on the 20th.

This is how I learned of the death of my father and the birth of my nephew. With as much jewelry as I handle it is not unbelievable or unreasonable that I would visit a safe deposit once a month or more.

From the bank I drove to the ocean. At the end of the pier

I said a small prayer and hoped the goddess of the sea, Oya, would accept my offering. I was overcome by grief as I watched the shoebox slowly sink into the sea.

From the burial site I drove to the airport where my jet was waiting to zip me to Oujda, Morocco. Once airborne I began to cry, permitting my mind to fill with smoke, my thoughts of Jack and Adam intertwined.

It appeared, for those who were watching, as if I'd checked into my room and fallen into a desolation-induced slumber. The images of exotic marketplaces, street cafés, Jack, and the purest of blackness drifted to the surface of my mind.

Those were the only thoughts I allowed to be viewed as I boarded a ferry bound for Spain. Only thoughts of Jack, as I flew from Spain to France. Once in Paris, my free thoughts turned to smoke and blackness to ensure my actions would not be detected.

Our contact point was at the Musée de la Chasse et de la Nature. The museum was actually inside a hotel, and I learned she had already checked in. I found her in lost in thought in front of a painting by Rubens.

"Hey Dragonfly how was your trip?"

"Its Adam, isn't?" she asked, unable to control her tears.

IV

ome said her beauty was unearthly, and the word "witch" was the last word one would have used to describe her, even though she did have a black cat. Her smooth, sable skin was pampered by the finest of European spas, and her long tightly curly hair was the same shade as night.

The only adornment that she allowed to rub against her obsidian skin was the ruby. Her gems were wicked and treacherous in their beauty, luring even the most pious of women to feelings of greed, lust, and envy.

The gems she demanded blazed with such a deep flame they could have been cinders glowing in Satan's private hearth. These stones, so large and flawless, were openly hostile in their opulence; burning against the slightest light with such a radiant flame it was as if the stones themselves were proudly supporting blasphemy.

But what were truly bewitching were her eyes – deep Mother Earth forest-green eyes that shone like bright stars blazing against a night sky and made avid astronomers of all who viewed them.

When she flashed her wicked, drop-dead gorgeous smile people assumed she was using the charms afforded to all beautiful women, but she wasn't. The African sorceress was a powerful and dangerous master in the dark arts. She studied spell-casting rites, curses, hexes, cures and rituals from all cultures, both past and present, and she was fluent in all.

Her father, an African shaman, a remnant of a once very powerful and secret religious order, originating thousands of years ago from ancient African civilizations, was known only as "The Dark One." He sailed from West Africa to Brazil. Once in port he traveled north until he reached the Caribbean Sea. Seafarers took him to Santo Domingo and from there he walked to Haiti … his journey to spend just one night with her mother took 300 days.

Her mother was a Haitian voodoo priestess, and she became her pupil when she was only three. When she was eleven it was apparent that her powers were much greater than her mother's. The child had summoned a force stronger than anyone dared to name in order to learn the forbidden arts her mother refused to teach her.

Whisperings rolled through the village like fog.

A fatal mistake was made to rid the village of the mother and child. But the mamaloi had been warned, and took her child and fled towards the sea. The day-and-a-half head start did not quell the witches' pursuers; in fact, it only emboldened them.

They were caught at the shore. The mother had just enough time to place the young sorceress in the boat and push her to the safety of the rip tide, which carried her child out to sea and away from the bloodthirsty hands of the mob.

Her child watched, screaming from the boat that was drifting further and further away from the beach as her mother was pulled back ashore. The child felt within her, her mothers' calls to goddesses of disaster, disease, vengeance, plague, famine, and war, and she heard her mother scream the name "Inanna!"

Her mother's pleas fell on deaf ears because she did not know what she was doing and the calls were made in fear and anger, in hopes of protecting her child. Her child, however, knew exactly what to do and who to summon, and it was there that the true nature of her powers where revealed.

The little girl stood in the rocking boat, allowing her small body to sway with the rhythm of the sea.

She raised her outstretched hands over her head in the form of a "V" towards the heavens, closed her eyes against her tears, and began to chant. In this trancelike state, she felt her mother's last breath brush against her face like a kiss. Her tears then could have quenched the Sahara.

The tiny witch destroyed every man, woman, child, dog, cat, bird and bug residing in the only world she had ever known.

The little girl had the power to shape shift. She had done it before when she was playing with a beetle and it beckoned her to follow him into a small crevice in the side of a tree. That beetle was the only thing she had left from her homeland, because the beetle was nested safely within her pocket. As she collapsed in the boat the only thing she shifted was her name. To Inanna, the last word she heard her mother say.

There was no way, at age eleven, that the girl could have known the goddess named Inanna was the powerful, all-consuming force of attraction. She couldn't have realized, at such a young age, that as much as she is sexual attraction, the goddess Inanna is rage, strength, and raw power. But once she was made aware of who it was her mother had been calling, the little girl who had been protected by the sea did everything in her power to live up to her namesake.

She drifted for days before the cargo ship heading to Europe found her. The captain fell under her spell immediately, carried her around the ship on his shoulders, and did everything within his power to make her smile.

When they returned to port, the Captain took the girl home and gave her to his head servant, to replace the child of theirs she hadn't been able to carry to term. Since leaving her homeland, this woman was the first person Inanna had seen with the same color skin as hers and the same type of hair as hers, and though she did not speak this woman's language Inanna clung to her. In these strange lands, with strange people, and strange smells, this woman was the only thing somewhat familiar.

Inanna was raised in privilege, highly educated, and spoiled beyond reason. She learned the languages of her surrogate parents, and through tutors learned twenty more. She was a quiet girl who spent a lot of time with one tutor in particular, not really a scholarly tutor, for this man worked in the kitchen, but he was Inanna's tutor nonetheless.

When he returned from sea, the Captain was concerned to learn the amount of time this man spent with his daughter, and vowed aloud that he would have the man drawn and quartered. But his lover and the substitute mother for Inanna cooled his temper and explained that she watched his every move, especially when he was with their daughter.

None of that was necessary; for Inanna had become strong enough to cast a controlling spell over all those around her. No one was walking around like a zombie with no free will – it wasn't that kind of spell. It was more like a malevolent love spell, where everyone had an uncontrollable urge to please her, to protect her, to do things for her. Basically the spell made everyone around her want to provide her with whatever she wanted – and she wanted for very little. The very last thing she wanted was to be was harmed.

What she did want, however, was knowledge, and the cook Inanna chose to spend her time with was no ordinary valet. This man was a warlock who had been sent on the winds of the the night to ensure the child that Inanna's makeshift parents had conceived would never be born. Sent to ensure there would be so much sorrow, so much grief, so much longing, that Inanna's place in their broken hearts would be but all guaranteed.

For this man had seen Inanna through an oracle, and – with no sons of his own – she was to be his sole beneficiary.

The great wizard had been alive for so long that no one remembered how dangerously powerful he was, and his name was only whispered among mortals in the retelling of nightmares.

He was called Myrddin. One man in the long line of forefathers who bestowed Myrddin his birthright was known in Arthurian legends as Merlin. Yet another was John Dee, a wizard with such great power that the archangels Uriel and Michael taught him a system of magic called Enochian, which allowed a wizard to make a spirit carry out his spell.

It was this magic, under the cover of night and in the shadow of the most ancient of Scotland's stone circles that Myrddin taught to Inanna. Under his careful teaching, Inanna was allowed to practice her craft, channel her energies, and become proficient in her skill. The first lesson that he taught was the myth of idol gods.

"Make no mistake about it," Myrddin told Inanna. "The gods worshipped here at Stonehenge, by the Aztecs and the Egyptians; the gods who fought alongside the Norsemen and walked among the Greeks, were not idol ones.

"The gods of antiquity are the angels that were banished from above after the Great War they waged was lost. After the fall, the immortals divided the earth amongst themselves.

"Those defiant angels who wanted to be gods, the beloved ones, had no intention of wasting eternity in servitude. They chose, instead, to have legions of men on their knees before them.

"It was the high priest and priestess, the witch if you will, upon whom they bestowed the knowledge not intended for man. The mathematics to build monuments, the astronomy to read the stars, and the language to create empires was given to us to dispense as we saw fit.

"The earth-bound gods reigned supreme for millions of years until the descent of the Son. Now they reign in shadows, assisting only those who have the knowledge to seek their help and the wisdom to pay homage."

Myrddin did not look like the stereotypical wizard, with long white hair and matching beard. He was beautiful. His skin was of a darker hue, as though he'd spent eons exposed to the sun's angry glare and in the stinging whip of the winds. His weathered face boasted lines and ridges like worn leather. Myrddin stood six-foot four, but his presence was much, much larger than his height, and the irises of his eyes were purple in color.

Myrddin's eyes were not the soft violet shade that blessed Elizabeth Taylor. No. The colors of his eyes were a deep, bruised, angry bluish-purple. He hid them behind dark shades to conceal the fact that his irises were always moving, swirling like twin typhoons that were dangerously close to slamming ashore.

When the greatness of Myrddin's power was first realized the powerful church of his village, with the blessings and authority of Emperor Constantine the First, condemned him to death. As a lesson for the church's futile interference Myrddin cast a spell on the entryway of the church so that all who crossed it became sick. The ill suffered a fate worse than those who had the plague – for those who fell to the plague eventually died. Those who suffered the wrath of Myrddin were marred with blackened skin and bursting boils, and were damned to walk the earth for 150 years.

When the Captain died Inanna was distraught, and tried for five days to bring him back to the realm of the living. It was thought she had gone mad with grief, and in a way she had. Although the bond between the Captain and Inanna was not by blood, the connection was just as strong.

The Captain acted like her father, and was the only person whom Inanna did not manipulate through wizardry. For one, it would have consumed an unfathomable amount of energy to control him once at sea, but more importantly she did not have to.

As long as the Captain could draw breath, Inanna knew there would be no mob, knew she would never have to flee in the middle of the night while being chased like prey. With the Captain, Inanna had the protection of a father, and she loved him like one.

In so many ways he reminded Inanna of her mother. The Captain was unreasonably over-protective, just like her mother. The Captain encouraged, comforted, and gently persuaded her to accomplish the things she was afraid to try. Like the time he bought her a large red stallion. The beast was the largest animal Inanna had ever seen, and she wouldn't go anywhere near it. The jealously she felt as she watched her brothers gleefully gallop off in the distance was not strong enough to catapult her onto the horse and chase after them. It took nine weeks before the Captain could instill enough confidence in Inanna for her to saddle-up and ride. It was the very thing her mother would have done, and the loss of him was more than she could bear.

The Captain was at the helm of more than just his ship. He was a shipping tycoon with more than sixty ships in his fleet. Inanna inherited the largest part of the fortune, even though the Captain had a wife and nine children. No one protested the unfairness of the Captain's gift because, still under her spell, everyone was too worried about Inanna, and hoped that she would eat, rest, and stop crying.

The shipping heiress reinvested her fortune and flew west. Once in the lush, languid city of New Orleans, Inanna fell into a depression. The entire city – with its exotic and bewitching luster – was infused with traces of her mother. The same rituals and customs practiced by her mother were also practiced here. To her surprise most people spoke Creole, and because that was Inanna's first tongue she reverted to speaking almost exclusively in the Haitian language.

Everything she heard, ate, touched, or smelled in this new city reminded her of her mother, and every time she thought of her mother she desperately missed the Captain. Inanna became suicidally depressed and stayed crying in bed for months, the scene of the day her mother was killed on the beach replaying over and over in both her dreams and waking moments.

One day, Inanna was jarred out of her slumber to the sounds of drums. Haitian drums, the drums of her *mother's* people.

Inanna rushed to the window and, when she opened it, was assaulted by bold fragrances of the incense her mother used to burn during rituals. And over the drums she heard her mother's song.

It was Carnival.

She couldn't control her tears as she ran down the flights of stairs and out into the crowd. She ran at full speed and slammed herself against the woman who was singing, so hard that the woman had to take a few steps back to regain her balance. Inanna buried her tear-streaked face into the woman's bosom and cried. The woman wrapped her arms around Inanna, comforting her as she continued to sing while gently rocking back and forth.

Under the guidance of the wizard, Inanna had been trying to conjure her mother or others who might know where her mother was, but she had been unsuccessful. But now, on the shores of a land so far away from her own, she felt her mother's presence everywhere.

Out of all the cities in the world she could have gone to, she had chosen New Orleans, rich with her mother's conventions. It seemed to Inanna that her mother ultimately brought her here, and here is where she stayed – for nearly ten years. And it was here in the ever-present shadow of her mother that she truly mastered her skill.

Like in Africa, the West Indies, and Haiti, people who practice Voodoo in New Orleans draw veves, ritual ground drawings used to invoke the Iwa, or the gods.

Inanna grabbed a handful of cornmeal-based powder from a bowl and held the chalky substance in her tight fist. She loosened her grip just enough to allow the flakes to slip through her hand, to draw a line on the ground.

She drew the first line from north to south. The first line drawn in a veve is the most important because it guides the spirit that is being invoked down to earth.

The next line drawn is from west to east. The very core of the veve resembles the Christian cross.

The drawing of the veve has nothing to do with the crucifixion of Jesus; however they stand for an equally exalting vision: the circling of the souls about the north to south "power line" the linking of heaven above with the dead below, and the intersecting west to east "border line" forming the boundary between the living and the dead.

It is not meant to be a cross but a wheel, The Wheel of the Cosmos. The cosmos wheel represents the four moments of the sun: dawn, which is birth; noon, representing efflorescence; the setting of the sun, signaling fading; and midnight, equaling life in the other world and the promise of return.

At the point where the cosmos wheel meets in the middle, Inanna drew an "X", so that there where now eight outward points to the wheel. Inanna coiled the tips of her "X" so that each tip curled inward, and then she drew a circle around the eight points, creating a true wheel.

On the outside of the wheel, from the four points of the power and boundary lines Inanna drew two lines that curled inward, that looked like the antenna of an ant. From there the design became very intricate and complex.

Veves are used to call down the gods by drawing the god's individual sign or emblem, however the veve Inanna drew had never before been seen.

While in New Orleans Inanna grew stronger, deadlier, and arrogant, and her strength became like that of a deity, so she changed her last name to the voudon word used to invoke one – Veve. The veve she created was her own.

When Inanna felt she could become no stronger in New Orleans, she traveled further west to a larger metropolitan city.

Once settled in a large condo with views of both the bay and the city, she took to prowling the city streets at night, visiting the market, paper stand and coffee shops until she found what she had been on the prowl for. It was a beautiful, large, male specimen standing in line at the methadone clinic. All she had to do was smile. There was nothing he could have done to escape even if he wanted to. He followed her to the hotel room she had reserved months before, and she used him in a human sacrifice to call up a scholar like no other from the depths of fire and brimstone.

The acrimonious instructor appeared covered in white crackling flame with shooting gold sparks and grey smoke. It was as if this genie she had called forth was not from a glass bottle but from a burning block of magnesium submerged in water. The demon gave off the same electrical charge felt in a thunderstorm, but much stronger, and his presence filled the room with steam and ash.

For her sheer boldness Inanna's newest professor pummeled and clawed the entire length of her back until it was bloody, swollen and scarred for life, and due to her unbelievable insolence Inanna prolonged her own suffering for days. Inanna however did not break and defiantly pledged her absolute obedience.

He left her then, and returned weeks later ... and the lessons began.

V

hen the child dragged himself from the grips of sleep, he found himself in another cage. This cage had an open top; he touched one of the bars that ran along the side. The barrier of this confinement was soft – not steel

The floor of the cage was very soft and warm, as it was lined with thick cotton blankets and soft pillows.

There were other things in the cage with him. His Teddy was there, but there were other teddies too, and all kinds of other toys that – in the next few days – the child would learn the names of.

This room was about the same as the room where his other cage had been. The walls were brightly colored and there was strange equipment about, including several cameras positioned throughout the ceiling. Looking down on him was a girl. *Her name is Christine, and she's 26 years old,* thought the child.

"Hello little one, did you sleep well?" She used the same singsong tone Wilson had used. This was the second person who had spoken to him, and again he was moved to tears. Christine smiled and brushed his trembling, poked-out bottom lip with her thumb.

"Awww baby, don't cry." She pushed a button on a little black thing that she picked up from the table and caused a constant and calming sound in his ears.

The child's eyes widened and he started to shake, as he tried to look everywhere at once to try and figure out where the noise was coming from.

Christine smiled "Don't be afraid," she comforted. "It's

okay, it's just music. This music is called classical." And as strings of Vivaldi filled the air the child blinked, blinked, blinked, and slept.

The child woke up in the dark. He slowly sat upright in his new cage and knew he was alone. In absolute despair the child wailed such a heartbreaking cry that it could have chilled the flames of hell.

As the tears were streaming down his flushed cheeks, the door to the room where he was confined flew open with a loud bang, overhead lights flared on, and Christine 26, Ernesto 20, Dr. Astor 56, and Dr. Anderson 60, spilled in and rushed to his cage.

Ernesto picked up the child, held the baby close to his body and began kissing his forehead and whispering "Shhhhh, now, shhhhh." Then Ernesto slowly started to sway back and forth, while the rest of the group stood almost surrounding the child and Ernesto. Christine reached over Ernesto's shoulder to wipe away the child's tears.

At nineteen months, this was the first time the child had ever been kissed. The child's eyes widened to frighteningly large sized disks, the sensation being almost too much for him to bear. His entire tiny frame began to shake, and the child cried.

The child did not know why he cried. Nothing was wrong. In fact everything was right. At last everything was right.

As Ernesto continued to rock the child, the others were cooing soft words to soothe. The child clung to Ernesto the way he had been clinging to Teddy, and started to drift back towards sleep.

Dr. Anderson noted that the child was grossly malnourished, with muscle underdevelopment to the point of being criminal.

"This is a child for Christ's sake!" he cried. "This is not some goddamned barren wasteland where our children cannot be fed."

Dr. Anderson had begun to yell, his face red with anger. No one could blame him, for this was the first time he had seen the boy, and the boy was hard to look at.

Dr. Anderson and Dr. Astor walked to the table and began to put together a diet and exercise program designed to put weight on the boy's frame and strengthen his muscles, starting with the core.

Dr. Anderson wanted the child to be mobile under his own vigor in three months. "Whether it be scooting, crawling, or walking, I don't give a damn. I want this kid to be moving. And fatten him up, do you understand me?" Dr. Anderson really wasn't giving any particular person an order; he was just blowing off steam. Dr. Anderson always yelled when faced with an uncomfortable difficulty.

It was Ernesto who answered, "Don't worry Dr. Anderson. Christine and I will have Adam up and running around this place in no time. Isn't that right, Adam?"

Everyone was looking at Ernesto in perplexed silence. Ernesto wasn't paying attention; he was still looking down at the sleeping child he was rocking in his arms. Finally Ernesto looked at Dr. Astor, as if drawn by his gaze.

"Ernie, why did you call him Adam?"

Ernesto hated being called "Ernie" and quickly glanced at Christine, who was still standing by his side. Dr. Astor made Ernesto nervous, and under his peering eye, Ernesto would always make mistakes. Dr. Astor reserved the pet name "Ernie" for when he believed Ernesto did something stupid.

Christine rubbed his shoulder for encouragement and Ernesto dug up the courage to answer Dr. Astor's question.

"Well this is the 'Genesis' project, and I ... well ..." Ernesto stammered. "Adam was the main character, the most important character, and I thought ... no, I didn't think, 'Adam' just felt right." Ernesto slowly raised his eyes to meet the eyes of the man who granted him his internship, and held his breath for the dressing-down he was surely to receive.

"Bravo Master Ernesto," the tyrant commended. "Bravo."

Ernesto breathed a sigh of relief as his chest puffed up with pride. But not too much puff or pride because Dr. Astor was still watching him. To do something productive Ernesto decided to draw the baby a bath. Thus the child became Adam.

Over the course of the next 120 days Adam's mental development and body strength rapidly accelerated at alarming speeds.

A television was placed in front of Adam's playpen so that he could view programs designed to enhance early childhood development, curriculum like Baby Einstein, Sesame Street, and Dora the Explorer.

At two weeks after Event Relocation, Adam had developed enough muscle strength to stand in his playpen, hold on to the rail, and bounce to the music played on the screen in front of him; Adam had gained ten proud pounds. After four weeks he was able to make simple vocal sounds.

Six weeks after E.R., Adam had learned to manipulate people in the most basic ways – using his smile and his tears.

Because there was so much more activity in The Skyward's facility than at The Foundation's,

Adam's mind reading abilities received the most stimulus and thus developed and strengthened faster than everything else.

After seven weeks Adam pointed and said "Bird," while looking out the window. At eight weeks after Event Relocation Adam took his first tentative step, thirty days ahead of Dr. Anderson's projected deadline. Four days later he was walking.

At ten weeks after Event Relocation, Adam started taking interest in toys other than teddy bears. He would retrieve them mentally, though when Dr. Anderson noted this behavior he returned the toy and told Adam to go get it, suggesting that Adam required the physical exercise.

It was suggested that Adam should have a few hours of uninterrupted "Alone Time" after lunch, so that he could play and have some time to explore his surroundings. One side of the playpen was lowered so that Adam could enter or leave it at his leisure, which of course he did. He roamed about the room and inspected things within reach. He opened drawers, finding the things that were hidden inside for him to discover.

In one drawer he found crayons and markers, so he used them to draw on the wall. His first drawing was a crude helicopter (or dragonfly depending on whose interpretation it was). Everyone came to look at the art Adam created, took pictures of it, and argued over it. Adam liked that so much that he drew on the walls every day. When the walls were covered with Adam's masterpieces he was brought an easel, small canvases, paper and finger paints.

One day Adam opened a drawer and found small, bright-colored rubber balls. He immediately plopped one into his mouth. The door burst open with such force that it startled Adam.

Though he didn't understand what the term "alone time" meant; he had simply memorized the routine of his schedule, so he wasn't expecting anyone to come see him.

It was Dr. Cassidy, age 47. He rushed to the boy with a frown on his face, and with his thumb opened Adam's mouth and retrieved the ball that was resting there. Dr. Cassidy shot a furious glace at the ceiling camera in the left corner then set to the task of removing the rest of the small balls that were in that drawer.

Dr. Cassidy snatched opened drawers that Adam could reach inspected, and then removing things he deemed dangerous from the rest of the drawers, before slamming them shut while Adam followed along behind him, singing his slurred A.B.C.'s.

As much as anyone could be as a captive, Adam was happy. There were doctors whom he liked better than others, but no one made him want to do to them what he had done to Dr. Morgan. In fact he could barely remember the time he had spent in that cage. Sometimes in the middle of the night he would remember and cry himself awake. But someone always came to wipe the tears away, and turn on the night-light.

Adam really liked Ernesto – Ernesto was his favorite.

One day when Ernesto came in, Adam greeted him with a cheerful, "Hola, Esto!" Stunned, Ernesto stopped in mid-stride and slowly turned to look at the ceiling cam in the left corner, which everyone did when Adam performed some magnificent feat.

Though Adam had been vocal, he really wasn't talking, except for the few words he was able to pronounce here and there; words like "no," "mine" and "cake."

Adam had been in the habit of singing the alphabet, but there were a lot of letters that he still could not pronounce.

He would just mumble through the difficult parts of the song, especially "L, M, N, O, and P." Dr. Anderson had been quite displeased with Adam's silence, since he was almost two – an age when most children are chatterboxes.

This was Adam's first sentence and he had chosen to speak it in Spanish.

"'Hola Esto?'" Ernesto echoed in question, his brow creasing. Then Ernesto smiled so wide he felt his cheeks starting to hurt. "Did you just say my name?"

Adam reached up, wanting to be picked up and held, and Ernesto obliged. "Hola Papi," he said, and Ernesto continued to speak to Adam in Spanish.

From that day on, they would greet each other the same way. "Hola Esto!" Adam would call. "Hola Papi," Ernesto would answer. Adam found it much easier to say "Esto" than to say "Ernesto," and Ernesto didn't mind the nickname. He thought it was cute, and so did everyone else. Within a week everyone on the project was calling Dr. Astor's' assistant "Esto" everyone except, of course, Dr. Astor.

The next person Adam called was Dr. Astor, omitting the title that had taken nearly a decade to obtain, and pronouncing "Astor," as "Astar." Dr. Astor refused to overlook this slight oversight. When Adam called him Astar, he was sternly corrected, "Dr. Astor. I refuse to be addressed so informally by one as young as you, Master Adam. Dr. Astor." If Adam addressed him six times by "Astar" in the course of an hour, Dr. Astor would correct him six times in the aforementioned way.

Dr. Astor was Adam's favorite male doctor, despite his being the most rigid and unforgiving in terms of his experiments and expectations. Dr. Astor gave Adam tasks to as simple as matching shapes or as complex as solving insanely intricate numerical puzzles or charting maps that were reserved for astronomers.

The bedtime stories Dr. Astor read to Adam were of Aristotle, Socrates, Nostradamus, the Torah, Koran, and the Old Testament. Dr. Astor determined that since Adam wanted to learn other languages – as he had indicated by speaking

Spanish with Ernesto – he would indeed learn other languages. Dr. Astor brought Adam texts in Hebrew, Arabic, Greek, Japanese, German, Russian, Aramaic, and others for Adam to study.

When Adam turned two, Dr. Astor bought Adam a blue cake with glittery silver dots on it.

"What the hell is this?" Dr. Cassidy asked, as all stood around frowning at the choice in Dr. Astor's cake design.

"Gemini," answered Adam. It was Gemini, but not the way you're used to seeing it drawn as a zodiac symbol. It was in its true form, the way you'd see it in the sky.

Adam was always aware of his surroundings. Even during REM sleep, Adam knew who entered his room and what they did, and usually he slept through it. But now he sensed someone new, and felt the person close. Adam woke up as fingers were lightly brushing dark curls from his face.

The first thoughts he captured from the doctor were, "His hair is too long." Usually Adam could pick up the name and basic information from a person he first encountered, but this time he couldn't do it because he was flooded by the storm of emotions that rolled off this doctor like a surge.

He knew that she was the reason he was there and that this doctor was important, like Dr. Astor. But the only thing he cared about was that she was the reason that he was here.

Adam uttered a word that he had never heard before, but Adam knew that this was the word he would always use when talking to this doctor who had saved him.

"Mommy."

Adam felt something inside her break and spill out to wash all over him, as a large tear fell from her eye and on to his forehead. She kissed away the tear that fell. She kissed both his eyes. She kissed both his cheeks, and she kissed his forehead even though she had already done so. And Adam memorized her face as he fell back asleep.

Adam spent most of his time with Mommy now, though other doctors and Ernesto still came to visit. Adam learned that Mommy would let him do anything, and get away with even more if he so much as threatened to poke his lip out. And if Adam had to deploy such heavy weaponry as tears his victory was assured.

Adam didn't like the vitamins that Dr. Cassidy made him take, so Adam made Mommy yell at Dr. Cassidy, while he clutched her leg and smiled up sweetly into Dr. Cassidy's astounded face.

Adam's tantrums and manipulation tactics became paramount. He learned to fling phrases like "I'm telling" with the deadly precision of an assassin. This went on for almost two years, and the team of doctors was pushed to the pinnacle of their patience.

The team was more annoyed than alarmed, until the day Adam opened the locked door to his room, while standing three feet away. Dr. Anderson and Dr. Cassidy were in the surveillance room watching Adam and taking notes, and both men were on their feet before the first sirens began to sound the bells of warning.

Because Adam had become such an unpleasant spoiled brat, they had forgotten that Adam was found in a steel cage, they had forgotten the accelerated pace at which Adam's skin and bones had healed. They had forgotten the accelerated pace at which the boy learned and retained information. They had forgotten the results of blood tests and tissue samples. They had forgotten Adam had the power of telekinesis. Most importantly they had forgotten about Dr. Morgan and how truly dangerous Adam was and or had become–until now.

Dr. Anderson pulled the lever to reseal the door remotely, but Adam as if sensing what was to come, bolted through the door on wings borrowed from Mercury just before it snapped shut, and ran into a world that he had yet to explore.

Both men were left to track his progress on the surveillance equipment and both scientists prayed that Adam was carried by the speed of youth and not the speed of anything else.

VI

My sister learned of my Genesis Project and the things I was hoping to accomplish over dinner when we were vacationing in Paris. I told her the things we had seen through the eyes of VR56 and how we were planning to use the information to relocate the child from their site and to ours. For a long time she said nothing.
She just sat looking at me.

"You think just because you've taken the fruit from that tree and cultivated the seeds to plant another tree – the tree that you're gorging yourself on – somehow that makes it okay. Well guess what? It doesn't. Because it's the same fucking tree. What you're doing is dangerous. Do you really think that you can defy God? Adam tried and was banished from the Garden. Nimrod tried it and caused all mankind to be divided by different languages and customs. Listen to me: the artificial production of life carries with it dire consequences."

"Really," I arrogantly interrupted, "tell that to all of the parents who conceived a child artificially …"

"I'm not talking about that!" she screamed. "I'm talking about what you're doing! There's a huge difference, so don't you dare sit there and try to justify what you're about to do. The fact that you're even considering taking that child, for a lack of a better word, out of its laboratory …" She let the word laboratory hang in the air.

My sister doesn't yell so her emotional outburst left me feeling attacked and stung. I remember how Jack sat trembling in my lap; his little head swiveling between my face and hers, not understanding why there was so much tension between us.

"He's just a baby," I tried to explain.

"No! No that's not a 'baby.' It's something that was created in some laboratory, created in the laboratory of the very organization that you've pledged to destroy. And now you want to nurture it?

"You haven't a stitch of data. You don't have any records indicating what tests were conducted. You already know what type of living conditions it was housed in, but have no idea what it was fed, and more importantly, no idea why this thing was created in the first place.

"If this 'child' has a fourth of the abilities you think it does, do you really think you'd be able to control it? How do you discipline a child who is capable of mind control?

"What happens when this brat throws a fit? Will he twist your body into a knot? Or maybe he'll make you commit suicide. And all in the blink of an eye! I mean who knows what that little monster will do.

"You witnessed his tantrum first hand. You have a responsibility to society, or have you forgotten that? Why don't you try approaching a large stray dog that's baring its teeth and foaming at the mouth? You'd have better luck trying to pet that animal than you will trying to control this abomination.

"You're so fucking full of yourself, calling this project 'Genesis.' You should pick up a bible and go to fucking church!"

I didn't even have a chance to respond. She hurried from the table and was on a flight back to The States before I'd even had a chance to close my mouth, let alone our tab. That was ten years ago.

She brought with her recent pictures of the family. Her son was already seven! And she brought homemade cookies and a letter from mom. I nearly revealed my mental whereabouts in a moment of absolute despair, as I wondered how I'd plunged so far from heaven and the light, and so far away from love in the form of homemade cookies with a hug in every bite.

We left the museum and strolled the streets for several hours while I did all the talking. We ended up resting on the concrete steps of a church, and it was there that I confessed all my sins through a torrent of lamentations, though I knew there'd be no absolution.

"He's angry at you for abandoning him."

"What?"

"It was you who sat Adam on your lap and read to him. You're the one who cradled him in your arms and sang him to sleep. No one but you brought the Disney movies for him to watch. You gave him a kitten for God's sakes!

"Your maternal instincts held more sway than your scientific interest. You didn't run any tests on him because you were too busy wiping his nose."

My warmhearted laughter both surprised and relieved me.

"Don't laugh," my sister said with a smile while wiping my tears away. "I'm being serious. But where were you when the people you trusted most tried to kill him? Where were you?" She held her fingers to my lips as I tried to speak. "No, don't answer me. You're going to have to answer *Adam*."

VII

here was a brief moment in which Adam revealed his capability to mind read. Dr. Cassidy was with him, and Adam deliberately made Dr. Cassidy angry. God this kid is such a fucking brat, Dr. Cassidy thought to himself.

No sooner had he thought that than Adam shouted, "Me not brat!"

To which Dr. Cassidy retorted, "Yes the fuck you are."

Dr. Cassidy had immediately begun trying to rub his headache away. After a deep dramatic breath, he said "Listen, Adam. You are going to take these goddamned vitamins, because you are iron deficient. We would not have to do this every day if you would simply eat your vegetables. But I am beginning to think you quite enjoy infuriating me, but for what means I am not sure.

"Now you can either swallow them or have them injected. Which will it be Adam?"

He defiantly swallowed the vitamins, while glaring at Dr. Cassidy over the top of the box of his juicy juice.

Dr. Cassidy was so beside himself over Adam's behavior that he missed the significance of what had just happened. Had Dr. Cassidy remained professional and observant things might not have turned out so horribly wrong.

Adam gleefully ran and shouted through the twisting corridors of The Facility. There were scientists and engineers who were not aware of the Genesis Project, due to the various levels of security clearances. So the cause for concern that Adam generated as he sailed by different labs reached nearly a fever pitch.

Something akin to a riot ensued as Adam burst – unchallenged – through the hermetically sealed doors of Dr. Hogue's workspace, dubbed the Germ Lab. He slammed against the stainless steel table, tipping it over as the entrance doors shut behind him. In the private sector the research facilities working on the world's most dangerous microbes (facilities such as the Center for Disease Control, the Central Intelligence Agency of Science & Technology, and the National Institute of Allergy & Infectious Disease) work in Level 4 Biosafety containment research labs. These labs are designed to prevent microbes from being released into the environment, and to provide maximum safety for the scientists who worked inside them.

We have own rating system here at Skyward. The research lab Adam invaded was rated a Level 6.

Later, upon reviewing the footage of Adam's entry into the germ lab and comparing it to the footage of the death of Dr. Morgan, Dr. Anderson surmised that Adam had gained entry by creating an electromagnetic pulse.

Upon Adam's impact with the table, Dr. Hogue, who was in a yellow full-body protective suit that contained its own air supply, grabbed the edge of the table to right it, but he was not fast enough to stop the Petri dishes from sliding off and crashing onto the floor. They broke open and released the deadly virus held captive inside.

Dr. Hogue deployed the first steps in The Decontamination & Containment Procedures.

With a push of a button, large powerful vacuums in the ceiling kicked on and began drawing every particle toward the incinerators. The suction was so powerful that it lifted Adam a few feet off the ground Adam thought that was fun.

Dr. Hogue approached Adam and began removing all articles of the boy's clothing so that they may be burned. With only his socks remaining Adam had enough.

He pushed Dr. Hogue with his mind, using hurricane wind strength, and tried to leave the germ lab. If Adam had been patient, Dr. Hogue would have exited them to the emergency scrubbing stations and sealed the room behind them. To insure the highest levels of control, entrapment, and containment, there was only one way in and one way out of the germ lab.

The entrance doors of the germ lab were designed to open inward. Their opening activates six jet vacuums positioned just inside of the doors. The suction draws in all the surrounding air from a foot and a half away, preventing the escape of any air particulates within the germ lab. It's the same concept as the large blowers that dry your car in the last part of an automatic car wash, but instead of blowing they draw air in.

The only way out of the germ lab was through the emergency scrubbing stations. There you would be showered and scrubbed by the haz-mat team, equipped with an anti-bacterial soap so concentrated as to remove even the most beneficial of human bacteria.
Then you would have to wait within the temporary containment chamber for the results of blood tests, to ensure you had not been infected.

Because Dr. Hogue had activated emergency containment procedures, the entry doors would not open. They were on a time lock, and would not open for another twenty-four hours. That was the second step in the Decontamination & Containment Procedures, put in place to prevent any type of foolish rescue attempts that might release an escaped agent.

Adam was mad now, and he started smashing and destroying equipment by merely looking at it. He wanted out.

Like the comic book hero the Incredible Hulk, Adam was only able to tap into his capabilities when he was truly angry or in extreme levels of stress. And, as Dr. Anderson correctly guessed, Adam's powers always displayed themselves in the form of a push or pulse.

Because Adam had been living in relative comfort and safety he never felt threatened. Since arriving at The Facility there was no need for Adam to create the protective energy pulse and therefore were too infrequent to study.

This was only the second energy pulse that Adam produced and both resulted in the death of a scientist.

If the energy pulses had displayed themselves enough to be studied, or if Adam had been taught to access and control these energy pulses, to learn to push and *pull*, or if he had the ability to push harder, he would have been able to open the doors to the germ lab.

If Adam had been able to get out at that moment he would have brought with him the Apocalypse, for the germ that had escaped the confinements of the Petri dishes was a manmade super plague for which there was no cure.

He started to cry, but for the first time since arriving at The Facility nearly two years earlier, his tears did not help.

Dr. Astor, Dr. Lott, Dr. Collins, Ernesto, Christine, and nine others were at the window, helplessly watching Adam throw a fit and Dr. Hogue die. Adam tried to break the glass to escape. The window splintered but held.

Step Three in the Decontamination & Containment Procedure is to chill the room to subzero temperatures. This step forces anything the vacuums miss into their dormant state, and this step is twelve hours in duration.

Adam saw Mommy at the window. He could see that she was screaming his name, but he could not hear her.

Dr. Hogue was alive but hurt, and it was clear to those watching that he would not be alive for much longer. His entire left rib cage was pulverized, his lungs punctured, and his back and neck broken. Dr. Hogue's mind, however, was intact and he wondered if this germ disguised as a child was a direct result of his research; wondered for the first time in his sixteen years of investigation and experimentation, if he had gone too far.

Dr. Cassidy had once told Dr. Hogue that he would never achieve greatness, would never have anything named after him, would never be mentioned in textbooks, because, as Dr. Cassidy told him, "You think too much." Dr. Hogue had chuckled at that and had not given Dr. Cassidy the satisfaction of a response.

It was no secret that Dr. Hogue never missed Friday Mass and never missed a confessional. Everyone knew that Dr. Hogue was deeply torn between the things he was taught in Catholic school and the things he was doing now.

It was because of Dr. Hogue's convictions that he was promoted to the position of Senior Director of Research. From that day of his promotion, young jealous Dr. Cassidy had not allowed Dr. Hogue a moment's peace in his ceaseless, yet futile, attempts to undermine Dr. Hogue's position of authority; and now Dr. Cassidy stood with the others and watched Dr. Hogue die.

If Dr. Hogue had been the SDR at the time Dr. Astor's footage was being viewed Dr. Hogue would have vehemently opposed the acquisition of Adam. It seemed almost unfair that Adam should be the reason he should perish.

Father Hogue, yes Father, for he had reached priesthood, called on a higher power for the strength to utter his last prayer.

"De profundis clamavi ad et Domine—out of the depths I cry to you O Lord. God is truly good to Israel, to whose heart is pure. As for me, my feet almost strayed; my steps were nearly led off course, for I envied the profligate, I saw the wicked at ease …" Blood spurted from Father Hogue's lips, his ears were bleeding, but he continued to pray.

"It was for nothing that I kept my heart pure and my hands innocent, seeing that I have been constantly afflicted, that each morning brings new torments had I decided to say those things I should have been false to the circle of Your disciples."

Drawn by the sound of the man's voice, Adam went to lie next to Dr. Hogue. The boy had expelled an incredible amount of energy, and he was upset and getting sleepy. Adam wanted to be held, wanted to be comforted by the cadence of Dr. Hogue's prayer and calmed by the labored semi-rise and fall of his chest.

Father Hogue coughed up more blood. The weight of the small child on his chest was insufferable, but he continued to pray.

"So I applied myself to try and understand this, but it seemed a hopeless task. Till I entered your sanctuary … You held my right hand, You guided me by Your counsels and led me toward honor. Whom else do I have in heaven? And having You, I need no one here on earth.

Father Hogue used the last of his strength to lift and drape his arm around Adam to offer the small child the comfort he was so desperately longing for.

"My mind and body may fail, but God is the Rock of my mind, my portion forever. Those who keep far from you perish … but as for me, nearness to God is my good. Lord Jesus Christ, have mercy on my soul." With that final plea seeping from his lips Father Hogue died.

When the room started to freeze Adam was already asleep. Adam's body responded to the change in climate by going into a state of suspended animation. His heartbeat slowed to two beats per minute, he only required a breath or two every hour and did not stir until the doors of the germ lab opened and the first wisps of warm air caressed his bare body.

When Adam's eyes fluttered open the first person he saw was Mommy. She was on her knees in front of him with a blanket, and she was crying. Ernesto was behind Mommy, and he was crying too, but Adam sensed that they were happy.

Dr. Cassidy, Dr. Astor, and Dr. Anderson were there too, but they were not crying and they did not seem happy. Dr. Astor wanted to take samples and run tests, and he suggested that Adam be quarantined until the effects of his exposures to the infection and subfreezing temperatures could be realized. But Mommy said no.
Dr. Astor and Mommy were screaming at each other. They always did when it came to Adam. Then Mommy took Adam to his room.

By the time the warm bath was ready, the blue tint to Adam's skin was gone, and after the bath Ernesto helped Adam put on his favorite Spider Man pajamas, and Mommy let Ernesto give him a cup of hot chocolate with a Snickers bar melted inside.

Mommy told Adam that when she came back she would be taking Adam 'home.' This was a word he had never heard before. She described what it would be like: it was a place where he could meet other kids, go to school, and have a bike.

Adam listened to her voice as he snuggled into the warmth of his bed. Mommy had given him a kitten a few days before. It was soft like Teddy, but warm. Nestled between Teddy and his kitten, Adam drifted to sleep thinking about a place called 'home'.

VIII

Remember when I told you that my team tried to warn me that I was under Adam's influence and that I had become unprofessional? Well they were right. When Dr. Astor first showed me the footage of Adam in the lab of The Foundation I was disturbed beyond sleep. Well later I became outright possessed.

Our firms were in mad competition to secure and or complete projects that would guarantee us an unfathomable amount of research funds and resources.

We had been using adult subjects, and apparently The Foundation was using children.

After viewing the footage of Dr. Morgan's death, I called a meeting of the founders. As far as our scouts could tell, this child was The Foundation's only such subject. With the stakes so high no one could understand why The Foundation had just one child, but speculation as to that merely created a backdrop for our decision to "liberate" the boy. Regardless of the reasons, taking the child would push back their research by years.

It was guessed that Adam had been created to become a super solider. The production of such a combatant would guarantee the firm that produced a solider like that the holy grail of reputation, contracts, and money. However, with the success of the things we were working on, to acquire a contract such as that would have been gluttonous. And that's exactly why we took him.

Every project under Skyward had six teams of scientists working on the same project. This was done independently of each other, without data sharing and without knowledge that there were five other teams working on the same thing. The only people who knew about the duplicate studies were the founders.

Dr. Davidson suggested that we move our most sensitive projects to the remote location because as soon as we removed that child, it would be an open declaration of war. All present felt that any setback we could cause to our archenemy would be worth any collateral damages.

Years before, we had taken steps to reduce or eliminate the casualties of this war that was surely to come. The very first project that Dr. Astor chaired was called "The Project of the Prophets." Every project that followed in his career had some type of seer or oracle at its core. Indeed, Dr. Astor created a method of intelligence gathering never before dreamed of – which is why all of Dr. Astor's projects were funded by the military. Seventeen of the thirty-five seers from the Prophets Project had gone on to attend the best Ivy League universities on the planet and had graduated in the top 2% of their class. By the time Adam was created, they were gainfully employed at various security levels within The Alpha Omega Foundation – so there wasn't much of what The Foundation was working on that we did not know about.

The founders supported the idea of a move, and so Dr. Davidson set in motion the arrangements for moving twenty teams of scientists, their assistants, their equipment, and the data compiled without creating the appearance of a mass exodus or a sense of anxiousness. No one was to have the faintest idea what we were about to do. It had taken months to accomplish.

Dr. Astor and Muhammad Quaseem, the Director of Gathered Surveillance, prepared for the first sequence in the Genesis Project, which would culminate in what we called "E.R." (Event: Relocation). They watched the footage produced by RV56 countless times, to find weaknesses in The Foundation's method of security and to prepare a team to remove the boy.

The weather was becoming favorable on that part of the continent, so I decided to fly ahead of the first teams that would be arriving to ensure that the facility was up and running and had a staff that could quickly accommodate such a large party.

After several weeks at the remote location, I flew to Switzerland to attend a conference.

After the conference I went to see a jeweler in the Mediterranean. The Byzantine pieces he was creating were jaw dropping. While lounging on Grecian beaches I decided to take a holiday in Europe.

It's the city, I swear, for little dogs. Jack loved being in Paris, where he used to strut around in his tiny diamond collar and little Coach rain jacket – barking gay greetings to other little dogs, as lavishly adorned or otherwise.

He always seemed so happy there. If I'd known that was the last time Jackie would travel to Paris, I don't think I would have ever left.

The last leg of my vacation proved to be not worth taking: I discovered that a bracelet created by one of my designers had been forged and was being sold at a third of the price, and had to start legal proceedings to stop its illegal manufacture; Jack ate seven richly cream filled pastries that made him sick; and due to recent terrorist activity the *Gendarmerie Nationale,* the military institution in charge of public safety with police duties among the civilian population, practically had the city under siege.

As soon as the vet said it was okay for Jack to fly, I came home. Jackie was in a pissy mood the entire flight, so I ignored him by focusing on responding to e-mails and reading progress reports of the projects I had left behind.

When I vacation I tend to do just that, leaving my work at home. I was alerted that the Event Relocation had been successful and that the child had been at The Facility for five months.

On the tarmac I changed the destination for my driver, instructing him to take me to The Facility instead of home. I had been traveling abroad for half a year, and being back in my native city greatly improved my mood. I rolled the window down and let the fat raindrops wash in.

Dr. Astor was waiting for me when I arrived at The Facility. He escorted me to the area that had been remodeled for the small child, while bringing me up to speed and giving me updates.

He explained that Dr. Anderson had placed the child on an exercise and diet program and that everyone on his team was instructed to teach and encourage him to play and explore his surroundings. That Dr. Lott and his team had begun touch therapy and that everyone who was on this project was to spend eighty percent of their research time touching, hugging and holding Adam but never, under any circumstances, to strike him.

"Adam?"

Dr. Astor explained that his assistant had given the child the name "Adam," and that Adam was quite taken by Ernesto.

"Master Ernesto figures since this is the Genesis Project …."

"Well it's fitting, isn't it?"

"I believe that under Dr. Hogue's influence, young Ernesto has become rather pious."

"There's nothing wrong with a little moral substance," I said laughing. "Speaking of Dr. Hogue, what do you think about Dr. Hogue as the Senior Director of Research?"

"I can think of nothing better. He's in here. Good night."

"Good night, Ken."

I took the files he handed me and entered the room where our Adam lay sleeping. Though he was alarmingly thin, he was beautiful and his dark hair fell into his face. I lowered one side of the playpen, sat next to Adam, and brushed a lock of hair from his face. His hair was too long and needed to be cut.

Adam woke at my touch and gazed at me with large, sleepy green eyes that sparkled like emeralds. He had me wrapped around his finger from the moment he opened his eyes. I fell in love with him right then and there.

I was sitting there for a long time, looking at him and wondering what kind of men could leave a child in a cage, when out of the blue Adam called me "Mommy."

It was in that moment, that I was lost. My eyes welled up with tears. One tear fell lazily to his forehead, which I kissed. I kissed him on both of his emerald jeweled eyes, then on both of his cheeks, and then I sat with Adam until he went back sleep.

My team and I were to work in pendulum with Dr. Astor's team in trying to discover the depths to which Adam had been genetically altared and engineered; to learn which capabilities Adam obtained, and which of those we could develop, strengthen, or suppress.

I did not conduct any experiments, didn't run any tests. I did nothing, and my team lounged around idle with nothing to do, eventually taking direction from Dr. Astor.

I was given looks of concern, I was whispered about when no one thought I could hear, and an intervention was attempted – all to no avail.

I cannot explain what happened to all my years of training and experience as a scientist, into what abyss my careful observation and data collecting skills had fallen. My unhurried method of discovery and analysis, the quick way I was to challenge someone else's theory … all gone.

Instead I spent most of my time playing silly games, making up stupid songs, rocking him to sleep, and ensuring I was there when he woke up. I bought clothes, toys, and books, and I rescued a small black kitten for him from the animal shelter.

I hindered my own project by monopolizing Adam's time, and I vetoed other experiments, bloods draws, or food servings that made Adam cry or that he did not like.

Dr. Astor and I had brutal fights every time we saw each other, which was several times a day. The other founders were patient, until of course I told them I was taking Adam home.

"You will take him nowhere!" Dr. Astor spat those words as if they were thunderbolts "If you'd been conducting the tests you were supposed to be conducting and analyzing the reports that were given to you, you would realize that removing him from this facility is not up for discussion because It. Is. Not. An. Option."

Ken had followed me into my office and was standing in front of the door, which he had slammed behind him, prohibiting any attempts from me to escape his external voice of reason – for the voices in my head had failed me.

He was desperate and angry, a deadly combination, and shaking with rage. If there'd been anything in my office that could have been used as a weapon I'm sure he would have killed me.

Sensing that I could have been in real danger Jack jumped out of his Louis Vuitton carrying case, growling, and barking. He charged at Kenneth with such speed that it appeared as if Jack had exploded through the barrel of a cannon.

Kenneth angrily swept Jack away with the side of his foot as if Jack were nothing more than a soccer ball, and my poor little dog tumbled over five times before regaining his footing. Jack came back swinging, and so did I.

"I will not stand here and allow you to suggest my commitment to this group – our group – and the projects we are working on has slackened or weakened! I believe Adam should be studied in a more natural environment."

Jack was able to get in a bite before Dr. Astor picked him up and tossed him into the hallway, where Drs. Lott, Davidson, and Anderson were keeping tally on this latest quarrel over Adam. I noted Dr. Anderson rubbing his temples before the door of my office was re-slammed.

"Studied?" Dr. Astor laughed without the slightest flirtation with merriment, "You have done no such thing."

I was beyond reason. "Move!"

"You will take him nowhere. Such a move would require

a vote of the founders. Are you in such a state of delusion that you actually believe the die will be cast in your favor?"

Check and mate.

It was as if I had been slapped. No, I surely wouldn't get a favorable vote from my colleagues. There was no way for me to respond, so Ken continued to try and reason with me.

"Dr. Hogue was a great man of science, religion, and philosophy. He was our friend, and the loss of him was not worth the risk, Dr. Hogue was too great a loss. Dr. Morgan, too, was brilliant, a palpable loss to the scientific community. However the loss of a simple man, a common man that we wouldn't even speak to on the sidewalk, would be too great a loss. Adam cannot leave."

I sat down at my desk and held my head in my hands. He was right Adam had killed two people. My heart shattered into a million pieces at the thought of Adam never feeling an autumn breeze on his face, never walking barefoot through warm sand on a beach.

Kenneth read my mind. "Artemisia, the love you have for this boy could not keep him safe in society. This is the safest place for Adam. The love you have for Adam, the love we all have for Adam, will make him as comfortable as possible and keep him as safe as possible."

"We have to find a way to control his temper and outbursts. I think I need to distance myself from this project. I'm not thinking clearly."

"You are now, and I think the separation anxiety Adam would suffer if you were to withdraw yourself from this project would take too long for Adam to overcome.

"I do not believe you have anything to punish yourself

for. Furthermore, who else but you can bring about the discipline that Adam so sorely needs?"

We both laughed at that.

IX

Dr. Astor had just left the office of his irrational colleague. The fight they'd had was the most vicious to date, but he was finally starting to get through to her. His dear friend had listened to him, had at last *heard* him, and agreed that it would be too dangerous for Adam to leave The Facility.

Dr. Astor placed a call to a structural engineer and an interior design firm. If Adam was to live there for the rest of his natural life he should be made more than comfortable.

For the first time he could remember since Artemisia had been on this project Dr. Astor felt relief. He knew that if she were to remove the child from The Facility he would never see either of them again. He loved Adam just as much as she did. Hell everyone on the project loved Adam; so how fair would it be for her to take him away from the rest of the team?

He was having a hard time understanding what underlying phenomenon was causing everyone on this project to march down the path of emotional attachment and the risk of unprofessional conduct. It was fascinating. This phenomenon had to be studied, he told himself. So no, Adam could not be allowed to leave.

He couldn't image what it would be like to not be able to hear Adam laughing and the last thing he wanted to think about was how Adam's absence would affect Master Ernesto.

Having made his phone calls, Dr. Astor prepared to visit young master Adam. He wanted to get his vitals, take some blood and tissues samples, and just sit and talk with Adam to learn how he was feeling and recovering from the freeze. Maybe he would allow Adam a cup of cocoa with the alarmingly high amounts of sugar created by the addition of a chocolate bar and marshmallows.

Dr. Astor smiled on the reflection of the day Adam talked him in to drinking a cup as well.

The onslaught of sugar that invaded Dr. Astor's body led him to believe he was having a diabetic seizure. He couldn't believe he had allowed the boy to talk him into drinking such a concoction!

Dr. Astor's feelings of nostalgia and relief melted away so quickly he suffered a slight case of vertigo as he opened the door to Adam's chamber and discovered that both Adam and the kitten were gone.

Dr. Astor rushed to the security room and demanded to review of the security tapes. He found that a block of time immediately following Adam's bath had been carefully removed, and that all security cameras in and around The Facility, including those monitoring Periodic Element AU, had been disabled for a period of six hours. The video feed the security guards had been viewing was a continuous loop of previous footage.

Dr. Astor consulted the Director of Surveillance and requested that the images be pulled from the main server that was located in another state. Hours later Dr. Astor was informed that the system had been hacked. The only thing that had been taken was the block of time that Dr. Astor was requesting.

Dr. Astor returned to his office and paged his assistant. Preparations were to be made to conduct a quick experiment; an experiment in which Dr. Astor would turn the all-seeing eyes of his remote viewers inward.

X

ominick stood over the crib and stared down at the sleeping kid who looked like his nephew. He was beginning to wonder if ten grand was worth it to knock off some kid. Dominick looked down at the smaller man seated near him, and voiced his concerns.

"Ya' know what man, I don't know. He looks like my sister's kid, and he's just a kid."

"How hard can it be tough guy? With the things you've been charged with, this should be easy."

"If it's so easy then you do it yourself." Dominick started to leave, but Dr. Cassidy called his cousin back.

"I'll give you twenty grand ... each." That certainly held the attention of the four men to whom Dr. Cassidy was addressing. Dominick was a mid-level crime associate in the business of drug and weapons trafficking. He had made countless adversaries disappear and was rarely seen without bodyguards.

Dr. Cassidy was frustrated at his cousin's sudden, lofty moral stance. But twenty thousand dollars is a lot of money.

Dr. Cassidy was seething as he watched his cousin carefully wrap Adam and his flea-infested cat in a blanket. He was glad to be getting rid of both.

As his cousin and his henchmen were leaving with Adam gently embraced in his cousin's arms, Dr. Cassidy did something completely out of character.

"Hey Nicky ..." and as Dominick paused to glance over his shoulder at his cousin Dr. Cassidy finished what he started to say. "Be careful."

Hey Nicky, be careful.

Dominick tuned out the ceaseless chattering of the men in his entourage as he drove along the wooded area where eight of his former associates were buried.

Adam's senses were off, and he could not read minds while his body was in a state of recovery. He did not realize that he was in danger.

If Adam hadn't been recovering from an elevated hibernation state, or if his body hadn't been busy destroying the airborne virus he was exposed to in Dr. Hogue's lab, Adam would have killed Dr. Cassidy and the men who had entered his room before fully waking up.

For now Adam was excited by all the new experiences: he was sitting in the front seat of a car, looking out a window, and asking so many questions that Dominick was starting to feel interrogated.

He was also starting to get a headache. There was a feeling in the pit of his stomach that was telling him this job was all wrong.

He glanced over at Adam, who was now standing and talking to the three men who sat comfortably in the back seat of Dominick's European luxury sedan. Dominick momentarily looked at the speedometer, eased off the accelerator and then looked back at Adam. He was once again bothered by the fact that Adam was not in a car seat.

He slowly pulled his car to a stop. Adam, who had been told to sit down several times during the drive, did just that as the car ceased to move and Adam discovered that he now held Dominick's undivided attention.

If Dominick had been a combat soldier, his commanding officers would have been alarmed at the ease with which he could take a life. It didn't matter what life: man, woman, child, or pet.

Dominick was a sadistic man who liked to be up close and personal with his targets. He preferred knives or various methods of strangulation over a gun because he liked to watch the life drain from his victim's eyes; however Dominick had no problems handling a gun, so he could not understand why this job was causing him so much anxiety.

The assassin glanced in the rear view mirror at his right hand man, Derek he had been with him on the very first job, when both of them were only twelve. Derek knew what Dominick was thinking.

"We could drop him off at the emergency room or at the doors of a church."

"Yeah, this is all fucked up."

"Hey wait a minute," Mark was new to Dominick's inner circle. This was his second job and he was eager to prove himself. "We were offered twenty grand. I won't let you back out of this." He whined while looking back and forth between Derek and Dominick.

Blake who had been with Dominick almost as long as Derek reached for his gun as he kept his eyes on Mark.

"You won't 'let' us? Who the fuck do you think you're talking to?" demanded Derek.

"I'll give you the fucking money out of my own goddamn pocket, if that's all you're worried about," offered Dominick. "But we are *not* going to kill this kid. Do you understand me? Now get the fuck outta my car."

With an explosion that sounded like a sonic boom, Mark's bullet entered Derek, and Adam began to scream. Blake was all over Mark in an instant, but Mark was stronger and in a better position. Dominick took advantage of the distraction, grabbed Adam, jumped out of the car, and ran.

They made it well into the forest, before Dominick was able to stop and calm Adam down. He set Adam on the leaf strewn ground and placed his hand over the child's mouth while holding a finger up to his own, asking Adam to remain silent. Dominick then took the gun from the holster at the small of his back and removed the safety.

He positioned Adam behind a tree and took aim in the direction from which they had fled. He'd heard two shots boom from within the car and wondered whether it would be Blake or Mark who gave chase.

It was cold enough to see the vapor of his breath, and the only sound that Dominick could hear was the chattering of Adam's teeth. This was Adam's first time in an uncontrolled environment, and he wasn't wearing any shoes.

Adam could feel the rage that flowed from Dominick like lava from a volcano, and Adam could sense the heat of Dominick's vehemence against his tender skin, even through the barrier of the tree. He moved from behind the safety of the tree and wrapped his small arms around the assassin's leg to warm himself within the heat Dominick's fury.

For the first time since leaving The Facility Adam made an effort to use his power of telepathy. What he was reading from Dominick was hatred. Never in his young life had Adam encountered this emotion, not even with Dr. Cassidy. Adam couldn't name the hot blackness, just like he couldn't put a name to the feeling it invoked in his tiny body… terror.

If Mark was alive, Dominick was going to make him suffer. Adam pried into the depths of Dominick's mind, and the things he saw there made him shiver with fear.

Dominick knelt and wrapped Adam in his jacket.

Adam was terrified, confused, and silently crying. "I want my Mommy, I want to go home."

"I know you do kid, I know."

Adam heard the rustling before Dominick, and quickly returned to the safety of the other side of the tree, but then ran back to Dominick because he did not want to be alone.

"It's Blake," Adam whispered.

"It better be," Dominick stated as he raised his gun.

Blake lurched into a small clearing, blood profusely dripping from his chest and stomach.

Adam began shaking so badly that Dominick believed the kid as having a seizure.

"OK brother hang on, hang on!" Dominick's rage whipped into a frenzy as he went to help his comrade stay on his feet, Adam stayed close beside him. Both of them were showered with blood and brain matter as Mark hit his intended target.

As Blake's lifeless body crumpled to the ground Dominick pulled the trigger. His bullet was wasted. As Adam was being showered with warm droplets of blood his push caused

Mark to suffer from *commotio cordis* that stopped the beating of Mark's heart.

The night's events had overwhelmed Adam with negative stimuli, and he turned and fled deeper within the wilderness of the forest. Dominick let him go and wished him luck, as he returned to the car to get a shovel.

Adam ran aimlessly for several hours in the cold and dark. He had cuts and scratches on his face, hands, arms, and feet from running through twigs and thorn bushes, but Adam's oldest abrasions had already begun to heal. All traces of them would be gone by the time the sun rose.

A horned owl launched itself from a tree, and Adam thought the bird was a monster. Startled, he tripped and fell down an embankment, landing face first in a shallow, icy creek.

Adam sat within the shadow of a large rock and coughed up the water he swallowed. Adam looked up at the sky and saw the zodiac constellation he was born under, and screamed out Astar as loud as he could.

Adam got up and started wandering once more, "Mommy! Esto! Astar! Where are you?" Adam cried so hard and yelled so loud that his throat hurt. His cries went unanswered.

That is until his calls attracted the attention of a mountain lion that seemed to materialize from the gloom. Adam would have made a tasty treat for her and her cubs. The great cat roared, displaying razor sharp teeth. Propelled by self-preservation, Adam ran. The adrenalin coursing through his body activated his bionic cells, which enhanced his speed.

If Adam hadn't been genetically altared, the big cat would have easily overtaken him.

Adam ran even though he didn't know where he was going. Adam ran even though he wasn't watching where he was going.

Adam burst through the forest's edge and into the path of a speeding car.

XI

he visit with my sister left me feeling relieved but exhausted. The only thing that filled my thoughts as I returned to Morocco was my tiny companion Jackie, and I cried a lot. He was so full of bravado. He thought himself as fierce and powerful as a 120-pound Bull Mastiff. Jack was such an amazing little guy and now he's gone.

Once I got off the ferry, I roamed around for a while, concentrating on erasing my trip to Paris. I wanted to replace what I had done with what I was seeing, and in my current state of sorrow it took more effort than I was comfortable with. I wandered further and further from all the tourist attractions until I found myself in a place where English was spoken less and less. I stopped for tea under a tented souk and became insanely distracted by the bracelets worn by the Gypsy girl who served me.

As a jeweler, it was the perfect distraction, and the timing couldn't have been better. The girl's jewelry gave me something else to concentrate and focus on.

Thoughts of the Gypsy girl eclipsed all that I was mentally trying to conceal, and I let the very being of her invade me. Under this tent on the outskirts of a Moroccan bazaar with a kaleidoscope of sounds, sights and smells, she was all that I saw.

Her sheer hijab was the color of the setting sun, and was worn more to protect her from the blowing sands than for any religious doctrine – as you could clearly see her face. The matching veil along the rest of her garments where heavy embroidered silks that covered the girl in reds, yellows, purples and gold's to protect her skin from the sun. The girls' complexion was just the same as of coffee with milk, and her brown eyes seemed translucent.

The girl was beautiful, but paled in comparison to the jewels with which she was adorned. The girl's left arm was encased in bracelets from wrist to just-below-the-elbow: heavy silver bracelets embedded with jewels, hammered copper bracelets with flower etchings, large-linked golden bracelets with colorful jeweled baubles, knotted wooden bracelets craved from exotic trunks, and thin glittery pink bracelets of unknown origins.

The bracelets on her right wrist weren't bangles and she only had four. These bracelets were a dark blue that looked as if made with braided twine. Each was linked together with a string of little cowbells, and the jingle they made was very pleasant.

What caught and held my attention was the thick glass bangle she wore on her left arm. It rested between the four pink bracelets and two wooden ones. It wasn't fine crystal, or even high-end etched glass. Her bangle had a slight green tint to it, as if it were made from the glass of a Coke bottle. From what I could see it wasn't chipped or racked, I couldn't even see any tiny dings in it. I was bewildered, wondering how this nomadic desert girl managed not to break a glass bangle.

From that moment on I knew I wasn't leaving this desert until I found that girl's jeweler. I started to feel foolish. I was watching the girl's every move with such a lascivious grin on my face. Anyone watching me watch her would have come to the wrong conclusion.

Though I was mentally exhausted I decided to take a walk. The pavilion I was sitting underneath was three football fields in length and four times as wide. The market was a delicious symphony for the senses. As I strolled deeper within the market I saw several camels on the ground resting, ancient images of Christ, vegetable and fruit stands, and the production of natural raw silk. I bought three prayer rugs, and Islamic and African art.

I slowly walked by or stopped at every stand, and through it all I found my mind drifting back to that glass bangle. I aimlessly evaded the packs of dogs, goats, and children that roamed unabated.

I made my way to every jewelry vendor I could find and slowly inspected their inventory. It was all to no avail: I could not find the glass bangles anywhere. By the time I made my way back to where I had started it was dark out, and the gypsy girl who had started this obsession was gone.

I ate from a street vendor who served me flavorful spiced meat wrapped in flat, moist buttery bread, piled high with cucumbers, sweet onions, and tomatoes, and garnished with cilantro. It was so tender the meat melted in my mouth. I washed it all down with four big gulps of Coke so cold it made my eyes water and left a burning sensation in my ears. The Coke bottle made me think once again of the gypsy girl. I threw the Coke bottle in my backpack and headed back towards the city.

I used my satellite phone to call my lawyer. It would have been cheaper to use the phone in my room, and I was nearly there, but I was filled with such a sense of exhausting urgency that to wait the mere half hour would have killed me. I explained to my attorney that I wanted to find the jeweler who had created that bracelet and commission him to reproduce it exclusively for Periodic.

The firm that represents me is globally connected with the nastiest slit throat lawyers money can buy, which means that anywhere on the face of the earth I need legal representation (from criminal to land use and zoning) I can get it. This also allows me to get out of any jam or any country in a matter of hours after the initial phone call.

I was still on the phone when I got back to my room, Jake said he knew just the person I needed and would have them pick me up in an hour. I pulled the Coke bottle out of my backpack and set it on the nightstand then placed the rest of my spoils on the bed and went to take a shower. I fell asleep after dressing and was wakened by the chambermaid, who told me I had a visitor in the lobby.

XII

nanna was flying in the wee hours of the morning through the outskirts of the city. Not on a broom, but in a red Jaguar. She enjoyed driving at night. It allowed her to think. Her nightly lessons had ended months before, making Inanna the deadliest Obeah priestess … ever.

The fiend who marred her body was now trapped in a box at the bottom of the sea, where he would remain for the next 100,000 years. Her long shapely legs, small waist, firm bottom and full breasts made it appear as if she was some CEO's trophy wife, and the red Jaguar and the jewels helped support that illusion. She was still pissed that he had flawed her body, and that there was nothing that any spell or plastic surgeon could do to fix it.

Because she looked eighty years younger than she actually was, and it would be hard to make anyone believe she was even thirty-five (which is what she told people) Inanna knew she could get away with sporting a tattoo, especially since her appearance would not change for the next eighty years.

With her skin so dark she wasn't sure that a tattoo would even help, but late in the summer Inanna made an appointment with an artist named JB in a place called The Permanent Mark. Inanna chose this emporium for body art because of its name, for her marks were to remain permanent, for the entire world and the adjudicators of Judgment Day to see.

The poor man was so smitten he could barely speak, but over a period of months, JB adorned her raised scars with thick, black, delicate, beautiful tribal markings.

Snow was falling before Inanna was able to stand in the full-length mirror to admire the completion of JB's work. It appeared as if the ink work and scarring were intertwined, and

Inanna stood in awe. JB hadn't used the tattoo to cover up the scarring; instead he had enhanced the scarring with the placement of the tattoos and made it appear as if the scarring was placed there on purpose.

Her body art brought back memories of the ritual scarification or cicatrisation status markings worn by high society women, who were considered advanced priestesses in the hierarchy of priesthood, markings that she had seen on her grandmother as a girl.

It made Inanna feel that her tattoo was honoring her mother and all the women before her who had passed down their gift – and luckily for JB, Inanna was pleased.

Inanna hit the "S" curves at ninety miles per hours and let the engine of her Jag roar. Her intention was to red line the big cat and fly back to the city at 120mph, but as she sped around the second curve, lined with tall dense evergreens and ferns, she slammed on the brakes with both feet and slid into a full-panic stop. It wasn't a deer she was trying to avoid, but a person.

A child.

Inanna jumped out of the car and ran the very short distance to where the child was standing, but before she could approach any closer, she felt the small child trying to push within her and stop her heart. Inanna stopped in her tracks and laughed a laughter that sounded like water trickling over bells.

Oh this kid was strong, and yes, that surprised her, but he was unskilled and Inanna practiced every day. The boy was no match, and Inanna was no longer amused.

She seized the child around the neck without even touching him, folded her arms across her chest and carried the boy the across distance between them while tapping her foot with annoyance. She held him at eye level. The kid was struggling, and this made Inanna angry, for she was not to be challenged. No one until now had even shown the will to resist.

Inanna decided she would have no earthbound rival so the boy must die. Before she could snap her fingers to make it so, the boy responded to her thoughts with a question, "What's a rival?"

Startled, she looked at the kid again; really looked at him.

He was frightened and cold, and he clung to a tiny hissing cat – which at first she had thought was a stuffed toy – as if it were a lifeline. He was wearing Spider Man pajamas that were muddy and ripped, and his feet were bare and bloody.

His large green eyes where the same shade as the Captain's, which made her believe the boy was some sort of trap. Inanna called upon all the dark forces that were at her disposal to learn which of her enemies had dared to send this ploy. A thousand whispers of the night answered, "This boy is yours."

Furious Inanna called upon the winds, the rain, the thunder, and the sea, and demanded an answer once more. All things in the darkness, no matter where in the world or below it, even if in shadows in the full bright of the day, answered the witch while cowering against her fury, "The boy is yours."

Inanna's attention returned to the boy hovering before her. He was terror stricken, crying and surely in shock, but he asked again, "What's a rival?"

The witch had been considering taking a pupil. The deal she had made with the dark master allowed many years on earth, but not eternity. She had decided that if she couldn't live forever, she would live through a daughter, thus beating the devil after all! However the powers from above had denied her. A spawn from a witch as powerful as Inanna would turn the balance of things in the wrong direction. There are a few who can beat the Devil, but the master in heaven cannot be overridden.

Inanna realized that though she wanted a girl, this was the child she so desperately longed for. In this child her legacy would live on, and her legacy would live forever. "Where you are concerned boy," she said answering his question, "there will be none."

This was her protégé. She reached to cradle him from where he was suspended. She held her child in her arms and wiped his dark hair away from his face. He allowed her to comfort him, and through her touch she learned that this boy was four years old and that his name was Adam.

XIII

The woman waiting for me in the lobby looked younger than me, far too young to be a lawyer with any experience, and I was instantly irritated. Despite living among Middle Eastern beliefs she was dressed as if in New York, wearing designer jeans that were at the very minimum $300 U.S. A crisp, white button-down shirt with the top four buttons undone to show off a healthy cleavage that immediately sparked envy.

She was sitting in a leather, wingback chair and flipping through an African fashion magazine, and didn't notice me when I first walked in. She glanced up while turning a page laden with shoe advertisements then stood up to greet me. I was astonished to find she was three inches taller than me.

Everything about her oozed power, royalty and confidence, and my initial feelings of irritation began to wane. Her ink-black hair tumbled down her waist in big unruly curls that she made no attempt to control. She had paprika skin and large dark eyes the color of almonds.

"Artemisia? Hi, I'm Anahita. I'll be handling the negotiations between you and the tribal jeweler, to ensure this bracelet will be created for Periodic Element AU and no other. Let's grab a bite to eat and go over all the details."

Anahita didn't tell me her last name, but when you're named after a goddess and stroll about like a queen, last names seem to diminish things.

Anahita was explaining that she had made reservations at a café with the best views of the sea and that she doesn't discuss business on an empty stomach, as we walked to her car. She made me comfortable and I found myself smiling at her jokes.

Anahita drove a grey convertible Porsche 911 turbo

cabriolet and she drove it entirely too fast. I felt like I was on a roller coaster. The city blurred past me as she zipped through the narrow streets, racing towards the restaurant that promised hot food and stiff drinks.

She parked next to a Bentley sports coupe, and announced that we had reached our destination. We walked past other high-end luxury cars as we made our way to the entrance. The café was more like a nightclub for the young elite than a restaurant, and Anahita's name was gleefully called from several different directions in unison as we walked in. I found myself smiling at that.

We were seated at the window, and she was right. The views were sweeping. I let myself relax a little as I bobbed my head to the music and looked over the menu.

Over the seductive, spicy Arabian-tinged and African-accented meal, I found myself both alarmingly infatuated and totally distracted by Anahita. She was enchanting. Her exotic accent wasn't exclusively Middle Eastern, and I found it hard to concentrate on what she was saying because I was too busy trying to place the undertones of her enunciations.

She must have known. "My father is Iranian and my mother comes from Belize," she explained. "I learned to speak both Spanish and Farsi at the same time, when I was very young I mixed both languages as one. And that is still the way I speak with my brothers. My Farsi is equally as strong as my Spanish due to the fact I grew up in Iran from the age of nine. However my brothers and I, my father too, speak to my mother in Spanish.

"I was educated in Spain and was able to enjoy speaking wholly in my mother's tongue for six years, except of course, for the times I rang home, which was nearly every day. In Spain is where I learned to speak English."

Yes, that was exactly it. Her South American way of speaking was in the center of her very Middle Eastern accent, and the fact that she had learned to speak English in Europe helped to place the royal tone in her dialect. Anahita's smile was infectious and deviously flirtatious. I couldn't help but flirt back.

Our plates were being cleared away when Anahita began to talk about the reason she was hired. "The region where you saw the gypsy girl is very isolated. They are an uneducated people – at least uneducated in the traditional sense of the word. Their language is an ancient one that doesn't have an alphabet; their entire history is oral, passed down from father to son. We are in luck. There is a linguist at the university who has agreed to meet us at the souk tomorrow, to help us find your gypsy.

"Speaking of which, it's late. My flat is closer than your hotel. I think you'll find my accommodations far more comfortable so I'll doubt you'll mind staying the night." She winked, as she said this, leaving no uncertainty in my mind that she was flirting.

The race back to her apartment was at quantum speeds that left me feeling queasy; I was actually relieved as I got out of her car and stood on solid ground.

On the way up to the penthouse suite that Anahita called home, I learned that she owned the building in which she was living as well as quite a few other apartment investments and two resort properties Still, I was unprepared as the elevator doors opened.

If she was hoping to impress me it was working – I was smitten. The doors opened onto three steps that descended into her living room, which she had chosen to decorate in the iridescent colors of peacocks. Floor-to-ceiling windows greeted us as we walked in, and they framed a superior view of the sea.

The windows were draped in Egyptian cotton so fine they could have been mistaken for silk, they were billowing softly inward, pushed by the breeze from the bay.

There was an off-white Italian leather sectional off to one side, and it's being the only piece of furniture in the gathering room made the room feel open and airy. There were lush, live plants behind one part of the sectional, their health, and enormity boasting the benefits of the vital spirit of the rising sun.

Anahita appeared from nowhere and handed me a glass of wine, and then my hostess began the private tour of the rest of her fl at. I was too tired to drink, and I almost requested a Coke instead, but I allowed myself a few sips before handing the glass back to Anahita.

We walked down the hall to where I would be sleeping. The small chamber also boasted an aquatic view, and was just as sumptuous and dramatic in décor. The only furnishings this room held were a dark burgundy, velvet chaise that was large enough to comfortably sleep two people, and the tiger skin rug that it was sitting on. Sheer drapes hung staggered from the ceiling, with no other purpose than to sway in the zephyr.

I imagine that this is what a room belonging to the favorite concubine of a sultan's harem would look like, because not a dime was balked at in regards to creating a space of abundant luxury, beauty, and comfort. The tiger rug was softer than I had expected, but as I had expected, it was authentic.

The adjoining bathroom had a mosaic tile floor with a large capital "A" in the center. A large sunken bathtub sat to the right, and to the left was a shower that boasted nine shower heads – six that swiveled, two that pulsated – to spray different parts of the body.

I took a long hot shower, promising myself to remodel my bathroom when I returned home. Anahita brought me silk pajamas and threw the clothes I removed into the wash while I was bathing. By the time I emerged from the steam-filled bathroom my clothes were tumbling in the dryer.

I came out of the bathroom to find a fire roaring in the fireplace that I had failed to notice when I first came into the bedroom. Anahita laid out blankets and handed me a cup of hot, spiced tea. After a few moments of idle chatting, she left me to my dreams, which were nothing but smoke and glass circlets.

The heavy breakfast Anahita fed me left me feeling sleepy, but as soon as she put her car in drive I was more than alert.

When we arrived at the market, Anahita's professor was already there and in a heated conversation with several of the local merchants.

"Alright?" boomed the professor disengaging himself from the political conversation he was having and using the British shortcut that meant both "hello" and "how are you" at the same time, as he spotted Anahita. He came to greet us.

I liked him immediately. He was very animated and chatty, and had a tendency to end a sentence with a laugh. He was explaining that he had located the gypsy girl and had taken the liberty of arranging a meeting, when the girl appeared from behind a kiosk. She had been bending over and I hadn't seen her until she stood up.

With a smile she joined our party, along with a woman who was older than her but undoubtedly from whom she received her beauty. The matriarch spoke to the professor.

He answered then translated. Then we all followed the women through the large tent, finally exiting through the rear, into the serenity of the desert. We followed awhile along a footpath, yielding to merchants traveling in the opposite direction, until we came upon a village that melted into the landscape.

The homes that were perched perilously on the cliffs looked as if the only materials the architects had used were paper cups, sand, and beach water, but these sandcastles were much larger than the one's children make on the shore, and far more relevant.

Once we were closer we could hear the little city's movement: women singing, children running around in reckless pursuit of play, dogs barking, clothes flapping dry in the sun. The gypsy's castle was a moderate one, bigger than most but not among the few largest. It was considerably cooler in the sand castle, and it was refreshing to be sheltered from the glare of an angry sun.

The floor was covered with ornate Arabian rugs, and around the cylindrical walls of the home were thick wool blankets that been folded and stacked four high so that you could sit in relative comfort off the hard surface of the clay floor.

Uneducated my ass!

The negotiations continued until late in the afternoon, but in the end I got exactly what I wanted. I was to pay the gypsy's family $50,000 U.S. for fifty-five units of assorted bracelets, earrings, necklaces, and anklets.

I didn't care how many of each as long as the total pieces of jewelry equaled fifty-five. The merchant father had the audacity to suggest a pair of earrings equaled two units. The nerve! I would only pay the gypsy family. I didn't give a damn about the tribal leader, and I was not to be extorted. I was pushed to the very edge of my patience before all parties agreed to the terms of contract.

The fifty-five units would be introduced exclusively for my "Desert Tribal Collection" and the price tag on the smallest piece would be no less than $15K.

On the walk back to the souk I was giddy. I could barely keep up my end of the conversation. We dined under the tent and watched the sun fall behind the terrain. Anahita offered to drop me off at the hotel and I declined. I was feeling pleasantly intoxicated, not by drink but from the deal that had been made in the desert, and I did not want it shocked out of my system by traveling at breakneck speeds.

I lingered in the city, taking in all the sites, enjoying the music played at cafés and laughing at tourists, but as I got closer to my hotel I started to feel nervous and watched. I hadn't slept well since arriving in Morocco, and that had been almost two days ago. I was so tired I was slipping towards delirium, and this heightened sense of emotional distress threatened to plunge me into a full-fledged state of panic and paranoia.

I tried to gain control of my outgoing thoughts, tried to fill my mind with diversion, but fear shoved reason aside, and I couldn't remember my last guarded thought.

I stood across the street from my five-star hotel. I could see the window of my room from where I was standing. The shades were still open and the light was still on. People were milling around at the lazy tempo of the locals. Nothing was out of the ordinary.

I crossed the street, entered the elevator, and waited for what seemed an eternity as I was pulled to the twelfth floor. I stepped out of the elevator, froze, and held my breath. Nothing out of the ordinary. I walked down the hall and made a right hand turn. No one was waiting for me in the hall. I quickly glanced over my shoulder ... nothing. I started to feel light headed and then realized that I'd still been holding my breath. I allowed myself to breathe as I walked past seven doors to my own, glancing over my shoulder and jumping at every little sound. I stood in front of my door.

It was closed and locked, nothing out of the ordinary. I inserted my key, released the lock, and stepped inside, just a door's length over the threshold. I quickly scanned my room. Everything was as I had left it. I hurriedly shut and locked the door behind me, turned off the light and drew the shades.

In the darkness I was able to regain my calmness, sensing that I was alone. I turned on the bedside lamp, and immediately felt dizzy and nauseous. On my pillow was not chocolate, but a bloody glass bangle wrapped in torn silks the color of the setting sun. The protective barrier I had draped over my mind broke like levees as I realized my mistake. I don't know how long I sat staring at that bracelet, only a half of inch away from my own disaster.

Slowly and methodically I began to re-patch and don my tattered cloak.

I wasn't scheduled to leave until the next afternoon, but after making a few calls I knew my plane would be ready by the time I got to the airport. I washed the blood and skin off the bracelet and was still distracted by its beauty, even after all this.

I packed the bloodstained pillow and the gypsy girl's torn clothing with my belongings and put the glass bracelet on my left wrist, where it softly banged against my diamond Rolex.

Then I called for the porter to come and get my luggage. I threw my backpack over one shoulder and went down to the lobby to meet my driver.

XIV

Adam was in shock. He was mentally and physically exhausted, and slightly traumatized from the sheer violence stemming from the night's events. He cried so hard, once he was safely in the car, that he was having trouble drawing breaths.

Inanna cast a light-sleeping spell to calm and regulate Adam's breathing. For all the things in the occult that Inanna had submerged herself in, she found that at the end of the day nothing was more beneficial than a good night's sleep.

When Inanna returned home Adam was still sleeping, exactly as she had intended. She carried Adam into her home and walked through the living room, with its heavily-carved wood furnishings and African and Haitian artifacts, down the hallway with which the walls were adorned with tribal masks and into the room reserved for sacrifices and rituals. She placed him gently on the floor.

Inanna pierced Adam's skin to draw blood and did the same to herself. She sealed the boys wound with the wound of her own, mingling his blood with hers and bonding them together forever.

She poured the drops of blood into a bowl and added talcum powder, gunpowder and chalk. Inanna mixed these ingredients and added a few others before she used what was in the bowl to draw a large pentagram in the center of her black lacquered floor. In another bowl she used a different set of elements to create a powdery substance. Inanna used this second mix to draw a veve in the center of the pentagram.

Inanna selected several botanicals, for the hidden properties they possessed, and blended these ingredients into a third bowl.

She enhanced this concoction with some essential oils then added warm water.

Inanna removed Adam's clothing and used the infused warm water to remove the dirt and blood from his body. As she gave Adam this sacramental bath, Inanna deepened the sleeping spell. She did not want Adam to wake during this ritual.

She carried Adam and placed him on top of the veve. Inanna set ablaze incense on the western and eastern points of the pentagram.

Inanna stepped outside the pentagram and traced it with the protection of a circle of salt. She sat within the space of the circle and 5-pointed star and placed beside her a black candle, a lighter, and an ink pen.

As the scented smoke began to whirl around the both of them Inanna began to chant within its mist. The smoke of the incense intertwined between the pentagram and the veve, and formed a vaporous portcullis that floated over Adam in a different plane.

"Hear me knights of past, knights of the ancient law," commanded Inanna. "whose blades and axes caused rivers and seas of blood. Hear me knights of lost souls. This night I invoke you."

From the depths of below she conjured five souls, the most powerful warlocks that the earth had ever known.

Kibuka Mombo – an African Juju so viscous, so vile, that his days on earth were covered in darkness. Because he was just as brutal and had the same name, he was often mistaken for the god of war.

Lung Pao – a Japanese Shaman who ruled the blue emperor, whom he kept on the ends of puppet strings. Under his advisement the ground thundered with the march of armies and the earth was scorched with the flames of warfare.

Erryk Sjoestedt – the son of a priest, who served the Viking gods. He arrived wearing molten armor, white-hot from the flames of the inferno. He had learned his father's magic then used it on the battlefield to become the cruelest general in military history.

Ixquimilli – An American Indian medicine man known as Chief Black Cloud. He was feared and appeased like a god because he came bearing the gifts of pestilence and death.

Sayyed Nasseem– a Mesopotamian wizard who assembled armies on the shores of both the Tigris and the Euphrates, controlled thunder and lighting, and meddled in the affairs of the gods.

Once Inanna assembled the warlocks, Inanna called forth five others.

"Hear me lieutenants of Satan, soldiers of the demonic law. I command thee Officers of Hell to make thy most evil appearance. Hear me warriors of anarchy, darkness and chaos. Hear me fallen angels, I summon thee, ye Apostles of Satan. I invoke you, thee commanders of mayhem and havoc."

"This night I invoke you. I order you by the beauty of my skin, by the beating of my heart, through the breath from my lungs, through the flow of my blood and the memory of my mother, to be here for my will and pleasure until my bidding is done."

"Lord Satan, by your grace, grant me I pray thee, the power of the ones I call before me and to execute that which I desire to do, the end which I would attain by thy help, O Mighty Satan.

From the depths further still monsters answered Inanna's call to arms.

Beelzebub – Lucifer's first lieutenant, Prince of Demons and the demon of pride.

Leviathan – next to Beelzebub, Lucifer's chief ally; the Grand Admiral of Hell, he is said to have seduced both Eve and Adam.

Baal – Commanding General of the infernal armies. He arrived on a chariot of fire pulled by thirteen tormented souls whose physical forms had long ago been disfigured beyond description. They were shrouded in flames and screaming in silence.

Amduscias – The Grand Duke of Hell, commanding thirty-six legions of devils, answered Inanna's call riding the back of Cerberus. Like that of a dragon Amduscias' breath was flame and smoke.

Leonard – Inspector General of Black Magic and Sorcery, the great Negro of the witches' sabot. He appeared as a giant black goat.

"In the name of my mother, in the names of my Masters the Angel of Chaos and his brother the Angel of Death, and in the name of me Inanna VeVe I bind you to the five corners of this pentagram in the order of rank until my bidding is done."

The gate to the portcullis lifted and the warlocks and demons spilled out in a wave of fire and smoke and took their respective places, hovering over the points of the pentagram.

The first time Inanna had called upon a fiend she had beckoned only one, and she had paid dearly. Tonight she mustered ten, and the high-ranking members of the "Southern Army" we're furious at being summoned and then bound.

The sadistic sorcerers were equally displeased and just as dangerous, and they glared at Inanna with lustful, vengeful eyes. All parties were angry, rebellious, and extremely treacherous. Any one of those she had summoned, if unbound, would attack and kill her. What she had done was exceptionally dangerous, and Inanna understood she was in grave peril.

Inanna spoke to the warlocks, "By your blade and axe I have invoked you. By your might I have invoked you. By your spirit I have invoked you. Now you will follow a new cause for which I have summoned thee. Hear me witch-kings of lost knights, now that you are at my aid and by my side; Cloak my child and hide his powers.

"Protect him from all clans of warlocks, from all covens of witches, from all channelers, from all mediums, from all oracles, from all psychics, from all mystics, and from all bases of power and families of magic, so that they will know not of the birth of this boy or the greatness of his strengths. I have invoked you. I have invoked you. Protect my child, protect my child, protect, and cloak my child … I command you."

With a clash of sword and axe the witch warriors entered the realm of the veve as if it were a battlefield. The ferociousness of the fighting increased with each hour that passed, until Adam was shrouded under the protection of the cloak.

Then Inanna spoke to the demons, "Hear me Masters of Hell. I have summoned thee to my aid and bidding for the protection of my child.

"In the name of Lucifer, I command thee, Great Ones of Darkness, to bestow the blessings of protection, strength, power and victory upon this child, my child Adam Veve. Hear me Lords of His Satanic Majesty. I command you that you must do my bidding and bequeath a protection and power spell over my child so that no harm shall ever come to him ... ever.

"Beelzebub, Leviathan, Baal, Amduscias, and Leonard, I command you give Adam Veve the gift of power of strength to move the heavens and earth, to command and control the air, and the use of the fires that swell and burn within me, bestow upon him the strength and knowledge to move bodies of water to reshape the earth. Masters of darkness I command that my will be done so that my child may learn the ways of the infernal and become a master agent of darkness."

The spell to provide Adam with demonic protection and power requested took nine nights to cast and was completed on the first full moon of the month."

"Your bidding has been done," spat Kibuka "Now release us."

"My bidding has not been done," sang Inanna.

"What else do you want?" demanded Erryk. His breath rolled from his lungs in puffs of black smoke.

"My will has not been done." Picking up the black candle and the pen, Inanna stood and began to dance. There was once a woman whose sensual dance was so powerful that as payment she received the head of a man on a silver platter. If any mortal were to see the dance of Inanna she would have been offered kingdoms. In the sensual throes of her dance Inanna sung and carved the names of those present in the soft wax of the candle.

"Stupid bitch, release me!" roared Kibuka.

"My name is Inanna Veve, and I shall not, for my bidding is not done." Inanna had made two nearly mortal mistakes when she first conjured a demon from the pit of flames. The first was that she did not bind him, and the second mistake that had almost killed her was the fact that she had released him. Tonight she planned to do neither.

Both demon and witch king alike knew what was about to happen but could do nothing, because they were still bound, and Inanna was strong and moved quickly. When Inanna carved the last name into the candle she lit it and cast her spell, which had to be repeated ten times.

"Come ye, as the charm is made! Queen of heaven, queen of hell, horned hunter of the night. Lend your power unto the spell and work our magic by rite. By all the power of land and sea, by all the might of moon, I call upon the Earth to bind my spell, air to speed it well. Bright as fire shall it glow, deep as tides of water flow.

"By air and earth, by water and fire, so be you Kibuka Mombo bound as I desire. By three and nine your power I bind and shall now be mine evermore. By moon and sun, and sky and sea keep harm from my young one and me, my bidding is not done."

Inanna held up her necklace to let the light of the candle bounce off the large ruby that dangled on a black velvet rope that was tied around her neck. "If harm shall come to me and my child, hold his limbs and stop his mouth, seal his eyes and choke his breath, wrap him round with ropes of death."

With nine spells remaining to cast Beelzebub laughed. The sound of his mirth would have burst the eardrums of man. "Very clever witch," commented Beelzebub "But the day shall come, Witch Queen, when you join us below, and there will be no end to your suffering."

"So it shall, but not now, for my bidding is not done. Return now all of you to your kingdom from which you have come, and I will summon you again when the time comes."

The war party departed in a riotous state. Their fury was uncontainable and their pride wounded by the fact they had been outsmarted and bound forever by an earth witch. The arrogance!

She had done it. Once those who had been called were gone, Inanna went to her and thanked those she worshiped, for her safety.

After prayer and meditation she wrapped Adam in a white sheet and took him to her bedroom, where she put him in the center of the bed. Then Inanna removed the sleeping spell so that he might wake naturally.

There was a phone on the nightstand but Inanna left the room to use the one in the kitchen so that she wouldn't disturb Adam while he was sleeping.

Inanna placed a call to the man who had first helped her to flourish. The warlock did not have many days remaining on earth, and this frustrated her because there was nothing she could do to prevent his expiration.

He was the only person on the face of the earth who knew her potential and encouraged it. The wizard was still a great master, and after all this time there were still many things she could learn. She knew that when he left the earth, she would miss talking with him, would miss his instruction. Now that she had sole custody of a baby wizard, this baby wizard that science had created with unknown potentials, Inanna found that she needed the instruction of Myrddin once again.

After an hour of conversation with her first instructor and all the arrangements made for the wizard's arrival, Inanna returned to her room. After ensuring Adam was tucked in, she fell asleep on the chaise next to the large window overlooking the marina.

XV

Logan is a descendant of a woman who was burned at the stake during the reign of terror in one of many dark periods of American history. If Logan had been alive during those fanatical times in the American colonies, she too, would have been burned.

The gorgeous girl with long flowing red hair, fair skin, blue eyes looked as if she'd been plucked from a Norse epic. Her natural abilities in clairvoyance were made stronger by Dr. Astor's manipulations. At nineteen, Logan was the strongest oracle Dr. Astor had ever encountered, and she was the very person he called upon in regards to the disappearance of Adam. Ernesto gently placed the electrodes on various points on Logan's body, while she sat on a heap of pillows on the floor in the yoga position of the lotus.

Logan located her center through meditation and allowed herself to enter a trance-like state. She was staring down at Adam's Teddy, which she was holding with both hands in her lap. As Logan's state of meditation deepened, her breathing slowed, and she closed her eyes.

"Tell me what you see," Dr. Astor prodded.

"Dr. Cassidy," answered Logan.

Dr. Astor and Ernesto looked at each other, and Ernesto took a step away from Dr. Astor as he registered the fury Dr. Astor wore on his face like a mask.

"Dominick LaShan," Logan continued. Dr. Astor shot a questioning glance at his assistant. Ernesto nodded his head and would later recount as best he could, the things he had read in the paper and seen on the news on the topic of Mr. LaShan.

Logan was shaking now, and Dr. Astor felt compelled to wake her, but before he could the girl spoke again.

"Gunshots." Logan started to rock swiftly back and forth "Dominick is running ... He's carrying Adam." Then she cried out, in Adam's small voice, "'I want my mommy! I want to go home. ... It's Blake." Her voice continued, "... an explosion of blood. Adam is running alone."

Logan looked up just as Adam had looked up at the sky. "Gemini," she whispered. And then in Adam's voice she shouted, "Astar!"

Dr. Astor bit down on his fist to keep from screaming. For the first time in his life he understood what it felt like for the human heart to break.

"Mommy, Esto, Astar, where are you?" Logan cried just as Adam had cried. As both men listened breathless to Logan's account, she continued. "A mountain lion, a mountain lion, a mountain lion!" Logan fainted.

"No!" Ernesto fell to his knees, overcome with grief and guilt that he hadn't been there when Adam so desperately needed him.

Dr. Astor wept as well, "Dr. *Astor*, Master Adam, Dr. Astor."

XVI

Dr. Astor entered my office without knocking, which is something he did all the time. "The time for the destruction of Dr. Cassidy has arrived."

"Has it?"

"Yes, I'm afraid it has come to that."

"Let me see it," I said as I opened the bottom left drawer of my desk. Dr. Astor handed me a writ that bore, in cooling wax, the crests of all twenty founding members of The Skyward Group … all the members of Skyward but me. When a decision is to be made that will affect our group, whether for good or not, it requires the seal of all twenty-one members. There is no veto or superseding of this rule. It requires all twenty-one.

I removed a jewel-encrusted golden box, lifted its lid, and retrieved from its velvet interior, a brass plate, which held the relief of my emblem. I picked up the heavily scented candle that was burning in a bohemian crystal candleholder on my desk and tilted it to spill several drops of spiced wax onto the parchment. Then I added my heraldic seal – Dr. Cassidy was to be destroyed.

Dr. Astor stood where he was for a few moments, then went to the wet-bar and helped himself to a glass of cognac from a bottle that cost $4,000. Glass in hand, he walked to the other side of my office and took a seat in the suede chair near the large gas fireplace.

"Do you wish to know the reasons?"

"No. I don't."

Since the loss of Dr. Hogue and the immediate disappearance of Adam following his death, I hadn't been myself.

I was reckless in my studies and my temper was short and violent. People withdrew from me as if I was a coiling venomous snake.

Normally I scrutinized the details of writs, checking the details on something as simple as a new equipment purchase or as routine as background investigations on a prospective doctor or his attendants, most times taking months to add my authorization. The writ to promote Dr. Hogue had taken three months before it carried the weight my crest, despite it was at my suggestion that he be promoted. This writ hadn't even been read, and it was to take a man's life. When I opened my drawer to grant Dr. Astor what he had came for, he couldn't restrain the look of alarm on his face. He sat by the hearth sipping his drink and gently petting Jack, who was sleeping in the other armchair.

"Do you wish to know as to the reasons why?"

"Can you find him? Please use a seer and find out where he is."

"It's already been done. Dr. Cassidy released the care of Adam to members of an organized crime enterprise. Artemisia, Adam is gone."

With a scream, I stood and threw a heavy flower vase onto the floor, sending shards of crystal, water and mangled narcissus and jonquils everywhere. I swept everything from my desk, then I overturned it.

I slipped in the water and fell on a piece of crystal that cut deep into my shoulder. I lay there and cried as Jack, Dr. Astor, and Dr. Anderson, who came from out of nowhere, were at my side to comfort me.

Dr. Anderson gave me a mild sedative and removed the glass that was embedded in my shoulder. It had broken into two pieces, and he prepped the area for sutures.

As Dr. Anderson was closing my wound, Dr. Astor called for my driver because the effects of the sedative were starting to show.

When I woke my desk was again upright and everything had been picked up from the floor, Jack was in my lap gazing worriedly down at me, and as always Ken was there.

"I want you to tell me what happened." I noticed my words were slurred as I struggled to sit up.

"Mr. Dominick LaShan, also known as Nicky, is Dr. Cassidy's cousin. Mr. LaShan seems to have a talent for making people disappear. He has had several mistrials due to lack of physical evidence and rumors of jury tampering.

"He took Adam into the woods just north of the city but then apparently changed his mind. There was an uprising within his party, which left all but Mr. LaShan dead.

"Mr. LaShan tried to protect Adam, but our dear boy was terribly frightened, and he ran from Mr. LaShan's protection. Adam ran into the path of a mountain lion."

"How will Dr. Cassidy die?"

"He will be injected with one of Dr. Hogue's viruses, then sealed away in a research chamber below."

That was the first time since the disappearance of Adam that I can remember laughing. I wondered if Dr. Cassidy would appreciate the irony. "There's something wrong with you," I told Dr. Astor.

"You're the one who's laughing."

And at that, I laughed more. "One must never

underestimate the healing power of revenge."

With a smile of his own Dr. Astor simply stated "Touché."

XVII

dam woke up screaming. Inanna woke up slowly. It was four in the morning, and she was still exhausted from the night's rituals.

Inanna tried to calm Adam, and though he stopped screaming he did not stop trembling. Inanna did not cast another sleeping spell because she wanted Adam to cry through it, though she didn't know what it was he was crying through.

The entire day Adam drifted-in and screamed-out of sleep, then was calmed to the point of softly weeping, before drifting back to sleep. He wouldn't eat or drink anything. His voice weakened and Adam became exhausted.

When the sun began to set Adam crawled underneath Inanna's bed and fell asleep. Inanna placed his head on a pillow and covered him up. She left him there under her bed, because it seemed like Adam had found a place of refuge.

When Inanna was certain Adam was sleep she returned to her ritual room to cast another spell. It was time for her to find out why a four-year-old child was running through the woods in the middle of the night, and how such a child had obtained the abilities to kill someone by just thinking it.

When the queen in the tale of Snow White demanded that her mirror to tell her about her vanity, she was using a technique known in the world of magic as scrying. It is a way of supernaturally seeing things or events, past or present. Some oracles use crystal balls; others use pools of ink, or even the liver from an animal, however like Queen Grimhilde, Inanna used a magic mirror.

But unlike the vain queen, who requested affirmations of her beauty, Inanna, sitting at her altar, requested visions of Adam.

Inanna gathered the required items and arranged them according to ancient law, then began to pray.

"In my great name, Inanna Veve, I demand that all things in darkness bestow their powers of prophesy upon this mirror, that I may use this magical medium to contact any demon or otherwise as I see fit, to scry upon the past and present for the revelation of secrets, and of knowledge that is unknown to me." Inanna was silent for a moment as she gazed into her mirror. After a few moments more Inanna resumed her request.

"In the name of my mother, I petition the Priestess of the oracle of Delphi, the Pythia, to bestow upon me the blessings of prophesy and all the powers related thereof upon this mirror. All of this I demand in my own name, Inanna Veve, times nine and three."

Inanna gazed into her mirror as she lit a candle. Once the candle started slowly burning, Inanna gazed into its flame.

"Candle flames, fire flame, on shifting sands and unforgotten sorrows, reveal to me what is left unknown. Adam Veve, this I must see to understand why this child was brought to me. Beings, who see, beings who say, aid me in this dark task I pray. From the corner of her eye Inanna noticed vapors forming in her mirror, and she leisurely turned her gaze from the flame to peer into the glass.

When the smoke gradually parted, the mirror revealed a mature woman of sensual beauty. The oracle had skin the color of cream with freckles splashed across her nose and cheeks, under chocolate-colored eyes. Her thick, red hair reached her waist and her head was crowned with a golden wreath. The oracle wore a flowing white dress of silk as sheer as gossamer, which flowed past her ankles. Strings of gold crisscrossed around her waist, and on her arm she wore a gold bracelet depicting a griffin. The oracle's long hair and garments blew around her as if she were standing on the bow of a swiftly moving ship.

"Mortal Goddess Inanna, I have heard your call and am here to provide you with the answers you seek."

"Priestess Pythia, servant of the Great Goddess Gaia, I bow to you in gratitude for granting me the answers I seek."

Four hours later Inanna knew the entire history of her son, from the men who had created him, to the woman who tried to save him, from the majestic owl that Adam believed to be a monster, to the mountain lion that had chased him into the path of her speeding car. She also learned of a young oracle who was not strong or skilled enough, and too emotionally involved, to see her visions through.

Logan was an oracle that Inanna paid special attention to, both while she was being shown her vision and again when she wrote the findings of her vision in her journal. For Logan was a direct descendant of the great witch Abigail. Inanna wanted to ensure that neither Logan nor her ancestry would become a problem.

After studying the notes she took from her vision, Inanna realized that the things that had terrorized Adam the most were the mountain lion, and his isolation. She also learned that when he ran into the street, Adam was actually trying to find Dominick.

Inanna went to check on Adam. He was still under the bed, and his tiny protector hissed at her. Inanna shooed the small cat away so that she could once again cover Adam with the warm, down blanket that he had tossed off in the throes of his nightmare.

Inanna went into the kitchen and made herself a cup of steaming tea. She ate a small meal to help speed the recovery of her vision quest. Checking on Adam once more, Inanna returned to her ritual room. In the final spell of the night Inanna sent Adam a series of dreams.

In the first dream Adam burst from the forest like he had on the night she had found him, but in the dream version, Inanna was sitting on the hood of her car calmly waiting for Adam. When the big cat burst through after Adam, Inanna thundered, "Stop! Now bow to your new king." When the wild feline did what it was told, Adam stood between them astonished, looking back and forth between the beast and this woman who was sitting on top of her car.

In dream two, Adam was on the narrow footpath where he had first encountered the owl. At first he was scared, but then he felt someone holding his hand. When Adam looked up, Inanna was with him. She looked lovingly down at him then looked at the great bird.

"This is your new king," Inanna told the bird.

"Hoo? Hoo?" questioned the owl.

"Adam Veve, your new king."

The bird slowly looked from Inanna to Adam, then swooped down off the branch and stood at Adam's small feet. There were four other dreams, three involving the puma and the last one of the owl. In each of them, Inanna instilled courage and sent a message that conveyed power and safety.

When Inanna finished her entries in her spell book and returned to her room, she found Adam still sleeping. Inanna sat in the chaise and looked out onto the harbor until she finally joined Adam in the realm of Hypnos.

When Inanna awoke she found Adam peeking at her from under the sheets draped across her bed, his large green eyes staring at her in wonder. She was amazed at how the color of his eyes where the very same as the Captain's. For a few moments they just looked at each other.

It was Inanna, who spoke first, "Morning honey, ya hungry?"

Adam nodded his head yes but made no attempt to retreat back to the safety of under the bed. He made no attempt to leave it either.

"OK, then Love. You can stay under there as long as you like. Gimme a minute and I'll whip up breakfast."

A half hour later Inanna returned carrying a plate of fried bananas topped with honey, sweet cream and nuts sitting on a bed of Haitian French toast.

Adam ate every morsel underneath the bed. Inanna didn't mind. She was happy that he was eating. Adam allowed Inanna to give him a warm, scented bath and then she returned him to his sanctuary under her large bed.

Myrddin arrived two days later, and after seeing the boy for the first time he suggested that Adam should be wearing a charm of protection.

XVIII

nanna knew exactly who she was looking for from the minute she stepped through the doors.

What pleased her most was the absence of sales representatives. The clientele here didn't waste time speaking to middlemen posing as customer service agents. No, each patron spoke directly to a jeweler, thus giving the customer a greater deal of control over their custom designs, from conception to completion.

Inanna knew who the jewelers were, and how beloved they were just by how many people they had gathered around them; but this jeweler seemed to have reached rock star status. Most of the people there where politely waiting to work with him – and those who couldn't wait clustered around him like groupies.

Inanna was handed a hot cup of strong coffee that she hadn't had to ask for, and she smiled as she took a seat, crossed her long, sexy legs and surveyed her surroundings.

The man she was waiting for wore large-framed sunglasses with purple rhinestones, despite the fact that it was dark and raining outside. She knew his mental state had not been chemically altared in any way. The only thing this man was high on was the attention.

He wore his jeans so tight Inanna wondered how he was able to breathe. His high-collar purple silk shirt was open to display a necklace weighed down by a large amethyst gem, and for reasons God only knew he was walking around in yellow fuzzy slippers.

By the time Inanna's jeweler came to sit next to her, an hour had passed and his sunglasses had been pushed up to rest on the top of his head like a crown.

"Hi, I'm Allen. I am so very sorry it took this long to see

to you, but I will forever be in your debt for your gracious, uncomplaining endurance."

His smile was as dazzling as his rhinestones. Confidence rolled off him like waves from the sea, and Inanna liked his flair for the dramatic. Allen's smile dimmed a bit as Inanna handed him her drawings.

"I have my own metal, but I need you to make the castings. When can I come pick them up?"

As Allen studied the sketched replicas of her veve and Myrddin's staff, his face wore a mask of concentration. "Do you mind if I ask what metal will be used?" Allen didn't look at Inanna as he spoke; he was tracing the outline of the veve with is finger.

"I'll be using gold for the large medallion and iron for the staff."

"Elements then, not alloy's … Hmmm." Inanna realized that Allen wasn't aware that he had spoken out loud. He was just vocalizing his internal thoughts. Inanna was impressed and pleased by Allen's observation. Allen studied Inanna's drawing for fifteen minutes before looking up from the sketch and back at her again.

"Do you think you can come back on Wednesday?" Inanna smiled and stood, then left the Atomic Weight 196 jewelry store without saying a word.

Inanna returned on Saturday. When she arrived Allen was prepared. He led her into his office so that they could speak in private. Inanna was surprised to find his office was not heavily adorned or jeweled. It was, in fact, quite the opposite.

The black and white photography that hung in Allen's

office illustrated blue-collar workers performing backbreaking work. Each photograph hung within a thick, black wooden frame. The camera had captured men whose faces were grey from dirt and sweat, had captured men pouring white-hot steel in foundries, had captured sparks and blue arcs created by the tips of welding guns and cutting torches.

But the most startling photograph portrayed the desperate look of men of various ethnicities, huddled together in a wire cage being lowered down a mining shaft. They were all looking up into the heavens, as if trying to memorize the warmth of the sun in case they should never see it again.

Allen's desk was a meticulously handcrafted antique Winslow writing desk from the early 1900s, carved from a single piece of mahogany. Inanna was invited to sit in a large, vintage, leather chair that allowed her to sit directly across from Allen, and enjoy the view of the park behind him that was framed by the large window. Allen then took his place on the other side of the desk; the only sheet of paper on Allen's desk was the sketch that Inanna had given to him the Thursday before. Allen was nervous, so he took a deep breath to steady himself before he started speaking.

"I know everything there is to know about metals. My father worked in a foundry, and later I worked alongside him, to pay my way through college. I earned my bachelors in Metallurgical and Materials Engineering from the University of Texas.

"I know a little bit about magic. My mom is a Wiccan, and I was always underfoot so I recognized that these symbols were sacred drawings. But I did not know they were powerful signs of protection until I showed them to my mom.

"But, for some reason, I think you know that. I don't think you picked me at random. I am very afraid of you, but not so afraid to be stupid enough not to create this medallion. Besides I don't think anyone else can do it but me."

Once again Inanna was impressed with Allen. Inanna's smile did nothing to sooth Allen's jittery nerves as she spoke.

"You need to tread lightly. There's a reason that pride is one of the seven. You're absolutely right. I didn't walk into this store by mere happenstance. I found you, and I had been looking for you for quite some time. And I agree with you. You, who are born of a witch and a master of metals, are the only person who can create this charm of protection. Now tell me what you had in mind."

Allen took a few moments to steady himself. With a shaky hand, he lifted a glass of water to his lips and took a sip. Then he took a few deep breaths before answering Inanna's question. "You said you wanted to use gold and iron, right? Have you ever heard of 'Grey Gold'?" He felt more confident now that he was back in the realm of his expertise. Inanna raised an eyebrow.

"Grey gold is gold that has been alloyed with about 15 to 20% of iron. When used in spells, both gold and iron alone are very powerful elements of protection, but if we cast them together it will combine their powers and strengthen the spell. Because there will be more than 75% of gold in this medallion it will still earn a classification of 18Kt. However people will not recognize its value because the finished product will look like industrial metal. Like something you would find on an engine, like brushed steel but not as dark. It will have a pale gray appearance, like the color of the moon."

Inanna was intrigued, "Tell me more."

"Well gray gold does have some disadvantages over normal carat gold alloys. For one, it will be a little brittle. It could be cracked with a sharp blow from a hammer. And another thing to think about is the production cost of a single piece orders. This makes it not so attractive financially."

Inanna was nodding her head, "Do you know anything about the ritual properties of color, Allen?" Allen shook his head, indicating that he didn't.

"The magical properties of the color gray are a powerful neutral. It acts as a liaison between the dark and the light. No matter the cost, I want this done."

"Here's the thing …" Allen was on the verge of collapse, because he was about to leave his comfort zone of metals and cross over to the realm of magic. " This is a very complex and competitive process. I hold the patent, and I will not tell you how to do it, so the mixing of the iron and gold must be done here. … That means your spell has to be cast here as well. You need to know that my mom will fortify this place with protection spells of her own."

Inanna laughed out loud at that. "A mother's love has no bounds! Nicely done, Allen. The spell will be cast here, but you will follow my instructions to a tee. If you don't your fate will be worse than that of Lot's wife."

As Inanna stood to leave the color returned to Allen's face, "Just one more thing…." Allen couldn't quite believe that he had just spoken so boldly to someone clearly very powerful. His mother had warned him to be very careful and he was about to be anything but.

Allen stood, because looking up at Inanna from a seated position made him feel vulnerable, but as he stood he realized it was not her physical size that left him feeling unprotected, it was the sheer presence of her power.

"Is this amulet for a male or female?"

"It will be worn by my son."

"And his birth sign?"

"Gemini."

They stood there for a moment with nothing but silence between them. Inanna remained patient because she knew Allen had more to say and was just trying to find the courage to do so.

Inanna really like Allen and knew he would follow her instructions to the letter. The warning from his mother had caused Allen to lose sleep, but the warning Inanna had just issued had the same effect as an epicenter that decides to make itself known in the middle of a large, towering, heavily populated city. Allen had been looking down at his feet and doing breathing exercises to calm himself. Finally, he looked up and into Inanna large green eyes and made his final request.

"May I please be allowed to remember? My mother told me to be extremely careful because she says you are very dangerous. But she is also very proud that you picked me. She's always saying that there has to be a balance, and she said that you chose me because I am a child of the light." Allen's face flushed as he realized he may have misspoken. He quickly added, "Not that I am saying you're a wicked witch or anything like that. My mom neither."

Inanna's smile widened and Allen just stammered on, "My mom says you simply cannot have one without the other. I guess kinda the way you were describing the power of the color gray. This piece will be the blending of the two."

Terrified at this point, he found the strength to continue. "My mom says that I am very capable to do what you are requesting, and I know that she's right. I know that I can do it."

Allen was speaking so swiftly in pleading his request that Inanna noticed he had forgotten to breathe.

"I just want to have the privilege to remember. I promise I will follow your instructions, and I promise not to speak of it to anyone, 'cept of course my mom, and I promise not to put your talisman in my portfolio. I just want to remember that it was me who you chose above all. I want to remember, but I do not want to sell my soul or be harmed. Please don't turn me into a frog."

Inanna laughed. She enjoyed Allen and decided it would be from him that she would purchase her prized rubies, but she thought he had seen one too many Blaire Witch type of movies for his own good.

"This is a custom piece is it not?"

Confused Allen said that it was.

"Do you think that your mother's son and mine are the only two who should be wearing protective charms child? Of course this will go into your portfolio, and of course you will not speak about this to others. There are those, like yourself, who will know its meaning.

"Your silence will ensure that the reputation you receive is that you can be discrete and can be trusted with secrets. And you will seek your mother's counsel, for she will keep you safe when you cannot do so yourself.

"I will grant you your request. You shall not be harmed by me or mine and you shall remember. And, on another note, I would never turn anybody into a frog."

Without another word Inanna showed herself out. Allen crumpled into his leather chair, then turned in it to look out the window at the rain.

XIX

On the morning that the stars were in alignment with Gemini, Inanna took Myrddin with her to see Allen and make preparations for the night's ceremony. They remained in Allen's office until noon before emerging to announce that things were ready. After lunch Inanna returned to explain to Allen the rules of her instructions.

The cast that Allen created for Adam's amulet had Inanna's veve centered over Myrddin's diagonal staff, with the tip of the wizard's wand pointing in the northeastern direction and the butt of the rod facing the southwestern direction.

On the floor, Inanna had drawn in chalk the emblem that Allen had created. The diameter of her veve was four feet, and it was six feet from the butt of Myrddin's staff to its point.

Three feet away from the top of the floor drawing was Allen's desk, over which Inanna had draped a thick velvet cloth. Atop it were tools Allen would need. What wasn't small enough to fit on top was made available within reach. Three feet from the bottom of the floor drawing was an altar draped in the same rich fabric. This held the tools that Inanna and her father would be using for the night's rituals, currently hidden beneath another layer of textile.

With alarm, Allen noticed that Inanna had changed the location of his mother's protection charms. Inanna felt Allen's anxiety and explained why they had been moved.

"I do not want dueling magics. The sage rod is now resting in the center of your desk. See it? Your mother chose the sage plant for its protective properties but even more for its abilities to heighten psychic awareness and increase your capacity for learning and wisdom. The other herbs that your mother has placed about have been rearranged around and near your work station, to concentrate her powers of protection around its intended target, which is you. The vessel of pepper, however, has been completely removed, and will be returned to you once we are done."

Allen felt somewhat reassured that Inanna had moved the herbs to a more strategic place in his favor, but he did not understand enough of what Inanna often referred to as "Kitchen Witchery" to understand the significance of the pepper.

There was no witch alive that could challenge the might of Inanna, so the appointment of the pepper – which is used to drive out negative energy – was nothing more than a slight annoyance, but Inanna removed it and sent a searing headache to Allen's mother just for the spite of it. It wasn't life threatening, it was sent just to prove a point and was nothing that a chamomile-based spell or two Excedrin couldn't cure.

During the rehearsal Allen was given the instructions that he was to follow later that night, and after the trial run was complete Allen was told not to reenter the office without being escorted by Inanna herself, which Allen found easy enough to do.

Allen stayed an hour after the shop closed, joking with his friends and co-workers. He locked the doors and accompanied the group uptown for dinner, only to return three hours later, half an hour before the scheduled time of return because he did not want to keep Inanna and company waiting.

He looked up from the accounting books just in time to see Inanna in the security camera, as she pulled into a parking spot behind the store, normally designated for employees. Allen closed the books, left the accountant's office, and went to open and greet Inanna and Myrddin at the rear entrance.

Inanna carried a sleeping Adam in her arms and greeted Allen with a smile to match the brilliance of the stars, and a sense of calm washed over Allen. He stood outside his office door and allowed Myrddin to guide him through it.

Just as practiced, Myrddin took Allen's right arm and gently guided him, to stand in front of his desk. Thick black curtains hung at Allen's window to block out the light of the moon.

Allen opened his hand palm up as instructed and Myrddin handed him a pair of soft foam earplugs. Allen rolled the soft foam between his pointer finger and thumb, one at a time, then gently placed one earplug in each ear. Next he was handed a pair of cuffed, NASCAR-like earmuffs, which he placed over his ears, plunging him into the dark world of deafness.

Iron in its pure form is rare and is only found in meteorites. Allen reached into the pocket of his jeans to retrieve the three pure iron pebbles that had been given to his mother by hers when she was only a girl.

Allen placed these iron chips in a small but very powerful puddling furnace. As the iron began to soften Allen also added a medium-size ingot of 24Kt gold. Myrddin then placed a lavender-scented blindfold over Allen's eyes, knowing that the aromatherapy of the lavender would help Allen reach a state of calmness. Allen took a steadying breath and reached out to touch the desk, to counterbalance the disorienting effects of a lost equilibrium.

As Myrddin was assisting Allen with the binding of his senses Inanna had carefully laid Adam on a thick blue blanket of woven wool. With Adam draped under a sleeping spell and Allen's sight and hearing abilities temporarily restricted Inanna and Myrddin were ready to begin the ritual. Inanna poured botanical contents from a black glass bottle into a bowl made of lapis. With a very sharp needle she pierced the skin of her sleeping child and squeezed seven drops of blood into the bowl. Inanna pierced her own skin to draw seven drops of her blood;

next she raised the bowl to her lips and spit into seven times. She handed the bowl to Myrddin who repeated the steps of his pupil.

The bowl was placed on her altar, where the botanical and bodily ingredients were mixed thoroughly with the tip of Myrddin's staff, while the wizard and his daughter chanted in a language unknown to man.

Allen's blindfold was then removed, and Allen dropped a quarter-sized block of metal, which is associated with the sun sign Gemini into the molten liquid. The entire mixture of blood, botanicals; and the electrum that now contained 78% gold, 17% iron and 4% chrome was poured from Allen's puddling kiln into the clay pattern that would later yield the jeweled medallion of protection which Adam would wear until the day he drew his last breath.

Allen's work was precise and methodical as he finished the final and most important stages of this process. His concentration was so absolute that Allen never once considered breaking his oath to turn and look behind him to see what the source of the muted sounds he was hearing. Allen lost himself in his work; unaware of all else around him. It was a quarter to the hour when Allen looked up from his labor. The thick curtains had been removed, and Allen was startled to see that the moon had begun her descent.

He called out, twice just to be sure, and then slowly turned around. The only evidence that Inanna had ever been there were Allen's mother's charms of protection (including the ewer of pepper) and the cooling gray metal on the desk behind him.

196 isn't open for business on Sundays and Mondays, and Allen took full advantage of the solitude to work on the newest jewel that he had been granted permission to add to his portfolio. Both of those days Allen worked a full twelve hours, until at last the amulet was complete.

The finished medallion rested on a thin bed of shiny chrome and was secured in place with a chromed tracing of the outline on the front.

In the center of the cosmos wheel Allen embedded a pea-sized flawless ruby that looked like a flame in the window of a boiler. He had selected the ruby not because he had noticed that it was the only gem he had seen Inanna wearing, but for the gemstone's magical properties of protection.

Allen entrenched the power and boundary lines of Inanna's jeweled veve with the fire stone obsidian. Born of the volcano, it is another powerful jewel of protection. For the entire length of Myrddin's staff, Allen's choice was to encrust it with the stone not only known for its powers of protection, but also its mystical reputation to infuse its wearer with physical strength and courage – the diamond. The hilt of the staff blazed with yellow gold, as did the very tip of the wand. Those were the only places Allen embellished, leaving the rest of the rugged grey gold exposed, to underscore and add an exclamation point to the strength of the masculine.

Complete, the jewel of protection was strung onto a thick cord of braided black silk and placed in a velvet-lined box to wait delivery to the person who would wear it. Allen placed the box in the safe, locked the store doors behind him, and then went home to sleep.

When Inanna returned to pick up the necklace, she was astonished, so much so that she had to be helped into a chair, for fear she might fall. This was first time she could remember that she had been stunned into silence.

The pendant was far more beautiful than Inanna could have imaged, and she saw in Allen's face that her earlier cautionary warning was being ignored. At that moment, for however brief a time; Allen understood that this powerful witch was wrapped around the pinky finger of a jeweler's hand.

Inanna took the charm of protection home, and carefully placed it around Adam's little neck.

XX

Adam stayed under the bed for several weeks. He wouldn't talk and answered both Inanna and the Myrddin's questions with simple head nods.

To familiarize Adam to the sound of her voice and prep him for the dark lessons to come, Inanna read to Adam every day for hours. She read from the Book of Shadows, the Book of Hours, various spell books. Inanna also read from ancient texts: the Egyptian Book of the Dead, the Emerald Tablet, the Rubaiyat of Omar Khayyam and the Seven Evils.

It was during the reading of the second tablet of the Epic of Gilgamesh that Adam came from under the bed and sat in Inanna's lap. Adam laid his head against her breast and looked at the pages from which she was reading aloud.

Inanna had waited nearly two months for this moment and now that it had arrived, she was unsure what to do. Adam looked from the pages and up to Inanna, "What happens next?"

This was the first time he had spoken, and Inanna couldn't speak for fear of crying. The wizard entered Inanna's bedroom at the sound of Adam's small voice. He placed a hand on Inanna's arm and began reading aloud, from over her shoulder.

From the second tablet of the Epic things started to assume a scene of normalcy. Adam started calling the wizard "Grandee," a nickname Inanna chose to use as well.

Inanna was the perfect person to instill discipline within Adam. The first tantrum Adam threw resulted in Inanna's onyx and alabaster carving of the West African water goddess Yemoja being smashed into a thousand pieces.

"You little … Oh hell no! I ought to whoop yo' ass!"

Inanna cast a binding spell instead. Adam couldn't move or talk. This was the first time anyone had checked his behavior.

"Was you raised by wolves or white folks? What I'm gon guarantee is, you ain't gon be tearing up my shit ... not in my house." With every particle of the former figurine she swept into the dustpan, Inanna became angrier. Because Inanna spent so much time in New Orleans her English had developed a southern accent, and that accent was most prevalent when upset.

"Little ass Yankee bastard... Boy, ain't but four years old. When I say no, I mean no! You're not paying not nar bill in this house and you gon throw a fit? Oh honey I got news for ya ... you gon learn, I betcha that! You gon learn. Bad ass little boy, keep it up, you hear me?"

And learn he did. If Inanna so much as thought Adam was about to have a tantrum she would bind him or simply say, "Don't you make me."

Inanna gave Adam plenty of growing room to push and challenge, but because she was not afraid of Adam and because she could quickly control him; she was able to administer discipline when discipline was needed. Adam's tantrums were reduced to stomping of the feet and pouting, like normal children.

His placement test for kindergarten revealed there was no choice but to enroll Adam in The Institute for Advanced Learning, because he was too advanced for the "See Spot Run" curriculum. Adam read at the tenth grade level, and could read in several languages.

Inanna spoke many dialects of multiple languages and a game she and Adam played was called "Around the World." Out of the blue Inanna would begin speaking to Adam in another language. Adam would have to answer Inanna in the same language and tell her where in the world the language was spoken. It was a fast paced game in which several languages could be spoken within half an hour.

"Boy it's really hot today," Inanna would comment in Awadhi.

"I think an ice cream cone from Uttar Pradesh sure would be a good way to cool off," Adam would answer.

"I think this is the longest line I have ever stood in," Inanna impatiently noted in Min Chinese.

"If we were in Taiwan we would probably be too poor for coffee."

"No, no honey, we're too rich to ever be poor. I'd have a sweat shop," in Belarusian.

"What's a sweat shop? Do they have those in Belarus?"

"Maybe they do in Russia," answered Inanna in Dari.

"I wouldn't want to live in Pakistan. That's where Osama Bin Laden lives."

"What do you know about Osama bin Laden?" laughed Inanna in Farsi.

"He's a terrorist."

"A terrorist to some, is a revolutionist to others," Inanna cautioned in Xhosa.

"I don't know what a revolutionist is, but I wonder if they have those guys in Mozambique," speculated Adam.

"Mozambique is close." When Adam missed his mark Inanna would stay in that parlance. "This language is called

Xhosa, spoken by the Transkei peoples of South Africa. And yes they do have revolutionists in South Africa. One in particular goes by the name of Nelson ... Nelson Mandela. Let's go to the library and learn all about South Africa, the people who live there, and the apartheid." Dr. Astor had given Adam a large language base from which to draw, and if Inanna stumbled upon a language Adam did not know she would teach it to him.

Inanna hired a servant from her mother's homeland to help with the boy. The girl did not speak any English so Inanna spoke to her in Haitian. Adam picked up the language fairly quickly and was speaking more in Haitian than English. When people saw Inanna and Adam together speaking in that African-laced tongue, they assumed she was his mom. After all they both had green eyes, just a different shade.

Adam loved dinosaurs. He knew the scientific name for each, which period they had lived in, and which part of the world they were first discovered.

"The legend of the dragon," Adam theorized, "was most likely started by an ancient farmer, architect, or anyone else who was moving dirt around who happened to dig up the remains of the pterodactylu, (the pterodactyl) from the late Jurassic and Cretaceous periods, or the ptersauria (the pterosaur) from the late Triassic, Jurassic and the Cretaceous periods. Every civilization has dragon legends, because like today's birds, the pterodactyl was following migration patterns, and some died along the way. How else is a man that doesn't know anything about science supposed to explain something he probably couldn't even pronounce, besides by making up a story?"

Submerging Adam into science, multitudes of languages and world events was deliberate. For one to understand and master the occult, one must understand the universe, understand themselves, and understand world religions. For one to understand another's religion, one must understand another's customs, and what other way to truly understand another's customs than to speak and truly understand their language? Adam was a quick study under Inanna's skillful eye and Grandee's careful instruction. He had the ability to read in several languages at the tenth grade level before starting kindergarten because Adam was required to study all things occult.

Many books in Inanna's collection were no older than third editions, cracked, yellowed, and curled with thousands of years with age. The Grimoire of Armadel, a book that taught the new sorcerer how to conjure up angelic or demonic beings, was one of Adam's most beloved, and he read it over and over again. Some of its pages had to be carefully separated from one another due to the peanut butter and jelly or chocolate and whipped cream that bonded the pages together.

Adam was in the second grade when, with the teachings from the Grimoire, and to Inanna's absolute bewilderment, he conjured a fairy from some magical epic told in school.

"Mama, check this out."

"Why?" Questioned Inanna with a baffled frown, as she watched the fairy.

"I wanted to see what it looked like."

"You couldn't see the picture in the book?"

"It doesn't look the same."

Inanna took a deep, slow breath as the two of them watched the fairy flutter around the kitchen. The fairy was the same size as a large dragonfly, with blue-green shimmery wings and a body of soft blue. Neither of them could tell if it was a girl fairy or a boy one. This was the first time Adam had conjured a being without Inanna and Myrddin present at the ritual.

The first book Adam studied from and the one he returned to the most was The Key of Solomon, which is considered to be the backbone of ritual magic. The first ritual that was taught to Adam, after he learned to draw a pentagram and the veve, was the Lesser Banishing Ritual. Inanna and Myrddin ensured that Adam knew this rite by heart before they proceeded to the next lecture.

The Lesser ritual is the most important lesson a person who conjures spirits needs to know. Performed correctly The Lesser Banishing Ritual invokes the Almighty and protects the one executing it with the power of God and his archangels. Any spirits or demons conjured would be expelled in the presence of God. Standing in his own protective salt circle (it wasn't perfectly round but he had proudly did it all by himself) with Inanna behind him in a circle of her own on the right and Myrddin in a circle on the left, the first extra-dimensional horror that Adam called forth took the power and skill of both Inanna and Myrddin to control and return it.

Though Myrddin was impressed by Adam's boldness, Inanna was startled by it. Adam did not try to flee from the creature. He stood within his lopsided circle, stomped his little foot and shouted a binding spell that probably wouldn't have caught a cat. When his spell didn't work Adam ripped his talisman from his neck and thrust it toward the monster, unaware that behind him, his mother and the wizard were feverishly working magic and casting spells to contain the fiend.

Within a year Adam was able to conjure and control demons ranging from the annoying to the devastating.

"It's almost time for bed. Finish your hot chocolate and send it back."

"Okay, Mamma."

"And don't forget your Banishing spell."

Year after year Adam grew stronger, learned more of his mother's skill, advanced under Grandee's tutoring and learned to control what had always been his own.

In the eleventh grade Adam started to resemble the Greek depictions of Adonis. His dark curly hair framed his broad face, and his green eyes were like the Mediterranean Sea against his honey-tinted skin. Adam wrestled, was on the rowing team, and fenced, so his body was the very definition of Greco-Roman athleticism.

When Adam turned seventeen he started to learn to drive. For his birthday the year before he had asked for a Ferrari, but he was just as excited when a year a later he was handed the keys to a brand new Audi – loaded with extra safety features. Living in the middle of the city with excellent public transportation and a personal driver, there was never a rush for driving lessons. Inanna was surprised at how well Adam handled a car. On a lesson one day, Adam pointed out a classmate while they were waiting for the light to turn green.

"Mom, see him in the red shirt? That's Thomas, I like him." Then Adam honked the horn to get the boy's attention and waved. The light turned green.

It was actually a miracle that Inanna didn't spill scalding hot coffee all over her lap. She was looking at Adam with her mouth open.

"What happened to Amanda?"

"Nothing, I like her too. I really like her."

With her free hand Inanna began rubbing her temples. After taking another sip of the calming double shot of caffeine she suggested, "I think it's time you and I had a talk about safe sex and how to use a condom."

Adam burst into laughter that was like the sound of singing angels as he accelerated to merge onto the freeway, "Mom, I already know how." Inanna looked away from her boy and rummaged through her handbag for the Tylenol. Though he'd had his first sexual encounter only the year before, Adam took his pleasures from both girls and boys. Inanna chalked it up to experimentation.

He used his beauty the same way his mother did, to control and manipulate. However the weapon Adam chose for total domination was the compliment, for which there was no defense. His first victim had been Inanna, and though she was on to him, he got her every time. He practiced the compliment until he became a master in the poetic verse. Adam once brought a transient man who was covered in scabies to tears of gratitude as he rummaged though his pockets to give Adam the change he'd collected that day.

"Shameless ass," was all Inanna could say as she ignored Adam's triumphant smile. He had been only nine at the time.

One day while playing the game Around the World, Inanna called Adam "Papi," and Adam burst into tears.

"Baby, honey what happened? What did I say, Adam? What's wrong?"

Adam's tears scared Inanna. Adam had cried before, but there had been precursors, like when he and Inanna fought. Adam cried when Thomas, whose dad was an officer in the army, received orders that took their family to Germany, and he would cry again when his Grandee would die a year later.

One minute they were washing dishes, she washing, he drying and relentlessly teasing each other in the languages of the world. Then the next minute Adam was crushed with tears. It didn't make any sense.

Adam immediately put up a wall to shelter his thoughts and feelings. He wasn't answering Inanna's questions, and this was something he had never done before. They told each other everything. She could have cast a spell and made him tell her, but she decided to let him have some privacy.

Adam went to his room and slammed the door. Inanna finished the dishes, replaying the highlights of tonight's game to see what she had said so wrong. Hours later, when she went to look in on Adam as he was sleeping, something she did every night before her ritual prayers, she noticed with alarm that Adam was not sleeping well.

There were many nights after that, that Adam did not sleep well, and more than once Inanna had that uneasy feeling in the pit of her stomach, the same feeling she would get when she noticed a new expression on Adam's face, or when she caught him lost in thought. Lately Adam seemed distracted and unfocused, but he would always flash his gorgeous smile when he looked up and saw her.

She hoped it was due to the way his life was about to change. This would be his last year in high school, and he had already begun applying to several colleges.

Inanna decided that maybe Adam needed a vacation before starting his senior year. She thought that the soothing waters of the Mediterranean Sea would do the trick.

XXI

he first thing I did when I returned to The States was to pay a visit to the C.E.O. of our private security firm. Without going into too much detail I explained that I needed to employ accurate, unflinching, twenty-four-seven safety measures.

This C.E.O. was six feet four inches tall and had the appearance of a U.S. Army Special Forces commander out of uniform. No doubt the military was where this man had begun his career. He wore an Armani Black Label suit, with $10,000 platinum and diamond cuff links that I could have recognized with my eyes closed because I designed them. They had come from my "Well Dressed Man Collection." He complemented his attire with dark grey, alligator skin loafers. He smelled like a million bucks; nonetheless I could not place the masculine fragrance. And though he was handsomely dressed I could not shake the feeling that I was in the company of a very dangerous man.

We left his mahogany-laden office, and he led me down a lushly carpeted hallway, past dozens of expensively framed photographs of Navy Seals, Army Rangers, U.S. Marines, and his own army of private security operatives in various stages of action. The C.E.O. walked with the confident, leisurely pace of man who had legions of armies at his fingertips.

The conference room he led us to strived to be like that of his office. The framed art on the walls were images of the Military Code of Conduct, the Geneva Convention, the U.S. Constitution, the oath of the Boy Scouts, and the Pledge of Allegiance.

Through the intercom, the C.E.O. summoned a Sgt. Dale. The man who responded was also dressed in a suit, but his appeared to be from a chain store. He wore a pale blue shirt that was the same color as his eyes. He wore his shirt buttoned to the neck, however this did nothing to hide the tattoos on his neck and hands, which appeared to indicate an allegiance with street gangs, military squadrons, and prison blocks.

He even had a tattoo on the side of his face, from the temple to the jaw line, which added a deeper level of his already large menacing composure. The C.E.O. explained my request in the form of instructions.

Sgt. Dale left the room and returned with a large purebred, 110-pound, two-year-old Rottweiler and stated, "This is Sentinel, the security partner that you have requested. He will never faltar, he will never quit, and he will never fail. He will protect you with his very life."

The dog was beautiful and I was amazed at how large he was. Sgt. Dale held Sentinel on such a short leash that it seemed like Sentinel was standing on the tiptoes of his front paws. I must have had a momentary break from reality because I actually stepped forward, leaned down, and attempted to pet this animal that I would soon be taking home.

The dog began to growl, issuing a deep, low, dangerous warning that made my blood turn to ice. I quickly withdrew my outstretched hand and slowly stood while taking two steps back, never taking my eyes off this obviously deadly and destructive animal.

"He doesn't like me very much," I stammered.

"He doesn't know you," corrected Sgt. Dale "And you are not yet his commander. Over the next eight hours here you are going to learn in the most basic way to handle and control this dog so that you'll be able to take him home tonight.

"You'll be back at O six hundred hours tomorrow

morning and every morning after that for the next two to six months. You'll be trained as a team to move as one unit, and over the course of the training exercises Sentinel will learn to anticipate your moves allowing him to provide you the highest level of personal security.

"One thing you need to understand," Sgt. Dale instructed, "is that an ill-handled or untrained dog is a weapon that can pull its own trigger. There's no point in carrying a gun around if you don't know how to use it. Come stand over here, on the other side of Sentinel." I did as I was told. Sgt. Dale handed me Sentinel's leash and then stood before us.

As I stood there holding the leash of my new dog I was overcome with emotion. I let my tears fall freely, not bothering to hide them or wipe them away as I thought of my brave little Jackie. He had given his life for me and here I was asking yet another dog to do the same thing, to guard my life with his.

From that moment I promised myself I would do all that was necessary to keep this dog safe because I could not bear to lose another dog. I just didn't have the strength.

Sentinel looked up at me, and then moved from my side to stand in front of me stretching his leash until it was as taught as a high wire.

Sgt. Dale did not have the patience for my tears. "There are four levels of K-9 training to consider when selecting a dog for personal protection. To select the correct level of training you must first recognize, identify, and understand the level of threat poised against you.

"The first level of personal protection when selecting a dog is the Watch Dog. Take a few steps towards me."

Sentinel turned his head slightly over his shoulder without

taking his eyes off Sgt. Dale, and when I began moving forward Sentinel did the same without allowing any tension to be removed from his leash. When Sgt. Dale held his right hand up in front of him, and then balled his palm into a fist, both the dog and I stopped moving.

"Watch Dogs are mobile, four-footed burglar alarms. They'll bark steadily and insistently when an entry is attempted, and they'll go to the point of entry to pinpoint it for you." That was my precious Jack a fierce little watchdog. I had to concentrate on Sgt. Dale to prevent more tears.

"The second level of personal protection from the canine is the Protection Dog. These animals have advanced obedience training and, on your command, they will bark and lunge at an aggressor, snapping at him without actually biting him. At your command they will immediately sit and fall silent. These dogs' training is oriented strictly towards a deterrent, a show of force. If the attacker persists however, this dog will fall back on their natural protective instinct and bite.

"The dogs you see on police forces are Attack Dogs. These animals have been trained to sink their teeth into people upon command or when their master is under assault. Once the resistance from the suspect ceases, a true Attack Dog will let go of him and will do the same under command, regardless of how excitement-charged the atmosphere, if, the dog has been properly trained and selected. True Attack Dogs normally will only bite if given the proper command or if the animal sees its owner or family member under attack.

"Now. Guard Dogs represent the deadliest form of canine training. These dogs either walk with a sentry or patrol an enclosed space. Their primary function is to apprehend and neutralize any human intruder. They do not stop biting when the suspect stops resisting. They stop biting only when the suspect *stops moving*. These animals are likely to be trained to go for the throat or the genitals."

I don't know where I'd drifted off to, but Sgt. Dale had to loudly snap his fingers to regain my awareness. "I'm going to need you to pay attention, understand? Guard Dogs are trained to kill and maim. Did you catch what I just said? To kill and maim."

Those four words ricocheted through my entire body and Sgt. Dale for once and for all held my undivided attention. "A properly trained Guard Dog is so vicious that it will usually obey a single handler, but now we are asking him to obey two, and eventually to disregard all the commands of his first handler." Sgt. Dale's frozen blue eyes pierced my soul until he was satisfied that I was fully aware of what he was telling me.

"The only legitimate use of a Guard Dog is in wartime, or when a human intrusion could result in awesome public danger and loss of life, such as a nuclear weapons facility, or let's say the apprehension of a scientist conducting research for our government."

The eight hours of training turned into ten, and tested my resolve that I could in fact handle such a large and powerful animal. When Sgt. Dale handled Sentinel, the dog walked beside him. When I handled Sentinel he would always walk in front of me. Sgt. Dale's commands boomed out with the authority of a general in wartime, in stark comparison to my commands, which sounded like soft-spoken suggestions. But towards the end of the day Sentinel began to respond to my soft-spoken commands, as he understood I was to be his new handler.

Walking back to my Range Rover I suddenly realized that I had nothing in my home for such a large dog, and again my heart sank as my thoughts returned to Jack. Sentinel brought me back to the now by grabbing his leash with his teeth and yanking it out of my hand with such force that the end of the leash cracked like a whip and left a welt on the back of my hand.

"What?" I asked as I took a few steps back. Sentinel raised his head and I actually ducked beneath the clear sky, as I looked up to see what he was trying to warn me about and prepared myself mentally to see aliens and UFOs. Sentinel issued an angry bark to get my attention; he picked up the trailing end of his leash and again raised his head.

"Oh," I laughed, "you don't want the leash." As I leaned down to remove it he licked my nose. Watching Sentinel walk you knew right away that he was a trained working dog, but you also knew that he was something much different than your normal hero, police, or rescue dog.

For one thing, he didn't walk beside me or even slightly ahead. Sentinel walked directly in front and at least a foot and a half ahead of me, and he moved like a lion. His head was constantly moving back and forth, actually scanning our surroundings.

Sgt. Dale offered that Sentinel chose to walk in front of me instead of by my side because Sentinel felt I required a greater level of security. He had chosen to create a security barrier if you will, placing himself closest to any potential threat that might arise. This would provide me with precious moments of lead-time that could mean the difference between my life or my demise. I couldn't help feeling a little jumpy watching the way Sentinel would duck his head down to look under the parked cars.

When most dogs hear a sound they look in the direction that the sound came from. When Sentinel heard a sound he would position himself between me and what ever made the noise – keeping me safely behind him until the source of the noise could be identified and eliminated as a threat. It was a little unsettling to realize that my dog was militarized. That he was on duty, guarding a perimeter and that perimeter and his mission was me.

On the drive home I rolled down the rear windows, remembering the way Jackie would bounce between them, hang out of them, and happily bark away at anything he saw. Sentinel chose to sit in the front seat, where he could peer through the windshield and conduct military reconnaissance operations.

I stopped at Pet Smart to pick up food, books on large-breed dogs, a dog bed, treats, and maybe a toy. Sentinel led me into the pet store with the same reserve as a member of a S.W.A.T. team forces entry. The glass doors slid open. Sentinel took maybe four or five steps into the air-conditioned chain emporium and froze.

Sentinel turned to look at me with an expression of utter horror and dismay, as if to convey the fact he could not believe his Brethren could hold such a lack of discipline and reserve, and I could not help but smile. Sentinel slowly turned his head back to the brouhaha that was being caused by his canine kin, eyeing it all, as if they were a group of brand new recruits thrust upon him –without the benefits of basic training – on the very night before they were to attack a mighty adversary. Annoyance, contempt, and actual exasperation were mingled in his glances.

At that moment a small brown dog came from around the corner, ran right up to Sentinel and dropped a sloppy wet ball in front of him, his small brown eyes gleaming with joy at the prospect of meeting a new friend and thus gaining a new playmate.

Sentinel did not move a muscle. He just glared down at the little guy with a grimace. The little dog began to bark encouragingly at Sentinel as if to say, "Come on, you can do this!" The little dog picked up the ball, ran backwards a little ways let the ball drop from his mouth, then using its nose he rolled the ball to Sentinel, happily wagging his tail.

Clearly Sentinel was not amused. He watched the red ball roll slowly to a stop in front of him. The terrier ignored, Sentinel marched forward into enemy territory to investigate the mayhem that unfolded before him.

There was a German Shepherd chasing its tail at dizzying speeds, and a chocolate lab puppy racing from one end of the store to the other. As I watched, he slid into a display of dog food that sent 12oz cans of beef flavored Atta Boy sailing through the air like grenades. There was an obedience class in session, but only the dog owners were paying attention. The dogs in attendance were out of compliance and did not share Sentinel's duty bound sense of "Honor, Respect, and Loyalty."

A perfectly groomed, white, standard-size poodle, wearing inferior black Tahitian pearls made by a competitor instead of a collar, was pretentiously standing away from the substandard behavior of the common dogs. Someone had the unfortunate job of meticulously painting the poodle's "nails" red.

A large mean-looking dog, the kind you see beyond the gates of a junkyard, bolted from class in the direction of the poodle leaving his owner to chase behind him shouting, "No. Fuck! Hey, stop!" Junkyard tackled the poodle and wrestled her to the ground. The poodle was unhurt but very angry, and she took a deep bite from his hindquarters as he turned his back to her. His eyes settled upon Sentinel with a look of psychotic excitement – and he charged.

An ill-handled or untrained dog is a weapon that can pull its own trigger.

Oh my God, was all I was thinking. Sentinel wasn't wearing a leash, and I doubt I would have tried to restrain him if he had been. The dogs clashed in what seemed like a blink of the eye. Junkyard was not socialized, and regardless of his formidable size, he was still a puppy. He was only playing. Sentinel, however, was not. Sentinel grabbed the young dog by his throat, flipped him onto his back, and pinned him to the floor. The puppy's eyes widened with terror as all of us stood watching in horrified silence.

After what seemed like a lifetime Sentinel released his

hold on the pup and, making sure that I was safely behind him, thundered out three resounding barks that I felt in my chest. It was as if he was announcing himself as the alpha male. His authority was not to be challenged.

No one moved, until the guy who was instructing the class walked over, wearing a nametag that proudly displayed the name "Skip." He was an even six feet, with sun-bleached blonde hair and a shade of golden skin that's impossible to get in a tanning salon, and absolutely unobtainable in a grey-weather city that rains eleven months out of the year, which left me wondering which part of the country he was imported from. Skip bent down, placing his hands on his knees and asked in his most cheerful voice, "Hey big guy, what seems to be the problem?"

Sentinel didn't growl, didn't bark, and didn't move. His body became as rigid as a gothic gargoyle perched atop an ancient castle to ward off evil spirits, such as this servant of Satan, who now stood before him.

Skip became uncomfortable and decided that kneeling within striking distance of such a powerful dog's fangs probably wasn't a good idea.

"Wow, he's not very friendly is he?" he asked as he stood.

"No. No he's not."

We strolled down the aisles as I collected the items I had come for and Sentinel completed security sweeps of each aisle that we went down. Sentinel selected gunmetal food and water dishes, which wasn't surprising. I never for a moment dreamed that he would eat out of anything adorned with paws, bones, and kitties.

For the first month after I received Sentinel I was a nervous wreck. Every ear twitch and slight turn of the head would put me on edge, as would watching the way he would concentrate on the most minuscule of sounds.

It took almost seven months before Sentinel stopped reacting to every new sound or smell by going into DEFCON 3. Once Sentinel started to relax his security measures I started to enjoy my dog's company.

I had created for Sentinel a chain mail harness of 22-karat gold. Some of the small rings that covered his chest held gems of rubies, others held peridots, and still others held yellow sapphires that blazed against his dark fur. When he sat at my feet, jewels and gold blazing, he looked like a dog of war, covered in armor, and prepared to accompany his knight into battle.

People would stop dead in their tracks, or move out of the way when they saw the two of us coming. People found it disquieting that Sentinel wasn't wearing a leash, and because he was such a powerhouse of supremacy and muscle, his presence served to add fuel to the fires of fear that people had of dogs. And if people were not afraid of dogs they found a way to be afraid of Sentinel.

Patrolling around with such a large dog I gently returned to the routine of things. I still worked on various projects at The Facility, but I was spending equal amounts of time working as a jeweler.

XXII

I inspect all the jewelry that the interns for Atomic Weight 196 create, and have the final decision on whether or not the quality is high enough to be sold bearing my name and status as a master jeweler.

There are six 196 stores: one each in Seattle, San Francisco, Arizona, Texas, Boston, and New York. Lately I'd spent a lot of time scrutinizing jewels and visiting the 196 stores. I'd just returned from Boston and was on my way to Arizona, where there were journeymen jewelers I wanted to pay close attention too, due to the quality of their creativity and workmanship.

Allen Jefferson, the head resident at the Seattle 196 was a phenomenal jeweler who wasn't making any money. Most of the interns at the Atomic stores weren't making that much money; just enough to live on, but they were earning reputations and would be earning much more once they made the transition from Atomic Weight 196 to Periodic Element Au.

Allen Jefferson now went by the name of Allen J. Alloy, and he engraved his initials in old English script on all the jewelry he created. Allen's specialty was ethnic-inspired jewelry. If you were a Norwegian your jewelry would look as if it had been past down from Viking forefathers. If you were black, the jewels would have seemed to be unearthed from beneath Nubian sands, and lately he had begun creating pieces that looked almost mystical. Allen sold his work in the three to five thousand dollar ranges, however his pieces cost between seven to ten thousand dollars to create.

When Allen was offered the chance of a lifetime, to create jewelry for Periodic, he refused. Stunned, I cancelled my Arizona trip and went to Seattle to speak with Allen myself.

I hadn't been in the Seattle 196 for nearly six months. The interns there were doing an unparalleled job. They weren't using inferior metals or gems and did not require my constant supervision.

Mr. Alloy had rearranged the entire layout of my store.

As I walked through the door I was greeted by two armed guards that looked like they had been plucked from the Roman Legion, one standing on each side of the entry. On the left, Allen had removed a display case to make room for an espresso stand, which was attended by two heavily tattooed and pierced girls. The black aprons they wore were embroidered with gold thread. The image sewn onto their aprons was the square from the periodic table that was the designation for gold. They served everything from double shot-hold-the-foam-with-soy to fruity iced teas – free of charge.

From the sound system pumped fast paced music, to match the elevated tempo of the heavily caffeinated clientele. The jewelry store was filled to capacity.

Gary, Allen's partner and a graduate from the Seattle Art Institute, was sitting on the floor in front of a couple seated on the leather sofa (something that hadn't been there the last time I was) and sketching their ideals of the perfect wedding bands.

I noticed that there were several sketch artists and they too were sitting on the floor in front of people sipping from Styrofoam cups, trying to translate into drawings what their customers saw in their dreams of jewelry.

There are eleven journeyman jewelers at the Seattle 196, and all of them were in front of customers. Most of them wore a frown of concentration as they were listening to what they were being told, and no one was mulling around unattended. I liked that. Once I got Allen's attention he raised his right hand and wiggled his fingers in his version of a wave, begged for forgiveness from the clients he was working with and walked over to greet me. He was wearing pink dress slacks that were a bit too tight around the bottom, a shimmery black silk tunic that was opened to reveal a heavy platinum chain that bounced against a yellow tank top; and a pair snakeskin loafers the same color as raspberry blue bubble-gum. Allen was dressed as if to give homage to the Bird of Paradise. You would think that all those different hues would be assaulting to the senses, but surprisingly the colors were nicely coordinated and pleasing to the eye.

"What a pleasant surprise. I was not expecting you here. Coffee?"

"That's fine. Allen we need to have a meeting." He reacted to the news as if he'd been slapped and was on the verge of tears. "What have I done wrong?"

"Nothing, really. Over dinner okay? Go back to your customers, Chris Ruth's at eight alright?"

Over dinner I asked Allen why he wasn't coming to Periodic. I explained that the caliber of his work would earn him a seven-figure income once he made the transition. Allen told me he wasn't in it for the money, but for the people who brought him their eleven hundred dollars that took five months to save and that they could not afford to spend. Allen explained that he loved the challenge of creating heirloom masterpieces with their very limited funds.

"It keeps me on top of my game. I can go toe to toe with Yayu Wells, create bold and brilliant pieces and give her a run for her money in chasing the prestigious 'Tama-No-Ya' award, sure I can.

"But I like working at 196, I like working for people who have to work hard for everything they have. I want to work hard for people like that. It makes me work harder. And everything I create means more to me because the people I work for hold me in such esteem as to trust me with their hard-earned money."

Wells, a central African goldsmith, produced jewels for the New York Periodic, and last year she earned nearly six million dollars in commission and won (for the second time) the Tama-No-Ya award. Tama-No-Ya is a Japanese god of jewelers, and the award is given to the most sought after jewelers in the world.

The International Jewelers Symposium, established sixteen years ago, was founded to oppose unsafe mining practices and the use child laborers. The IJS also awarded excellence within the industry. Out of the sixteen honors given, jewelers for Periodic were the recipients of nine.

When I offered Allen permanent employment at Atomic Weight 196 – Seattle, with a promotion to Master Jeweler and a salary of $130,000.00 a year plus 30% commission on all jewelry sold by his interns, which is something I've never done with a journeyman, he started crying.

The first pieces of jewels for my "Desert Tribal Collection" arrived six months behind schedule due to the loss of a child. I knew all this of course, because I'd been wearing the bracelet of their fallen angel.

I sent a letter of condolence, and the numbers to the bank account I'd opened on their behalf, in which I deposited another fifty thousand dollars. The first pieces of jewels were three necklaces, two rings, and two bracelets. I held an exhibition to celebrate the launch of my newest collection.

I sold the heaviest necklace for $125,975. The second went for $98,600. The third I kept for myself, and mine was actually the heaviest and most opulently adorned.

I sold both bracelets to the same woman for $28,000 a piece. One ring went to the son of The Russian Prince, (of course there are no kings in Russia, but here in The States, "The Russian Prince" is what his father – a real estate tycoon– was known by) which he wore on his pinky finger, to the tune of $15,550. And the other went to a man with a fiancée who was thrifty-five years younger than he. The price for that ring, a prenuptial agreement! No, I'm kidding. I sold it to him for $18,990. You see? The extra fifty thousand I sent cost nothing, and meant even less.

I made the mistake of lapsing into a false sense of security.

We were at the dog park, a baby Jack Russell was climbing all over Sentinel as he sat as still as a statue. Sentinel had grown use to senseless, undisciplined dogs and the mindless games they played.

I couldn't contain the tears as I watched the puppy having fun all by himself, the same thing Jack used to do. We had been in the park long enough for Sentinel to walk the fifteen miles of the park's perimeter and deem that no one in the park posed an imminent threat.

He was on duty, ignoring the puppy that used him as a jungle gym and watching the people who entered the park.

Sentinel had been watching something in the distance. He slowly rose and began to growl. Something he had not done in almost a year.

XXIII

The growling was barely audible at first. It was Sentinel's rigid body language that jolted me from my memories of Jack. The puppy continued to play for a few moments more before sitting in front of Sentinel and looking up at the dog who towered over him like the Statue of Liberty.

The owner of the puppy approached with apologies but was stopped in her tracks by Sentinel's growling which had become much louder and ominous. I was standing too, though I do not remember the actual act of standing, and I was holding the tug line to my dog's harness. I did not want my dog charging off into the unknown, but I wasn't sure how I was going to contain him. At that moment he was nothing but power and aggression, a champion gladiator.

The puppy was now standing under Sentinel and his owner was behind him. All the playing in the park had stopped as other dogs and owners seemed to sense something bad was about to happen. It was like everyone, man and beast was holding their breath. Even the birds had stopped singing it seemed, as people hastily made their way in our direction while throwing tentative glances to the shadowy place at the far end of the park that held Sentinel's undivided attention.

It's a fairly large park in an upscale part of the city. If I remember correctly, there were about forty people there that day. What you expect to see when you walk or drive past a park this big is dogs running around at top speed, sniffing each other, and barking wildly. I can't image what the officer thought when he drove past and saw all the park's occupants and their domesticated animals standing clustered at one end, nervously looking in the same direction. Or the elderly woman who always sat in her window that held sweeping views overlooking the park was thinking when she dialed 911.

The patrol officer made a wide, U-turn just as the

dispatcher radioed in the "disturbance" at It's a Dog's Life Dog Park.

I was so lost in my own turmoil that I did not realize everyone was standing behind me until the cop asked me what was wrong. I would have laughed at that moment if Sentinel's concentration hadn't been so absolute.

The cop also had a K-9, a large, powerful German Shepherd who was sizing up Sentinel. Something in the direction that Sentinel was glaring caught the Shepherd's attention and the dog issued six rapid deafening barks and took six bold steps in front of Sentinel. The police officer un-holstered and drew his weapon, and started to move towards the area in which his dog was barking, but an older gentleman holding a Brussels Griffon wrapped in a peach colored blanket whacked the officer on the shoulder with his walking cane. Because I was standing so close to him I was hit with the cane as well. It brought tears to my eyes and I nearly fell to my knees.

"Stop youngin', wait for your back up."

The cop spun around angrily and in pain and turned his fury on me, "What the fuck is going on? What happened?" It was a mess that was quickly turning into a nightmare. Sentinel lunged and snapped at the officer, inches away from his lower torso, then quickly turned his attention to the officer's dog.

The officer restrained his dog just in the nick of time, leaving both dogs to snarl and bark, pulling on their restraints and displaying fangs inches from one another's face. All the while the older gentleman was demanding to know if that's the way you speak to a lady and brandishing his cane.

I was mortified! This is the kind of distraction that causes disasters, and I kept looking in the direction where all this had started while desperately trying to control my dog. The older gentleman was able to smack the officer's dog on the tip of his nose with his cane before two other police officers arrived and broke us all up. It took hours for all the statements to be collected, and before it was all over two more sets of police officers arrived.

XXIV

A dam returned from the Mediterranean Isles with a tattoo of Apep. He was home for almost a week before his mom saw her son's body art.

Despite the fact Adam was about to enter his senior year in high school, for Adam, bath time was still playtime. He was singing and dancing in the shower when he slipped, got tangled in the shower curtain, fell over the ledge of the bathtub and crash landed onto the heated tiled floor. Adam hit his head so hard that the edges of his vision went white, and in a moment of panic he called for his mom. Ianna was in his bathroom before the last shower curtain ring hit the floor. "*Adam!*"

Myrddin raced to Adam's bedroom at the sound of his daughter screaming out her son's name, expecting the unspeakable. When the great wizard saw his grandson he burst into laughter.

Adam had managed to get to his feet; he was covered in lavender scented soap bubbles that were slowly dripping off of him to pool on the floor. Myrddin glanced at Inanna with a raised eyebrow and a knowing smile. When he shrugged his shoulder and smiled at Adam who was rubbing the growing bump on the back of his head, Adam smiled back.

Inanna snapped a look at the old wizard that would have brought a mortal man to his knees, and though the Great Myrddin was dying he was still much stronger than his daughter and remained on his feet. Annoyed Inanna returned her attention to her son's tattoo.

"Oh, you little Yankee ass brat."

Adam's smile widened because he knew she'd meant that in a loving way. By the tone of her voice Adam knew she wasn't mad at him, and even if she had been Adam knew with Grandee there he wouldn't get in that much trouble.

The tip of the evil serpent's tail hovered just above the adolescent's tailbone. From there the god's body traveled left, across Adam's gluteal muscle to his hip. Then the mighty snake began its ascent up the boys ribcage, looping its body up and over itself to form duplicate patterns of infinity, with the final loop coming to a stop right under Adam's armpit.

The snake-god draped the uppermost part of its body over the boy's sculpted shoulder, and finally rested his head on Adam's large chest. It was in this detail that the skill of the artist was undeniable. The snake's head wasn't lying gently on Adam's chest, but rather appeared to be rearing and ready to strike. Aiding this illusion was a shadow that the tattooist had included. The markings on Adam's version of Apep had his mother's veve repeated throughout the entire length of its body, and on the crown of Apep's head was Myrddin's staff.

As Adam dressed, Inanna voiced her concerns over Adam's choice of deities. As the personification of all that was evil; the Egyptian god snake Apep is said to be so wicked that the only thing the god thrived on, the only thing that nourished him was eating the tortured screams of his own anguish. Apep was not so much as worshiped, as worshiped against. "Is there something you're trying to tell us?"

"If you only knew the power of the dark side," Adam said, in his best Darth Vader voice.

"You ignorant little Yankee ass." Inanna was exasperated but Adam was laughing, as he did every time she called him Yankee. "The dark side?' No. There is no darkness in this house; only light and warmth."

Now both wizards were laughing. Myrddin had tears of merriment rolling down his weathered cheeks and had to sit down on the edge of the tub to catch his breath. Inanna turned on her heels and left both wizard's laughing in the bathroom.

Adam followed her out, "Come on Mom. I was joking. I like Apep because everybody was hating on him but he always came back fighting."

They'd made their way to the kitchen. Inanna was preparing to boil milk for Adam's hot chocolate. "*Was hating on him...* Boy I do not spend $11,000 a quarter for your education so that you can come home speaking like a street thug."

"Okay," Adam laughed. "Apep appeals to me because, first of all, it is written in the text that he existed from the beginning of everything. Someone or thing that's been around at the beginning of time has crazy knowledge. I think that's the reason they were fucking with him so much ..."

"Watch your mouth," interjected both his elders in unison as Adam handed his mom the chocolate.

"Knowledge is power," continued Adam, "and to know as much as you would if you were born at the beginning of everything is dangerous."

"That's an interesting interpretation Adam," Myrddin noted. Adam shrugged absently while he watched his Grandee slowly stir the simmering milk.

"Apep was bad ass, cuz."

"ADAM."

"What mom? He was. Apep was the only one strong enough to challenge the Sun god, and he was so big that his body wrapped around the entire world."

"Boy do you think I don't know what it says? I'm the one who gave you those books." Adam's face reddened as his diverted away from his mother to hide the fact that her tone of voice had stung him.

"Adam, your mother is upset because you are not strong enough to conjure such a demon. It would be foolish for even one such as me to do so."

"I wasn't gonna conjure him. I want to be as strong as him. Everyone banded against him, but he was so strong that he continued to exist. If he was killed he would just come back. His enemies never had a moment to rest because Apep lived forever, attacking his adversaries. If he was defeated and killed he would just rise and attack again.

"You cannot conquer an opponent that you cannot kill. When Horus' sons cut Apep's body into pieces, he was revived so that he could come back and fight."

"Adam your mother and I give you all that you desire. I'm not sure why you feel that you can identify with a malevolent creature."

Adam set his hot cup down to let the thick chocolate cool. He was looking at his mom despite the fact that it was his Grandee who had spoken.

"You had to fight for me," Adam let his gaze drift toward his grandfather, "and you're not always gonna be here." Tears were starting to build in Adam's large eyes, making them sparkle like two massive emeralds.

"I got a tattoo of Apep because I want his strength. You have to fight for everything because nothing will be handed to you. I wasn't born in a manger, and the guy who was didn't have it so easy either."

Grandee's powerful arms engulfed Adam while his mom wiped away his tears. The three of them stayed in the kitchen for hours afterward. They talked, cried, laughed, and were comforted by each other's touch. It was something Adam needed.

He knew that his Grandee was dying, but it was something no one ever talked about. If Grandee could die, that meant so could his mom, and that was something that truly terrified him. The sky was tinted with amber highlights announcing the arrival of the sun by the time Grandee tucked Adam into bed.

"Did you enjoy yourself in Greece?"

"Oh yes!" Adam spent the next hour excitedly telling Grandee about his summer vacation.

Grandee was smiling throughout most of Adam's tale, but his smile slowly slid from his face and something much more treacherous took its place. Myrddin wore his dark shades at all times because looking into his swirling eyes was unsettling even to Inanna who loved him most. Adam had never seen his Grandee without his dark glasses and he wanted to scream for his mother as he watched Myrddin remove them. "Now tell me about your trip to Morocco," demanded the wizard.

Staring into the twin hurricanes that surged within Myrddin's eyes Adam felt crushed. For the first time in his young life, he felt the absolute infancy of his own powers. The trio oftentimes communicated with each other telepathically, but Adam had been blocking some of the things he'd been thinking about – and most of what he'd been doing – from his mom and grandfather for a little over a year now.

Myrddin sat back in the leather wingback and crossed his legs, never taking his eyes off the boy. With the flick of a finger of his left hand, the wizard closed the door to Adam's room.

The boys' defiance was infuriating, and Myrddin had to go to great lengths to restrain his temper. He didn't want to hurt Adam, but there was a lesson that needed to be taught.

Adam's boldness was too far reaching in comparison to his age and skill. Myrddin decided to speak to the boy without saying a word.

Adam you must learn to realize that there are greater beings that have the strength of eons and who must never be challenged, even a woman like the one you're stalking could be more dangerous than any creature in the universe.

She is no fool and is very capable of taking countermeasures. Her knowledge, though not unfathomable, is great and as you yourself said earlier knowledge is indeed power.

"But I am protected." Looking into Myrddin's eyes sent shock-waves throughout Adam's entire body, and he could only muster a whisper as he reached to touch the charm of protection that dangled against his chest.

That very well may be true, however you've been sheltered. You are a mortal and can very well perish before me, and if you continue on this path of carelessness you will.

Tears welled in Adam's eyes at the reminder that Grandee's time was close to an end. The boy's tears did nothing to quell the wizard's displeasure.

I asked you a question Adam. Tell me about your trip to Morocco. Actually let's start year ago on that day in the park with that little dog. And while we're at it, let's not forget about the man you killed in the city.

Adam's head started to spin wildly as he realized that nothing had been hidden from this Great Wizard and that the only person blocking communication between him and his mom was the man Adam was now cowering before in a state of terror-induced paralysis.

XXV

The incident at the park left my nerves frayed. I had to stop by The Facility to have Dr. Anderson give me something to calm me down and help me sleep. I was still so upset that I poured the contents of the packet he gave me with shaky hands into my Coke and gulped it down in the parking lot; despite the fact he had told me to wait until I was home.

The powerful effects were almost immediate. I have no idea how I made it home that day. I literally stumbled through my door and collapsed just inches away from the sofa. Sentinel pushed the door closed, then stood watching over me. He turned and sat with his back facing me, so that he could be on guard with me safely behind him. I tried to pet him but couldn't lift my arm, and I crashed into sleep with one shoe on.

I was jolted from sleep in the throes of a nightmare. Sentinel was the first thing I saw when I opened my eyes. He was licking my face; reassuring me that things were okay.

I was mortified when I reached up to touch him and saw that my watch was telling me it was Thursday. I had been asleep on the floor for three days. My anxiety returned with such force that I thought I was going to vomit, as I slowly remembered what had happened days before in the park.

I had to sit up slowly because my entire body was in agony from sleeping on the floor, and I was feeling weak and dizzy. Once again I looked at my watch in stunned disbelief.

Once I had my bearings I called Kenneth and asked him if he could meet me for lunch.

Dr. Astor asked me if I was okay, while gently referring to the fact that, indeed, the hour of lunch had passed, due to the fact that is was eleven o'clock at night – not eleven in the morning. Dr. Astor suggested the Le Crystal Château, which is just north of the city because the top floor of the hotel boasts an upscale restaurant.

Dr. Astor called ahead to make the reservations, and I told him I'd meet him there within the hour. I had to lie back down for a minute while I tried to figure out how I was going to find the strength to stand up and walk what seemed like a mile to my bedroom to take a shower.

While I was on the phone with Ken, Sentinel had disappeared into the kitchen. He was now slowly emerging, gently carrying an apple in his powerful jowls. His attempt at carefulness made me laugh. I have no idea why he imagined he had to walk so slowly, and his thoughtfulness made me cry.

The first thing I do when I get out of bed in the morning is kiss my dog. Then I grab an apple and eat it while I stand in front of the large picture windows in my library gazing at the city below while I wake up. I've always done this, even with Jackie and Rusty before him. But both Jack and Rusty were small. Sentinel is the only dog I've ever had large enough to reach the basket of fruit I keep on the counter.

Sentinel let the wet apple drop into my outstretched hand. I kissed my dog, issued a playful "Eeewww," and took a bite out of my breakfast. Then Sentinel laid his head in my lap.

I was late.

I hadn't seen Dr. Astor in over a year. When I returned from Morocco, Dr. Astor had gone to Israel with Team 9 to work with a team of doctors whose techniques and research could greatly benefit the research and experiments we were conducting at The Facility. Dr. Astor was so impressed with the research, that after only four months on site he suggested a merger.

The Skyward group has a research and recruiting department that scours the earth for requests for medical research grants. They read medical publications to find other indications of scientists, doctors and research teams who are pushing the boundaries of convention – of people who are so desperately passionate about the projects that their working on, that they are willing to cross the line.

We watch and wait from the shadows until they have been ridiculed by the scientific and medical communities, shunned by friends and peers, and are truly frantic over the impeding destruction of their reputations and the halting of their life's work due to the lack of monetary recognition in the form of contributions.

Such was the case with the Israeli team. Dr. Astor must have seemed like the Savior, with the promise of unlimited funding.

Team 9 travels with a group of lawyers who are experts in international and domestic intellectual property laws. Section 4.21a, Part 6 of the terms of agreement clearly states that we, The Skyward Group, will have complete and total access to their projects, collected and or learned data, and the rights to research discoveries made during and one hundred years after the period in which we, The Skyward Group, provided funding – though they would not have access to ours.

It takes decades to cultivate doctors who are willing to conduct the type of research that was being performed by a team such as theirs. It would cost even more to secure a doctor with that level of skill who would be willing to disclose the information of a previous project. We have found that mergers are the easiest way to recruit new talent and increase our intellectual power throughout the world.

Just the sight of him brightened my spirits, and the smile he returned felt like the warmth of the sun, and I have to tell you he looked good.

The first thing I noticed was that he had changed his glassed from the circular wire rims to a chic square rim designed by Prada. His skin had a warmer hue to it, as if he'd just returned from vacationing in the tropics. He was dressed casually in dark khakis and a soft, pale green shirt. His hair had the luster of health to it, and he had gotten it cut, but it still managed to look as if he had just gotten out of bed.

He stood to greet me and as we embraced I told him I how much I'd missed him. The maître d' brought our drinks just as we we're sitting down, which included a glass of Camus Cuvée for me and a crystal bowl containing water from the French Alps for Sentinel.

"Nice job on your 'Desert Collection.' Absolutely stunning pieces. How was Morocco? Where's Jackie, and who's this big guy?"

"I want to know how Logan could have gotten it so wrong. Adam is furious and far more dangerous than any of us first imagined."

The last time I had seen Dr. Astor was during the emergency meeting in which we all realized that Adam was still alive. So I had to start at the beginning to bring Dr. Astor up to speed with what I was going through.

I started with how I had found Jackie murdered after returning home from the meeting and recited the letter I had found near his body.

I explained that the real reason I traveled to Morocco was so that I could sneak into Spain to give my confessional (and that was almost true), which led to the killing of the girl in the desert and finally to the stalking in the park. As I said it, I realized out loud that this was the second time I had been stalked like that at a park. As I spoke I watched the color drain from Ken's face. Toward the end of my tale I watched his eyes glide from my face to my bracelet and back to my face.

"You went all the way to Spain to give your confession?" He squinted his eyes and raised an eyebrow, "So you're Catholic now? Is Saint Barbara's not grand enough? You can see that cathedral from your window. If Spain, why not Rome? You're lying."

I shrugged my shoulder "Prove it. A priest is not the only person one can confess to."

"Peter was run down in the middle of the street. He was dragged underneath that car for twenty feet."

"Peter?"

"Petey was my partner."

I was shocked. "You have a … *social* life?"

"You're insufferable."

I didn't mean to off end him and I told him so while trying to suppress my laughter. I explained to him that I was just so surprised because it seemed like he was always locked away working in his lab oftentimes skipping meals and forgoing sleep.

I wanted to know how, if he didn't have enough time to eat, how in the world did he find the time to nurture a relationship. I asked him to tell me about his Pete and what had happened to him.

He explained that I was the reason they'd met. Every year I throw a gala called "The Display of Personal Embellishments." It's presented like a runway fashion show and I host multitudes of buyers and private guests from all over the world.

The models the jewelers use walk wearing the same outfit, identical shoes, the same pinned up hairstyles and no handbags. The only thing that differentiates the models from each other is the jewelry that they are dripping in.

The goal of such a show is to showcase all of my jewelers who have made the transition from being journeymen working at Atomic Weight 196 to the title of master jeweler and working for Periodic Element Au.

Kenneth told me that Pete was working with the girls who were modeling for Miss Wells. "I understand she's earned quite a reputation since that show. Such a brilliant artist she's become.

"Logan modeled in that show, remember? As you recall she was the only reason that I attended."

At that time Logan was not yet one of Dr. Astor's weapons in his arsenal of oracles. I refused to use professional models because those descendants of Venus are nightmares to work with; a lesson I had to learn the hard way and one I had no intentions of repeating. We found her, and everyone else modeling, through flyers that were asking if anyone wanted to have fun while earning $1,000.

Dr. Astor had heard of Logan months before and made sure that she received a flyer. Logan was using her psychic abilities to read palms and tell fortunes to pay her way through school.

"I went backstage to find Logan, and that's where I first saw Peter. I stood staring at him for I do not know how long, and when he finally looked up and saw me gawking at him he bashfully looked away. I noticed that he was blushing.

He found me after the show and from that moment one we were inseparable."

"Yayu transitioned to Periodic fifteen years ago. Oh my God, Ken I am so sorry." My heart was breaking into a zillion pieces, "Inseparable? So Peter knew about Adam, he knew about your work at Skyward?" I couldn't help it. I was getting angry.

"No, no. Calm down, I told him from the very beginning that there was a significant part of me that I would never allow him to know about. Of course he was angry at first and demanded to know if there was someone else. He thought that maybe I was still in the closet, or that I had a wife and a couple of kids out there somewhere."

Ken had a distant smile on his face, "I remember laughing at that suggestion and telling him if only it was as simple as that. His next suggestion was that I worked for the CIA, and I knew that was my out."

"I looked at him very gravely and said, 'If you so much as mention that to *anyone*,' then I grabbed his face and held it tightly in my hand for emphasis 'anyone, it will cost me my life and quite possibly yours as well. This is something we can never speak of again, and if you bring it up no matter how subtly, you will never see or hear from me again.' My poor Petey bought it, I think it excited him a little but it provided the cover I needed without question. No he did not know about Adam, but Adam absolutely knew about Peter."

"The man who ran Peter down says he does not remember anything. He says the last thing he remembers is waiting in line to get a latte, and the next thing he knew was that he was cuffed in the backseat of a police car.

"His credit card statement announces the purchase of the coffee was four days prior to the slaying of Peter, his wife called authorities to report him missing later that night.

His employer states that he is so dependable you could have set your watch by him, and nothing connects him with Peter. The car he was driving wasn't his. It was a rental. To add to the man's confusion the car he rented is a manual transmission, despite his claims that he doesn't know how to drive one."

Kenneth was crying now, and I couldn't comfort him because I was crying too. "When I went to identify his body and collect his belongings the only identifying mark was the tattoo on his middle finger on his right hand. It looks exactly like this."

Ken held out his right hand. I held it in mine and ran my thumb across the tiny Chinese character tattooed on his middle finger.

"There was an envelope in Petey's back pocket with my name on it. But it wasn't written in his handwriting, and the note inside wasn't from Pete. It read, 'You've abandoned me.'"

"Ken I do not want the cleanup crew to kill Adam, I want them to keep him alive, I just want my baby to come home."

"You what?" Ken rocketed to his feet, sending our table crashing into ruins. Sentinel stood as well and the only thing that could be heard in that moment of stunned silence was the rumbling in the back of my animal's throat.

XXVI

Once Adam became accustomed to the implications of danger in the swirl of Myrddin's eyes he was able to read within them more than anger – there was also disappointment; and that was more painful than any punishment that Grandee could dispense.

Adam knew he had to explain things, regardless of the fact that his grandfather already knew it all. Adam was extremely headstrong and dealt with his punishments fairly well, which of late had become more severe because he insisted on pushing the boundaries, but the look of disappointment that was stretched across Myrddin's face like a mask was more than Adam could bear.

"At first I thought they were just dreams. Sometimes people dream about the same thing over and over again, so at first I thought I was just dreaming. I didn't know I was remembering."

Myrddin slowly sheltered his eyes behind dark lenses then asked, When did you realize that you were remembering?

The booming of Myrddin's voice vibrating within the walls of Adam's head was deafening. Adam felt trapped and exhausted, and he hardly had the energy to speak, so he decided it would just be easier to exchange thoughts with his grandfather because Adam didn't trust that the sound of his voice wouldn't come out cracked and high pitched.

One day I was with mom and we were in the kitchen doing dishes. We were playing and she called me "Papi" and I had a flash of my dream. But it was a part I hadn't dreamt yet. It fucking scared me and I don't know why but I didn't want to tell Mom, so I just went to my room and closed the door. I thought she was going to bug me about it but she didn't.

The next day I went into Mom's room to scry.

Didn't your mother tell you to stay out of her room?

"She told me not to *take* anything out of her room," Adam's tone was filled with so much venom and defiance that the flash of anger that rose from Myrddin caused Inanna to rush into the room.

"What the hell is going on in here?" Inanna was ready to fight to the death to protect Adam, and fighting Myrddin meant just that. Inanna didn't know which was more unsettling, the thought of actually having to fight her mentor, the site of Adam trying to control his tears and the plea of help embedded in his eyes, or the radiation of calmness that rolled off the great wizard like thick ominous fog.

Inanna tried to move towards her son, but felt tangled within Myrddin's web of restraint. A quick glance at Adam's terror-stricken face made her as angry as a hornet, and she began to tap within her the well of dark powers and marry them to her maternal instincts.

Myrddin never removed his eyes from the boy, but spoke directly to his daughter without saying a word. Leave.

"I'm not going anywhere."

This time the wizard did speak aloud, "I said leave."

"I said no." Inanna was trembling with rage and fully prepared to enter this fight, which she would surely lose.

"Mom, it's okay. I'm okay."

Inanna looked at Adam, and he looked more frightened than ever.

"We're just having a man to man talk is all." Adam managed a smile that always had the power to wrap his mom around his finger, and Inanna stood down.

The defiant glare that Inanna blasted in Myrddin's direction was just as malicious as the tone of voice Adam had chosen, which had ignited this family feud in the first place.

It was no surprise where the boy got it from. Myrddin had half a mind to remind them both of who they were truly challenging, in a magnificent display of power and force. In the end, the wizard was able to keep his temper in check. He knew Inanna had great survival skills, and it wasn't her that he was worried about. It was Adam.

Once Inanna felt the binding spell that she was trapped in loosen she went to Adam and ran her fingers through his hair. Call me if you need me she instructed. She kissed her sons cheeks until Adam blushed, and she left the room as commanded, but not before throwing one last optical thunderbolt at Myrddin – which he thoroughly ignored. Left alone again with the mighty wizard, Adam tried to gather the words needed to give his mandatory divulgence.

"I saw her in the mirror," continued Adam, "and she looked just like she did in my dreams. Just the way I remembered her."

Even though Grandee had replaced his glasses to shield the boy from his eyes, Adam still felt the weight of his crushing glare. He found imaginary dirt under his fingernails to occupy his gaze while he spoke to his grandfather.

"Sometimes it's hard for me to understand what the mirror says, so it took me about a week to actually find her. She was coming out of a jewelry store and she didn't see anything but her Blackberry. Just the sight of her pissed me off, and that little fucking dog of hers.

"I followed her for a month or so before she even knew what was going on. Then that day in the park I made her look at me. I made her see me, and then I just ignored her. I felt her fear, but then she just looked away like I meant nothing, like she wasn't afraid.

But I knew that she was," Adam spouted triumphantly.

The warlock had heard enough, "You should have thanked her."

"Thanked her?" Adam demanded in astonishment. "Thanked her for what?"

"Adam, if it weren't for her you would not be lounging on this lap of luxury that you call life."

With a tsk Adam shrugged his shoulders then issued a brazen "whatever" in the form of an insult.

With the speed and devastation of a lightning bolt, Myrddin slapped him.

It was the first time in his life that Adam had actually been struck. With mouth ajar in surprise and the side of his face stinging from what felt like a thousand stinging wasps, Adam burst into tears.

"That will be the end of your insolence." With a whispered chant in an ancient language the wizard left the room.

XXVII

"What are you all looking at?" Ken's voice cracked around the edges with tones of hysteria as he scanned the restaurant. People lowered their eyes as Kenneth's swept the room. No one wanted to lock eyes with the deranged lunatic that now inhabited the body that, until recently, had been occupied by Dr. Kenneth Astor.

The tension was palpable and his anger was infectious. I felt my grasp on my temper slipping. I stretched my legs from underneath my chair crossing them at my ankles and lazily reached over to pet Sentinel, while surveying the wreckage around us.

I noticed my glass had landed upright with its precious cargo still safely inside. I picked it up and took a drink.

The server was the only person who was still watching our scene unfold. The story written across that kid's face told a tale of inner turmoil. He was caught between wanting to help a woman in distress and the fear of interfering. With his eyes darting between Ken and Sentinel, I couldn't tell which frightened him more. I hoped he was wise enough to know that this was not his fight-to-fight.

Ken looked around the room one more time before finally sitting down. He folded his arms across his chest, rested a leg on the overturned table, and glared at me in silence. For a while I said nothing. I just stayed within his company contemplating what I was going to say next. I wanted a chance to calm down because I wanted to choose my next words carefully.

"Dr. Hogue, my little Jackie, the gypsy girl and Peter – they all died because of me, and though I can't take responsibility for the death of Dr. Morgan, he should have been my first clue."

Ken was visibly moved by my admission and tried to say

something, but I didn't give him a chance to speak.

"This is all my fault, mine and mine alone. I was warned but I didn't hear you out. I fought you every step of the way and now look what's happened." It was clear that Ken was no longer angry with me; I was starting to scare him because I was rambling, but I couldn't stop myself. "He was right." I shouted as I stood up and thrust my upturned hands into his face.

"Who?"

The look of terror on Ken's face made me laugh. "The ocean doesn't wash it off, see?" Ken grabbed my hands and told me he couldn't see, and asked again who I was talking about.

"Don't you see? There's blood on my hands." My laughter turned to tears as I collapsed in Ken's arms.

The maître d' discretely brought me a glass of water and a silk handkerchief, and with the help of his associate they placed the table back on its feet. I asked our server to bring me something stronger than water and Ken advised against it, suggesting that I needed to get some sleep. I reminded him that I had been sleeping for three days.

"It wasn't a restful sleep, it was drug induced, quite a difference. This little episode is nothing. Things are going to get worse if you don't rest and find a way to reduce your high levels of stress, unless of course you want to share the fate of Lady Macbeth."

Then he added as the waiter brought me my drink, "Another thing you might want to take into consideration, all your daily values in a 2,000 calorie diet shouldn't come from cognac."

I shook my head, rolled my eyes, downed my glass and ordered another. "Don't worry, I'm not going to kill myself, but we all have to pay the piper. If Adam is hoping for retribution then I should be the only one punished. None of this should have happened. Peter shouldn't have died."

"I somehow need to let Adam know that his road to hell was paved by my intentions and that I never meant to lie to him. I need him to understand that I really intended to take him home. Hell anybody can tell him that."

"I suppose that's true."

I was surprised that he would agree with me, but his next statement hit me like a speeding truck. "If Adam thinks that we were trying to prevent that, and that's exactly what we were doing, then maybe all of his rage isn't directed at you.

"You told Adam you were going to take him home and we were the ones telling you not to. To Adam you were the person who was supposed to keep him safe, so he must be thinking that it was the rest of us that made sure you didn't."

"I need to explain."

"As your dearest confidant I have to advise against that. You need to eat something and go to sleep. I cannot allow you to make a decision such as this while you're drunk."

"I'm not drunk," I slurred.

"Yes, love. And I'm the Queen of England." Ken paid our bill, handsomely tipped our waiter, walked me to my car and drove us home.

XXVIII

dam sulked into the kitchen after being released from a nine-day binding spell, a reward for his bold disobedience.

The nine days of imprisonment had done nothing to cool the flames of Adam's anger. Quite the opposite. The nine days of solitary confinement were used as billows, to fan his flames into an inferno. He was angrier than before but after over a week without food or drink he felt like he was starving.

Adam poured a mug of milk into a pot to boil for hot chocolate. He selected a plate from his mother's finest china and placed upon it two slices of sweet bread. He took from the cupboard a jar of peanut butter and honey, and deliberately reaching over the everyday flatware Adam defiantly selected a sterling silver knife to cut his banana.

Adam spread the peanut butter on first, then added the banana slices, and then finally the honey. Without wiping the knife clean Adam dipped it into the honey jar, never minding the peanuts that were left behind, all the while glaring across the penthouse apartment at the closed door to his mother's bedroom, part of the reason he was punished in the first place.

After cutting his sandwich into four small triangles he turned his attention to the simmering milk. Adam added four scoops of powered cocoa from the Tiffany silver canister that his mom kept next to the range.

Reducing the heat Adam slowly stirred the chocolate into the milk. Adam took a Snickers bar from on top the refrigerator, gently placed the unwrapped candy bar into the hot chocolate, and stirred the two until the candy was completely melted. Adam spilled some of the chocolate as he was pouring the steamy drink from the pot into a mug large enough to eat soup from, and he didn't clean it up.

After topping his drink with whipped cream he carried his lunch into his bedroom, leaving the sticky knife on the counter next to the spilled chocolate. This was a surefire way to receive the wrath of his mother but he didn't care. She wasn't home anyway. If she had been she would have slapped Adam on the back of the neck with such force it would have cause him to drop the plate and cup to the floor, creating yet another mess that she would require Adam to clean up.

At fourteen Adam had begun to test and defy his mother's authority. Inanna allowed the boy some room to stretch his wings, but when Adam stepped out of bounds her iron-fisted punishment was swift and absolute. It left no room for challenge, contest, or protest. Three years later, this discipline from the wizard felt like a betrayal, as it was he who had allowed Adam the greatest liberties.

As Adam was returning to his bedroom he shot another glance at his mother's room. He knew he was going back in there, despite the fact his mom was going to be furious and the result of her fury would be something similar to a vacation in the seventh realm of hell. Adam was granted access to everything in this world as well as others, anything that his young heart desired. Anything that is except for a few ancient text and artifacts his mom kept hidden in her room.

Adam put his lunch plate on the floor. With his hunger pains temporarily forgotten, he went straight into his mom's room. He felt a little like Indiana Jones as he crept up to the door.

Though the light from the large chandelier was off, and the delicate silk draperies were drawn to keep the room cool against the autumn heat. Adam started to sweat.

The small amount of light that filtered through the rich draperies from the bright autum sun was reduced to a soft glow, and the crystals hanging overhead managed to capture and harness the light and cast radiate rainbows throughout the room. As Adam eased his way closer to his mother's closet he realized that this room was his favorite place in the world to be. When he was upset, sick, or scared, or just needed a quiet place to think, this is where he always came – to his mother's room.

When he had difficult exams to prepare for, or if Grandee gave him a spell to learn he would bring all his books, laptop, herbs or botanicals and sit in the middle of Inanna's triple down feathered bed to study.

Usually he would just fall asleep within the downs of his mom's bed, and he always felt better when he woke up. Adam smiled as he thought to himself that maybe he should just take a nap. Inanna's room was his favorite room in the house. Warming himself beneath all of her covers, which is something he did when Inanna was traveling for long periods of time, felt almost as good as a real hug.

Before he knew it he was standing at the door of his mom's closet, which was the size of a small apartment that one could rent in the city below. Adam plunged deeper within the closet and opened the mirrored French doors that led to his mom's shoe chamber. Removing twenty pairs of shoes that could have paid someone's tuition, Adam cleared the floor space, exposing the trap door. Adam pulled it open and gazed within the prohibited space, but this time he didn't touch anything.

It wasn't long before he remembered how hungry he was. As he was leaving he picked up an unfamiliar book that he hadn't seen on the way in.

Once back in his room he gently placed the ancient text on the floor. Adam studied the pages of the text for quite some time before taking a sip of his cold drink. He returned to the kitchen to reheat his cocoa in the microwave. Returning to his room and sipping from the scorching brew Adam began to study the writings.

He could read or recognize a multitude of languages; however he could not interpret the hieroglyphs he was looking at now, but he knew for sure that they were not Egyptian. He took a bite out of his sandwich and a healthy blob of honey-enriched peanut butter dropped onto the tablet in front of him.

With his thumb and forefinger Adam pinched up the peanut butter and plopped it into his mouth, then began tracing the images he was studying with his sticky finger. He wondered why his mom would keep such awesome writings locked away from him.

The color had faded from the pages but the drawings were deep and still clearly illustrated the scene. As Adam took another sip from his cooling chocolate he had a sense of sheer panic as he realized he was no longer alone. He nearly drenched the sacred text in chocolate as he bolted to his feet, spun around, and made a feeble attempt to block himself from his mother's undisputed wrath.

It was Grandee.

Adam was so terrified that he almost started crying. Adam quickly regained his composure and tried to be brave in the face of his personal apocalypse.

"You're just like your mother." The master wizard entered the room and slowly lowered himself into the chair at the foot of Adam's bed. "Finish eating boy. I believe you have something you wanted to say to me."

Adam wasn't hungry anymore, but he ate anyway. He sat on the floor and defiantly thumbed through the book he'd removed from his mother's bedroom while trying to look bored. Adam exaggeratedly broke off and chewed on tiny bird-size pieces from his sandwich and languidly sipped from his mug. Adam knew he was skating on thin ice and knew he was really pushing it when he felt the searing heat of Myrddin's anger rising like the sun from the east.

Adam looked up and expressionlessly held Myrddin's glare, then he managed to look startled, as if he hadn't know Myrddin had been in the room; a technique that he'd mastered that had infuriated Inanna. Myrddin, however, refused to be baited. Myrddin shifted in his chair and Adam flinched. With his performance of bravado shattered, Adam's eyes clouded over as his thoughts returned to his encounters with the first woman he had called mom.

"After practice I went to the jewelry store and waited for her to come out. She was wearing diamonds that day. She usually doesn't."

"It's amazing what a man remembers about a woman, isn't it?"

Myrddin's question made Adam blush, "It's not like that. Mom always wears rubies. I think I would notice if one day she wore an emerald or nothing at all, I would think that something is wrong. It's the same thing with her. She wears a lot of gold, but that day she was wearing diamonds. Besides don't you always tell me to pay attention?"

"Aye boy, but I always tell you because you don't listen." Adam laughed at that, and then got up from the floor to lay across his bed so that he could be more comfortable.

"She was waiting for her car. It was raining and I was standing across the street, inside the bus stop booth because I didn't want to get wet. I watched her step from under the awning and she lifted her head so that the raindrops could bounce off her face. Her stupid little dog did the same thing."

"Astonishing." Myrddin's face frowned in bewilderment.

"I know. When she had enough of the rain and opened her eyes I made sure that I was the first thing she saw. I stepped closer to the street so that she could see me, and I stared at her, but she didn't even know who the fuck I was."

"Adam ..."

"No! She didn't even fucking remember me!" Adam tried to calm himself down, but he couldn't do it. He sprang from the bed and began frantically pacing.

"Stop treating me like a *kid* Grandee I'm almost eighteen. Why is it supposed to make me feel better that 'if it wasn't for her I wouldn't be here'? She didn't care. I looked in the papers and police reports ... not one mention of a missing child, no Amber alert, nothing. How the hell do you just throw a little kid away?"

"Adam, relax," Myrddin spoke gently weaving a calming spell with each word.

"No!" Adam thundered while shrugging off the blanket of tranquility Myrddin tried to wrap him in. As soon as he heard himself Adam raised his hands in front of him, the way people do when they are trying to get something to stop, to let Myrddin know he didn't mean to be so disrespectful.

"If I came up missing Grandee what would you do? What would mom do? You know what she would do? She'd stop the earth from fucking spinning, that's what! So why didn't *she*? She didn't even fucking look for me, I could have ended up anywhere. She didn't even fucking remember me!"

"Adam."

"I hate her," Adam hissed.

"Listen to me Adam, though you are very talented, you are nowhere near strong enough to harness the power of hate and vengeance."

"I fucking hate her." It was as if Adam hadn't heard a word.

"Adam." The voice of the feminine smothered their conversation in a suppression of silence, as Inanna entered the room. Her glare went from man to boy then zeroed in on the book Adam had taken from her bedroom.

Mystery shrouded the whereabouts of any of the missing volumes from the Hermetic Text. Knights of the Order hunted these books down with more ferocity than they chased the Holy Grail. And here was one on the floor in Adam's room, pages sticky with peanut butter and honey. Written in a language only known to God, its ancient words were now blurred with fat droplets of milk sweetened by chocolate.

Trembling with rage Inanna raised her eyes from the sugar-coated book to her son. She didn't trust herself to speak. She slammed Adam with a hammer blow look that caused her son to look away in shame.

In the same instant Myrddin threw a thought towards Adam that Inanna could not intercept. Careful now boy, your mother knows nothing of what you've said.

Inanna saw the look between them and was infuriated, "You dare keep secrets from me in my own house?" The roar that issued from her was like that of a lioness. She snatched the book from the floor. With his eyes full of tears Adam took an instinctive step away from his mother. Myrddin rose and stood between them.

"Be patient my girl, the boy is only seventeen. These growing pains are natural for a boy his age. You knew this was coming, and that's precisely why you called me to this country." Inanna's anger waned as she considered Myrddin's point of view. The wizard read her thoughts as if reading pages from an open book.

"All of this turbulence, Adam's distance and these wild outbursts, though maddening are Adam's transition from boyhood to man. He has simply lost his footing and he has to find his way."

Inanna moved around Myrddin to stand in front of her son. She placed a hand on his cheek, and Adam held her hand so that she couldn't move it away. "I'm so used to you clinging to my skirt hems," she told him.

"He has to find his own way, Inanna."

"I know, I know. It's just that it's hard to think of my baby growing up."

"Mom, I'm a foot taller than you," Adam pointed out through his smile.

"The next time you take something out of my room that won't make a difference in this world or the next. You hear me boy, Yankee ass brat?" Inanna truthfully teased as she brushed his curly hair away from his smiling face. "Okay then," was all she said as she started to leave the room.

Adam's smile widened as he thought that Myrddin might be right. He couldn't imagine what his life would have been like if he hadn't ended up here with his true mother and grandfather. But then a dark cloud promising a storm rolled across Adam's thoughts as he was once again reminded that he could have ended up anywhere and that the other woman, his false mother, hadn't lifted a finger to ensure that he was safe. The change in Adam's attitude changed the temperature in his room, and Inanna had reservations about leaving.

Looking out the window at the sprawling park below Myrddin suggested a walk. "Don't forget your scarf, its chilly out." warned Inanna. "And before you leave this house Yankee, you better clean up my kitchen."

XXIX

The autumn air was crisp against Adam's golden Mediterranean-sun-kissed skin. The two were walking along the jogging path in one of the city's upscale parks, and the caress of the chilly breeze left Adam's nose and cheeks reddened by its touch.

Myrddin took long, confident strides and Adam had to quicken his pace to keep up. Myrddin felt that this vigorous exercise would keep the fight from the boy. "When did you leave the note for her, before or after you saw her in the rain?"

"After," answered Adam. "I wanted to jog her memory of me, but mostly I wanted her to know she wasn't as safe as she thought she was."

"Listen boy, you are still an apprentice. The thing you must realize about using fear, when you are strong enough to use it, is that fear can be overcome. You must never underestimate what a person can do when frightened; never underestimate what a person can do when in the throes of self-preservation."

"I wrote her name on an envelope, but I didn't actually write a note. It was dark by the time I stood outside her balcony and called to her dog. He came out right away, all pissed off, as if he could have done anything. She came out not long after and picked him up. She yelled down 'Oh sorry' but you could tell she really didn't mean it."

They stopped at a street vendor to order a lunch of hotdogs and Cokes then sat on a bench facing the pond that was not quite large enough to be a lake. They sat in silence for awhile enjoying the meal and each other's quiet company. Adam sat close to Myrddin and looked up at him as he did as a boy. Not to take anything away from his mother, Adam loved the time he spent was able to spend alone with Myrddin.

"I really didn't mean to kill her dog." Adam calmly remembered the episode as he threw pieces of bread to the geese. "I called her from a payphone and told her I couldn't control my feelings. I reminded her that as a doctor she wasn't supposed to do any harm, and then I just dropped the phone and walked away before she could say anything.

"I knew she would leave, so I waited by the garage gate. I knelt down like I was tying my shoe, and she didn't see me. I slipped in while she drove out, then I cast a sleeping spell on the guard and turned off the security cameras.

"When I opened the door to her apartment her little fucking dog bit me. He made me so mad that I kicked him across the hall. I didn't think he would be there, because she never went anywhere without him.

"He was hurt pretty bad and at first I felt sorry for him, because she had left him just like she left me. I was going to try and heal him, but when I tried to pick him up he bit me again, so I destroyed him."

"That's precisely what I am talking about Adam, when I say you still have a lot to learn. You should have been able to convey to the animal a sense of comfort and safety, but you were unable to."

Adam shrugged off any feelings of guilt, "I bet she won't leave anything else."

"No, I suppose she won't."

XXX

I woke up squinting against a sun that was piercing through the darkness of a nightmare that I couldn't fully wake from. The searing pain in my head and neck dared me to move. Of course I did no such thing. I was relieved to see that Ken was there. He had prepared me a breakfast of scrambled eggs with spinach, mushrooms, and feta cheese, a pile of bacon, toast, and a tall glass of sparkling Alka Seltzer.

Sentinel watched Ken's every move but did not leave my side or hesitate to let Ken know when he felt Ken was too close, I hushed my dog to allow my friend to get close enough to hand me the hot plate of food.

I could barely manage to prop my head up on my hand, so I ate lying down and was surprised that I was able to eat at all. I don't remember the last time I had drank that much, but Ken was right; I had to pull myself together if I really hoped to speak with Adam, something that Ken was vehemently advising against.

We talked awhile about the weather, my headache, Sentinel, and work, but our conversation always drifted back to Adam. The deaths of Dr. Morgan and Dr. Hogue could be overlooked and forgiven; however the murders of the desert girl and Peter were altogether different.

"I understand that you still love Adam," Ken observed "We all did. Even after Peter's death I still do. But sometime nature overrides nurture. You need to understand that there is a real possibility that there is nothing you can do."

"Where do you think he's been all this time?" I asked. "He was only four when we lost him. Never minding his altared genetics he didn't have the skills to acquire the basic four necessities of life."

"Food, water, shelter, and clothing," Ken added. "It's clear he's had much more than just that. I have no idea where's he's been, but I highly doubt he was alone."

"Logan is the strongest seer that you've cultivated. I just don't understand how she missed her mark. This is the only time she has ever been wrong."

"That was ten years ago. Logan was only nineteen, still an infant in her abilities."

I was still lying on the couch. Ken took a seat on the other end of it and I draped my legs across his lap. Sentinel had fallen asleep on the floor. Ken gently tapped my legs and I moved them so that he could get up. He stepped over my dog and walked across the living room to lean against the window.

"That's something that has been bothering me as well. Last year, when you convened that emergency meeting, I put together a team to comb through the records of police, hospitals, churches, child protective services, foster agencies, and even the morgue, searching records from the night he was taken from The Facility. We found nothing. I started to get a horrible feeling that whoever found Adam didn't want anyone else to know."

"How in the world do you hide a child?" I asked then noted, "You cannot send a kid to school without immunization records. You cannot immunize a child without a birth certificate. Why in the world didn't Adam just kill Cassidy, his cousin and his henchmen?"

"That's an interesting point." Ken was slowly nodding his head as if he was remembering something. "I don't think he could have. The day before his capture Adam was in Dr. Hogue's lab, exposed to a deadly virus, and then frozen, however our boy did not die. We were unable to conduct tests after the thaw." I winched at this because I was the reason no data had been collected.

"But a year prior we exposed Adam to varicella spores and though highly contagious chickenpox is a common childhood illness, Adam did not contract the attacking pathogen; but during the time his body fought off the invasion he was sluggish, and drowsy. During the first six hours after exposure Adam was disorientated and giddy and could not perform the simplest of tasks. It was as if he were intoxicated."

I smiled at the image of Adam being giddier than he already was, because the kid had a silly streak a mile long, but as the image faded I felt like shooting myself for not paying attention to the research.

"What else was Adam exposed to?" I asked, while silently vowing to comb though all the reports and footage of Adam.

"He was exposed to Human Parvovirus B-19, Rubella, Roseola Infantum, Scarlet Fever, Mumps and a multitude of other illnesses that affect children from around the globe."

"You injected Adam with Scarlet Fever?"

"Yes, we did. What was discovered during those experiments is Adam has four times the amount of white blood cells in his body than God intended, and that Adam's systems shut down to varying extents to fight off infections. If the infection was something as common as chickenpox or the flu Adam became a little loopy. If it was something more aggressive Adam needed to sleep it off – as the saying goes.

The virus Adam's body fought from the germ lab is one million times stronger than anything we exposed him to, so there was no way that Adam could have known he was in trouble when Dr Cassidy's men removed him from The Facility." Ken took a deep breath and looked at me with eyes full of dread. "There's something I haven't told you."

"What?" I could barely breathe and I didn't really want to be answered.

"Logan is gone."

XXXI

he woman who captivated their attention was so beautiful that she looked ethereal. The aura of her unapproachableness bathed her in a silvery glow, and the wind wrapped her honey golden hair around her head like a halo. Adding to her angelic appearance was her wardrobe, which were all shades of white: cream pumps, ivory trousers, winter white cashmere sweater with a matching scarf, an eggshell overcoat with real rabbit fur at the collar, and pearl earrings.

Her eyes were such a light blue in color, they almost looked white, like two orbs of ice – and they were seeing nothing but Myrddin. Looking at her filled Adam with such a pressing feeling of ominous doom that he felt like he was being crushed, and Adam started to get angry.

Myrddin placed his hand on Adam's chest to calm him. "Adam I need you to go home right now." His instructions heightened Adam's level of anxiety because the tone of his voice left no room for argument.

"Who is she?"

"Do not attempt to interfere," Myrddin responded without answering Adam's question. "There is nothing you can do and any feeble attempts made will result in precious loss of energy. Go home. Run."

The woman was only steps away from them when Myrddin and Adam stood in unison. Myrddin stood in front of Adam. With his grandson safely behind him he repeated his command once more and encased Adam within a shield of protection with so much force it felt like a shove and repeated his command once more. "Run!"

The woman lunged at Myrddin so fast that she looked like a blur. Her manicured nails turned into tiger claws as she grabbed and dug into Myrddin's shoulder. Her mouth opened to reveal large fangs, like that of a bear, as she bit into Myrddin's face.

Adam was screaming with rage. He tried to throw a protective barrier around his grandfather and a binding spell against the witch. With her thumb and middle finger she flicked Adam away as if he was no more than an annoying little picnic gnat. Adam was flung nearly the distance of the pond and landed in four feet of murky water.

He looked up in time to see the woman split into two. Not split in half but split into another. The second woman zipped across the pond and put her foot on Adam's chest to keep him down. With her hands in the pockets of her overcoat she was looking over her shoulder to watch the progress of her sister. Dismissed and submerged under water Adam was furious. The first two spells attempted resulted in failure. Incapacitated with rage Adam pushed upwards with a pulse so violent it caused most of the water from the pond to shoot skyward towards the heavens.

The woman was thrown back a few feet but before Adam could catch his breath and climb completely out of that chasm she regained her footing, multiplied herself, and the two of them pinned Adam against the shore as the water rained back down to refill the pond. Despite his fury, spell casting, and struggling, the women were not fazed. The one on the right was so confident in their ability to restrain him she momentarily held Adam with one hand as she swept her wet bangs from her face and tucked them behind her ear. Her blasé gesture infuriated Adam. He had never been angrier in his entire life, and he tried in vain to hurt her. Adam screamed so loud and for so long that he could no longer do so. The fact that they were all but ignoring him while watching the developments across the pond, added insult to injury.

The women across the pond had swarmed and multiplied into a dozen and descended upon Myrddin like a pride of lions. They ripped and devoured him in the same manner.

Myrddin was on the ground. He could hear Adam screaming "Grandee" over and over again but could no longer see him because his eyes had been torn out.

Myrddin knew Inanna was on her way, though there would be nothing that she could do.

When only his limbs remained the two holding Adam released him to join their sisters in the feast.

Adam tried chasing after them. The water was deeper than Adam could have guessed. Swallowing gulps of water while trying to call out to Myrddin Adam nearly drowned. By the time Adam reached his Grandee there was nothing left of him but his coat and staff. Clinging to both Adam screamed once more for his grandfather, hoping against hope that his cries would bring him back.

XXXII

hat do you mean 'Logan is gone'? Gone where?" That was the last thing I was expecting to hear and it hit me like a ton of bricks.

"If I knew where, she wouldn't be missing, would she?" he shot back. This was the beginning of an argument I did not want to have. Sentinel was awake and eying Ken as if he were an enemy combatant. I stood up so fast that I nearly fell and realized that I was teetering on the edge of still being drunk.

"Ken, did she *leave* or is she *missing*?" Ken ran his hand through his hair and led the way into my library before answering,

"She's missing."

I lost my vision for a minute while I tried to tell myself it wasn't as bad as it seemed, that surely there was a reasonable explanation. I went to my liquor console and drank from my bottle of Beauté du Siècle. Ken watched in silent horror as I poured thousands of dollars of cognac down my throat without the benefit of a glass. I regained my equilibrium as I felt my body warming in response to the liqueur's caressing touch. I told Ken I'd be back and I went into the master bath to splash my face with cool water.

When I returned to the study I was already starting to feel the effects of the alcohol. My Charles Eames lounge chairs frame the chess table and are nestled in the window overlooking the city's park, and that's where we sat. Ken belligerently advanced his knight to the middle of the board. Ignoring his opening I asked Ken to tell me what had happened.

"She didn't come into work over a weekend."

"Is that it, so what?" I interjected while Ken was trying to find the words to continue. I was starting to feel uneasy but tried to brush it off.

"She's only twenty-eight years old. She young and beautiful, a bit sporadic, with a very active social life. It's probably just a weekend get away with her friends or a rendezvous with a lover."

Ken was nonchalantly nodding his head in agreement, and I knew I was just being appeased. I watched Ken go to the liquor console and select the British Royal Navy Imperial Rum, and I knew that what he had to say was bad new at best. At 108.6 proof this isn't the rum for celebrations. Ken took two Cokes out of the small refrigerator and brought them, with the tall shot glasses of rum, back to the chess table. I closed my eyes and took a tiny sip of the rum. Without delay my mouth and nose were bombarded with intense zest of orange essence and earthy-peaty notes. I let the lingering flavors roll off my tongue before opening my eyes and countering Ken's move.

"And then I was contacted by a detective working on the missing persons report of Logan Dweller. I was stunned. I had no reason to think that anything was wrong because she had requested time off to prepare for exams." Ken stared absently out of the window and for a long time said nothing. "Logan meant to me what Adam meant to you, and now she's gone."

Have you ever ridden on a roller coaster? You know that feeling you get in the pit of your stomach as the coaster reaches the peak and then pauses? That was almost how I felt at that moment, except I felt so much worse than that. My posture was extremely tense. I was sitting very still and holding my breath because I did not want my coaster to teeter forward.

As if answering my unasked question Ken told me, "She's been gone now for ten months." *Almost a year.* I felt the click of the brake being released as my coaster began its descent.

XXXIII

The only other person to see the demons besides Myrddin was Adam. The last moments in Myrddin's life happened in a parallel plain of existence. The other park visitors were blissfully unaware of the death of the wizard.

A woman pushing a stroller waved down the police officers on horseback when she saw Adam. He was soaking wet, sitting on the ground next to the bench where he and his grandfather had shared their last meal. He was hugging Myrddin's coat, sucking his thumb, and rocking back and forth. The woman frantically explained to the officer, as he jumped from his stallion, that she had seen the boy earlier in the day, sitting with his grandfather on the bench.

Because the woman who was speaking to him was near panic, the boy on the ground was covered with pond water and obviously in shock, and the only thing remaining of the alleged grandfather was the coat and walking stick, the officer called the paramedics, and requested a dive team, and the city contractor to dredge the pond.

Adam wasn't responding to the officer's questions. He was looking through the officer with unfocused, glazed-over eyes. When Adam's eyes focused on something behind him, the officer turned to see what Adam was looking at. In the same instant he heard the boy say, "Mom!" and start to cry.

What the officer noted in relief was not the woman the boy had cried out for but the medic team behind her. The paramedics took Adam's blood pressure while he cried within the safety of his mother's arms.

Engulfed in Inanna's protection Adam sent her a thousand words telepathically as he tried to explain what had happened. The lead paramedic decided to wrap them both in a thermo blanket rather than try and separate the boy from his mom.

Let them believe what they see Inanna gently thought back.

People were beginning to mull around and whisper in small groups. One look from Inanna was all that it took to kill the cat of curiosity, as all around tried to find other places to be. The senior officer thought it was strange – almost unusual to see crowds of onlookers disperse without police encouragement, but he was glad to see them go.

The first diver was already below the surface when the senior officer approached Adam to gingerly probe him for answers.

"He fell in and I couldn't …." Adam was shaking his head back and forth as tears blurred his vision. Adam wasn't crying because of the lie he was telling, but the truth within it; he couldn't save Myrddin. The officer did not want to push the boy further but he wanted to prepare him for the inevitable.

"Listen kid," the officer began. His words were soft and comforting, which caused Adam to hug Inanna even tighter as if to prepare himself. This pond is deep, and the bottom, well it's kind of like quicksand." The officer looked at Inanna and the tears forming in her large green eyes were too much for the cop to bear so he cast his eyes downward before continuing. "He may never be found." When the officer looked up he saw both mother and child in tears.

Inanna was seething during the walk home. She saw the world through a veil of red as she listened to Adam recount his ordeal for a second time, slowly through tears, and in detail.

"Carrie," Adam explained towards the end of his tale. "I think her name was Carrie. She kept doubling herself until she was too many to count."

"Not Carrie," Inanna corrected, "Keres." Inanna explained that the female death spirits were Nyx's daughters, in charge of transporting souls to the flames of hell. The more Inanna explained things to Adam the angrier and more upset she became.

She understood Myrddin's time was coming to an end but she hadn't thought it would be so sudden or so violent – and in the presence of innocence! Inanna was angry because Myrddin had been stolen from her and ripped away from her son. She felt cheated.

Inanna was upset because Adam was becoming more and more inconsolable with each word he spoke. Adam felt shameful because he had been unable to save his Grandee. Inanna understood there was absolutely nothing her son could have done to save her father, and Adam's guilt shattered her like glass.

Adam cried so hard once he was in the safety of Inanna's arms that he was having trouble drawing breaths. Inanna hadn't seen him cry like that since the night she found him on the banks of the wilderness. Inanna started to tremble as she struggled to keep her temper in check.

Her son was suffering and she wanted to kill everything in sight. She hadn't felt like that since the night her mother was killed on the shores of Haiti.

What finally pushed Inanna over the edge of madness and caused her to have visions of violence, and want to deploy the scorched earth policy is when they got home and Adam did not want any hot chocolate with a Snickers bar melted inside – which until that day, had been Adam's cure for everything.

Adam went into Inanna's room, crawled under the down comforters without taking off his shoes, and cried himself to sleep.

XXXIV

When Adam woke up entangled in blankets that were infused with his mothers' expensive fragrances he thought for a moment that he'd just had a horrible dream. Adam knew Myrddin was really gone when he looked down the length of the bed and saw he was still wearing his shoes.

Adam slowly rolled over, tucking the comforter under his chin. His mom was sleeping on the chaise that was next to the window. He blinked his eyes against his tears. There was something comfortingly familiar about waking up like this and knowing his mom had fallen asleep while watching over him. Adam got up and softy kissed Inanna on her forehead and covered her with a clean blanket that had fallen on the floor. Adam quietly removed the silt and muddy sheets from his mom's bed, working slowly so the rustling of the sheets wouldn't wake her. As he took the sheets from her room and set them by the front door so that he could take them to the cleaners, Adam was thinking that he had to be strong for his mom because Myrddin was gone and he was all she had left.

Adam went into the kitchen and saw the tin of chocolate, a Snickers bar, a mug and a spoon lined up on the counter next to the range that held a small pot waiting to boil milk. Adam leaned against the refrigerator for support but slid down it in tears. He muffled his cries behind both hands and cried for what seemed like an eternity.

Adam crawled forward on his hands to peek down the hall. When he found the strength to stand he slowly walked back to Inanna's room, took a quick look inside, and found her still sleeping. After softly closing the door he walked past his own to stand in front of the door of Myrddin's.

He had never been in Myrddin's bedroom for it had always been forbidden. Inanna's bedroom was the first room in this house that Adam remembered being in. Her room always whispered the promise of warmth, comfort, safety, and the familiar and was the reason why it was the first place Adam went when something was wrong.

He had full access to all the rooms in their summer home in Manchester, as he did with the properties in Cairo, London, and Madrid. Though well-traveled Adam spent the majority of his life in this city, growing up in this penthouse, and had never been tempted to enter his grandfather's room because his mother's captivated his attention.

He opened the door and squinted as his eyes adjusted to the dark. From floor to ceiling and wall-to-wall, except for the doorway, was lined with books. Shafts of light forced their way into the darkness, past the volumes that concealed the window. Adam closed the door and trailed his hand across the bindings, and he breathed in the mixture of odors that is scent of old books.

He inhaled the unique charred aroma of books that had survived fires, and the scent of salt from books that had once lived by the sea – his fingers gliding over the textures of aged leather knowing the title of each just by the power of touch. The pleasant aromatic blend of leather, oil, wood, and ink engulfed him as he walked toward his Grandee's bed.

The four posters of the large bed that was on the left side of the room, looked to Adam like Roman pillars. The only thing that separated the bed from the wall was a long desk that looked like it had been carved from ivory and a chair made of the same.

He sat on the side of Myrddin's bed and took a visual inventory of the items that were displayed on his grandfather's huge desk. There were beakers and vials, three armillary spheres and two astrolabes, crucibles, an alembic and all kinds of boxes in different shapes and sizes.

Adam moved from the bed to sit at the desk. Once seated he touched or picked up everything that was on it. He ran his fingers along the deep engravings of intricate knot work on the face of the desk that he thought was Celtic that were tangled around hieroglyphs that looked Norse. On one end of the desk were twelve jars made of different shapes and materials, lined up in rows of two in front of the stacks of books.

Each container held exotic spices and unfamiliar powders. There was a brass candleholder supporting a large green candle. Adam used the matchbook sitting near it to light it, and the room was bathed in a soft amber light.

There were stacks of parchment that had curled and turned yellow with age. In the center of the desk a cauldron the size of a cereal bowl rested on top a Bunsen burner. On the left side of the desk was a small blue jar with a shallow pool of black ink and dipped within it were two feathers from a seagull. Behind the quill and inkwell was a picture of him and Inanna in a heavy brass frame. In the photograph, Adam was only five or six. He was wrapped in Inanna's arms, leaning against her chest and laughing with his eyes closed. Inanna's was smiling into the camera. Behind that picture was another one. A picture like the one of him and Inanna, but this one had captured a moment with Inanna and Grandee.

She looked very young. Her hair wasn't as long as it was now, only just past her shoulders and blowing in the wind. Inanna's hands where on her hips, head cocked to the side, and she worn a devious smile on her face. Myrddin was standing behind her with his arms folded across his chest and the hint of his smile was not directed into the camera because he was looking at Inanna. Adam picked up the crystal frame and watched the glass moisten as it caught his tears. Adam removed the other picture from the desk along with his grandfather's spell book, blew out the candle, and left the room.

Inanna was waiting for him in the kitchen, "How ya doing Yankee?"

Adam gave her a weary smile through his tears. Inanna never understood why he liked it so when she called him that. Adam hadn't learned the meaning of the word "Yankee" until he studied American History in the fifth grade. Inanna rarely called Adam by his name except during times of great praise or punishment, but she was relieved to see Adam smile.

Adam had never seen his mother look at him the way she was looking at him now. He answered her question with one of his own. "You okay?"

Inanna shook her head slowly in disbelief, "I can't believe how brave you've become. You fought against all odds."

"I know. Do you remember what you used said to me when I was little? As long as you can draw breath, you can fight. Remember that summer in Italy when I was thrown from that horse? I stood up screaming covered from head to toe in mud and you ran to me and picked me up?"

"Of course I remember. You had just turned seven."

"You were wiping the mud from my face and kept telling me that I was okay." Adam's voice trembled as spoke and he hugged the spoils from his grandfather's room close to his chest. "When one of the Keres was standing on me and had me pinned under the water I heard your voice telling me that I was okay."

Inanna was comforted that Adam was safe at home but she was also extremely upset by Adam's headstrong willfulness. Inanna ensured that Adam didn't intercept her thoughts but the fact of the matter was she could have lost them both yesterday.

Inanna knew she was going to have to find a way to keep his intransigence in check. She reached up to brush away a dark curl of hair that had fallen across his forehead.

"Go take a shower, Yankee and pack a bag. We're going to spend some abroad."

"School starts in two weeks."

"You'll start late."

Adam shrugged his shoulders and did as he was told.

XXXV

They spent six weeks in Amman, in a luxury villa overlooking the Dead Sea and the Judean desert. Adam cried every day of the first week they were there. Adam never saw Inanna crying but he heard her when she thought he was sleep.

After their week long mourning period Inanna spent most of her mornings deep within the Jordan Valley, bathing in the simmering waters of the Dead Sea under the beating sun and lapping up the thirty-five minerals that are essential for the health of the mind, body and soul. Adam chose to receive his therapeutic properties by praying and meditating amongst the ruins of the citadel, visiting archaeological discoveries, and traveling old roads that were the paths of kings, emperors, traders and prophets of antiquity.

They spent their afternoons over lunch, sipping on strong, sweet, and slightly scented Arabic coffee, and in one café they puffed apple-flavored tobacco from an ornate Argeelah. Watching Inanna inhale the sweetened smoke made Adam believe that there was something spiritual about smoking from a pipe so heavy entwined in this regions culture.

Adam's first attempt left him coughing for almost an hour and wondering where in the world the Surgeon General was when needed most. He tried again every day until he got it right.

Inanna and Adam spent their evenings before dinner exploring the city like tourists. They strolled through marketplaces selling intricate embroideries, antique jewels of gold, silver, amber and coral, heavily spiced teas, camels, and goats.

They browsed through every elaborate storefront bejeweled with mosaic tile and Arabic script. They rode on camelback to the desert castles scattered around the barren regions of the Basalts, and through it all Adam was despondent and distracted.

Inanna took Adam into a gallery displaying Byzantine art. As Inanna leafed through primeval images of Christ and walked past large mosaic tapestries, Adam stood absently at the window, with his hands in his denim pockets, gazing at the locals across the street at the café in the middle of the market.

Adam vaguely watched men play games of backgammon, cards, and chess. He distantly watched women smoking, laughing and gossiping, and others arguing over politics. Suddenly, he saw the reflection of a girl in the window who was standing behind him.

Adam slowly turned to look at her, and his jaw dropped. The Ethiopian girl was just as tall as he was, with honey colored skin, and molten bronze for eyes. She looked up and held Adam's gaze for a full forty-five seconds. Then with an appraising look from head to toe, she returned her attention to her patron. The slight smile she gave caused Adam to forget there were other people on the face of the earth.

Adam recovered his composure with a smile and glanced toward Inanna in time to see her raise an eyebrow and shake her head in mock disgust before pretending not to know him. Inanna was relieved that finally something had come along to distract Adam from his grief and open an umbrella against the cloud of gloom that he seemed trapped underneath.

Adam's attention returned to the girl, who ignored him while looking in his direction. She carefully wrapped her customer's merchandise in brown paper and twine while pretending that she didn't see Adam feigning for assistance. She walked her customer to the door then stood by Adam's side. "Can I help you?" the girl asked in English, with an accent that was as beautiful and relentless as the Horn of Africa.

Adam took a few moments to take her all in before

answering. The oukrat that adorned her exposed skin was more ornate than any jewel Adam had ever seen.

The traditional tattoos that she wore on her forehead and from ear to ear along the jaw line were cross-like designs in a bold statement of her creed. The six rows of sensuous tribal marking that graced her throat left Adam mesmerized, as the patterns fluttered against her heartbeat and rose and fell like the tide with her breath. Her shoulder-length braided hair held within it Cowry shells to represent her family's beauty and prestige, along with gold and brass beads to match her eyes in a flagrant waste of wealth. When Adam finally spoke he did so in the girl's native tongue of Amharic. "You are beautiful."

She took a step closer to him and replied with a coy smile, "I am told that everyday, sometimes twice." After a moment of consideration she added, "As if somehow I would forget."

Adam took a step closer to her feeling her tea-scented breath on his face. "Tell me," he flirtatiously demanded, "which Goddess are you named after?"

She took a small step back. "My name is R'bka Nishan."

"R'bka means to blind and Nishan is metal right?" Adam translated in English. "Blinding metal ... because of your eyes."

She smiled and took a step closer to Adam. Inanna loudly cleared her throat to remind them that they were not in the privacy of somewhere alone. R'bka Nishan bashfully rung up and wrapped Inanna's items while Adam stood staring at her from Inanna's side. Their infatuation with each other blossomed, despite the fact that R'bka Nishan was five years older than Adam. She was distracted every time Adam came around, which was every day. The shop owner grew weary of her daughter's giggly distractedness and finally gave her the entire month off, and Adam and R'bka Nishan were together everyday for the thirty-seven days that Adam and Inanna spent in Jordan.

When they returned to The States, Adam's mood was worse than before they had left.

The death of his grandfather changed Adam's happy disposition and silly attitude into something dull. The separation from R'bka Nishan changed it to something dark and brooding. His final year of high school was almost like the previous three. He was extremely popular and well liked. He competed in varsity wrestling, rowing, and fencing while receiving straight A's. Adam was the captain of the fencing team, science club and the debate team – but his competitive nature became brutal because Adam refused to lose no matter the cost. Adam no longer had any patience for anything; he was quick to anger and even faster with his fist. Adam added to his extracurricular activities, fighting and reducing peers and faculty alike to tears by reversing his power of praise to words of wrath. Adam's short fuse and hyper aggression alarmed the dean and compelled him to phone Inanna. The dean suggested that Adam be tested for the use of steroids.

Inanna met the dean for lunch because under no circumstances was she going to allow Adam to take any type of test that required blood work or a urine sample. The phenomenal results of such a test would be reported and generate the wrong type of attention. Besides she knew her son wasn't using any drugs, illegal or otherwise. With words that slid across Inanna's tongue like ice, she explained that the thing Adam needed most was grief counseling. Inanna watched the dean grow uncomfortable as she proceeded to explain Adam was not on drugs, his change in behavior was due to the drowning of her father and how Adam had attempted but failed to save him.

What she didn't tell the dean was that Adam practiced the dark arts in his grandfather's room every spare minute that he had, desperately striving to shed the title "sorcerer's apprentice," which he felt had cost Grandee his life. Having Adam see a counselor turned out to be a battle of wills and a test of patience. Adam spent most sessions glaring at the doctor with hostile suspicion. On the days there was not a staring contest, Adam would use the hour a day after school constructively – by ignoring the doctor completely and completing his homework assignments or taking a nap.

XXXVI

nanna was jarred from sleep by traces of a dream that depicted smoke, fire, and sand. As she sat up slowly in bed Inanna focused all of her concentration on the dream that was slipping away, and she saw a nomadic tribal girl and a glass bracelet covered in blood. The fleeting dream revealed flashes of a small dog being torn to pieces by hand, a man being run down in the streets like a dog, and a large dog snarling with fangs bared. The last thing Inanna saw before fully waking was Adam's face, and on it was the smile that had the power to wrap her around his little finger.

Inanna spent several minutes in bed, contemplating the visions in her dream. After drinking her morning tea and paying homage to angels of both death and chaos, Inanna went into her ritual room to make the necessary preparations to conjure the wizard who had summoned her.

The death of Myrddin transitioned him from mere wizard to demon. She knew Myrddin would not be allowed to manifest into the physical form for a period of one hundred years, but, as she did with so many things, she knew a way around that rule.

To speak with Myrddin Inanna would simply scry. The spirit does not manifest into the physical form … it manifests as a vision in the mirror. Inanna sat at her altar and began her request.

"In my great name, Inanna Veve, I demand that all things in darkness bestow their powers of prophesy upon this mirror, that I may use this magical medium to contact any demon or otherwise as I see fit, to scry upon the past and present for the revelation of secrets, and knowledge that is unknown to me."

This is the way Inanna began each of her vision quests, taking sometimes an hour for the one she called to answer, but as soon as she lit the candle on her altar the image of Myrddin rose in the mirror like the smoke from the freshly lit flame. Inanna was so startled that she cried out. The sight of him was not what she remembered or expected.

Myrddin looked his age, which was countless of centuries, and for the first time within the brutal purple of Myrddin's eyes she saw pain. Inanna covered her mouth with both hands as she began to cry because she knew he was suffering, knew there was nothing she could do to relieve his pain and because she knew she would never be allowed to touch him again. For the longest time neither said a word. Inanna cried and Myrddin just watched. Though they were within sight of each other they were worlds apart.

Despite the fact the great wizard was bonded and tormented he still had great strength, and he created an optical illusion, turning Inanna's room into the rolling green hills of the Western Isle of Scotland, where Myrddin first taught Inanna the secrets of Enoch.

Inanna felt the breeze dry her tears in the impression Myrddin sent, and he appeared the way she remembered him: tall, beautiful, full of vitality and strength. They walked arm in arm to sit against a stone that had been erected millennia before the birth of Christ.

It was there that Inanna asked about the visions of her dreams and why she was summoned. Weeks past as they sat in the fields of the Callanish village, and Myrddin told Inanna everything about Adam. Over time the vision faded, and she was sitting alone in her room. Only two hours had passed. Inanna took a deep breath as she sat back in her chair. As she remembered the things that Myrddin said to her she began to tremble. She felt her heartbeat quicken. Her body tensed up and she felt slightly jittery. Inanna closed her eyes and allowed herself to be absorbed by this sensation. She hadn't felt this way since her mother had put her in a boat and pushed her out to sea, and tears of rage pressed their way out from behind Inanna's closed eyes.

XXXVII

hat is it that we're missing?" I asked Ken. I opened my Coke and drank it from the can. I was done drinking for the day. I still felt off kilter from the night before and I was already starting to feel the effects of the rum, though I'd had very little of it.

I wanted to be alert, able to think straight, and react quickly. I wanted to remove myself from this situation emotionally and look at it through my scientific eyes.

Ken sat quietly for awhile as he considered what I had just asked before finally echoing my question and saying he wasn't sure.

"There has got to be something we are missing," I repeated. "Let's look at what he's done since he was removed from the facility. Jackie, the tribal girl, this bracelet, Peter, and possibly Logan." I counted them off, starting with my thumb, ending with all my fingers extended from my right hand, which I held up between us. "The way to solve this equation is to find out the why." I took another drink of my Coke and blinked away the tears as the carbonated caffeine raced down my throat. I shook my head in attempts to shake off the affects of the alcohol but knew it would take more than that as I noticed the blur around the edges of my vision.

Ken asked me, "Why the gypsy and not your sister?" He finished what was in his shot glass and took mine to replace it. Ken scrolled through his Blackberry and suggested that we have lunch delivered. He placed a call to a Thai restaurant and then called a bistro that specialized in gourmet organic dog food.

"That's exactly what I'm talking about!" I exclaimed, when Ken got off the phone. "He couldn't see my sister. When I talk to her I call her Dragonfly, and when I look at her dragonflies are all that I allow myself to see."

"So anyone looking through your eyes would see not her but dragonflies."

"Swarms of them," I added. "When I got to Morocco I wanted to be extra sure that who she was and what she looked like was protected. So I absorbed all that I saw, smelled, and heard. When I saw this bangle as the Gypsy girl poured my tea I saw nothing else. I was possessed by it, and the girl who was wearing it."

"Adam killed Jack, the server girl, Pete, and maybe Logan but he gave you this bracelet. Why, why would he do something like that?"

I took a bottle of water out of my refrigerator and started pacing. "Maybe he felt they were taking attention away from him. I doted on Jackie. He was my little partner in crime." I sat down on the floor next to Sentinel. I petted him then leaned against him to feel the essence of his protectiveness. "You were the same way with Logan, and Pete was your boyfriend and by your admission, inseparable. Adam must have felt that they stole us away from him."

"And him giving you the bracelet was his way of pleasing you. He must have seen how distraught you were to find Jackie that way. He definitely knew how highly you thought of that girl's bracelet."

"You're saying that Adam gave me this bangle to make me feel better after he killed Jackie?"

"Men who beat their wives or girlfriends give them flowers to apologize. It's not so unreasonable to believe that a boy who killed your dog would give you jewelry, especially when you're so preoccupied by it." I jumped as my phone rang. I answered it to the concierge who called to see if it would be okay to allow the delivery drivers up.

We all ate lunch on the floor of the library. Sentinel's meal came on a plate with a Japanese theme, his food having been prepared to look like sushi, lobster, and shrimp. The arrangement looked so appetizing I had to ask the girl who carefully unwrapped Sentinel's food and gently set it on the floor before him if it was, in fact, dog food. Ken couldn't help but pinch a piece from his plate with his chopsticks.

With a frown I asked, "How was it?"

"Not bad, not bad at all." Ken replied. He tried to taste another piece; however, Sentinel thought it was good too and growled at Ken as his chopsticks hovered over his plate. Both food and water shot out of my mouth as I burst into laughter.

We lingered over lunch for an hour before Ken took his leave. I changed into sweats and a tee shirt then left the house to take my dog for a jog.

XXXVIII

Adam was rereading and making the necessary corrections to his philosophy thesis when his mother opened the door, the doctor's receptionist frantically trailing close behind her.

"You and I need to finish the conversation that you started with you grandfather."

Adam's face turned crimson. He slowly, deliberately turned his eyes away from Inanna and bored them into the doctor. Adam's expression was so full of rage and rancor that the therapist felt guilty of breaching patient-doctor confidentiality, forgetting that for the four months Adam had been seeing him the boy had never said a word.

Inanna had instructed her driver to drop her off so that she could drive Adam's Audi back home. Adam stared out the front window without seeing. The forty-five minute drive was spent mostly in silence, which put Adam's nerves on edge. He couldn't even pick up anything telepathically, and that made things worse. Four blocks from home Adam finally looked at his mom and silently begged her to talk to him. Inanna drove past their block and on to the expressway that led to the outskirts of the city. As the city rapidly fell away behind them and the scenery changed from metropolis to farmland and from farmland to densely wooded forest Inanna finally broke the silence in response to Adam's thoughts

"So, *now* you want to talk? Well, go head Adam, I'm listening." Adam would have preferred being called Yankee at the moment. He knew from the way she had said 'now' that she was referring to the way he had blocked her out of his thoughts and hid from her his actions.

"What is it that you want from her? What can she possibly say to make you feel better? You've killed two people and her dog, and for what, what are you trying to prove?"

Adam's eyes filled with tears that refused to fall as he looked past his mother and out the window. The look of sorrow was replaced with a frown as Adam was seized by an unconquerable sensation of déjà vu.

Adam surveyed the surrounding area as Inanna pulled the car to a stop along the shoulder. Adam rolled down the window and drew a deep breath of the cedar-scented air. Inanna got out of the car, walked slowly ahead, and waited for Adam to get out the car and catch up.

It was comfortably cooler here in the woods than in the sweltering city.

As he walked beside his mother Adam could not understand why anyone would think silence was golden because the lack of noise was actually starting to make his ears hurt. He glanced sideways just in time to see the last traces of his mothers fleeting smile.

"What?" He questioned the shaking of Inanna's head.

"You're such a city kid." The four inch heels she wore brought her eye level to her son and she grabbed the back of his head, and pulled him close to her so that she could kiss him on the temple and brush away a dark curl that had fallen into his face. Adam placed his hand within his mother's hand the way he had done as a boy, and though he no longer had to look up at her, her presence still towered over him. They walked in silence for a while as Adam continued to survey the forest.

"This place is familiar to you, I can see that all over your face, but do you know where you are?" Adam stopped walking, let go of Inanna's hand and tried to peer through the dense darkness of the unmolested wilderness. The thickset forest denied the warmth of the sun.

The only place the red-golden rays could penetrate were along the forest's edge and even there the forest cast ominous shadows in attempts to challenge the light. Adam felt the darkness, or the unseen things within it, gather strength and brush against his skin – as the forces rushed past him in response to the great witch's voice.

"As far as I am concerned this is the place in which you were born."

Adam slowly turned to face Inanna with eyes and mouth open in awe. He had known the story of how she found him in the middle of the night but this was the first time he had been brought here.

"Make no mistake," she continued, "from the moment my mother was slain before me on the pristine beaches of my homeland I exhaled vengeance with every breath I took, and hatred was pumped through my body with every single heartbeat."

Though Inanna had started speaking in English, she was now speaking in the Haitian words that had been given to her by her mother.

"My mother was a mighty and powerful witch and the most beautiful woman I had ever seen. She could heal any pain with just a simple touch, and there was nothing in this world she didn't know, or so I thought when I was a child.

"Mamma was a witch of the light. She chose the path of patience and healing and forged a trail behind her upon which I could follow in her footsteps. But even as a small child I could see that her kindness was mistaken for weakness, and her knowledge thought of as sinister.

"Through my mother's teachings I learned the power of love and the depth of endurance. However I also began a supplementary course of study, because even at such a young age

I was able to understand the power of ignorance.

"My mother endured an insufferable amount of accusations and ridicule. The men who spit in her face at the market came to her under the cover of night to seek advice and guidance. The women who threw rocks at her and flung mud on her garments as we washed by the riverbanks would use the light of the moon to find their way to our house to retrieve the ointments to cure any wound and the teas that repelled any sickness, and never once did she expose the hypocrites or demand any reprisal for the abuse.

"My countrymen, my elders, my cousins and playmates chased us toward the shore because everyone knew there would come a day when the ridiculous treatment of my mother would come to an end. They understood that the day she handed me the reins of power, their mistreatment of her would be avenged and abolished – and it was no secret, none what-so-ever, that I was paying more than attention. And you can trust and believe that I was taking names."

Inanna had picked up a rock along the path and was wiping the dirt from the surface. Collecting rocks was something she did, and Adam had already found two that he thought she might like.

Inanna rarely spoke of her mother. Never before had he heard such pain in her voice. Adam was uncomfortable and uncertain how to comfort her so he continued to search the ground for rocks of unusual shapes, sizes, and colors that he could give her to add to her collection.

"My mother kept us out of the way as best she could. We lived in a small hut on the outskirts of the village. The creek that ran off of the river was our own water supply. We raised goats, chickens and had a small garden with vegetables, and we rarely ventured out into the commons unless it was absolutely necessary.

"There was a night that my mamma was summoned to the house because her services as a midwife were needed. The woman was in labor, a bad one, by the time we got there. It was clear to all that her baby would have surely died without my mother's help. After my mamma put that baby in its mother's arms we left without gratitude or payment.

"Three weeks later when the woman was strong enough she came to our home. When my mamma opened the door her sister threw a bucket of cow shit and river mud that covered my mother from face to foot.

"I was always right by my mother's side but she was able to shove me behind her to protect me from the onslaught. I peeked around my mother's hips to look into my aunt's face and what I saw there enraged me. It was the look of pride, of spiteful gleeful pride. But when she looked down at me that smirk on her face vanished, and I promised myself right then and there that neither she nor her newborn would live to see another full moon.

"Days later my aunt was working on her land with my tiny cousin tied to her back when she grabbed a place in her fence that had a nail poking out of it. The nail went straight threw her hand. She had to yank hard to pull herself free. When she did she tripped and fell, landed on her back. She hit her head so hard it knocked her unconscious. and.

"By the time someone found her, she was sick with fever and my cousin suffocated beneath her. The infection from her hand spread quickly, but she suffered greatly. When her family members, my family members, tried to reach my mamma to ask for her help I caused a storm and used a fallen tree to block the path to our home. She died the night before the moon rose full. It was days after that, that my mother woke me in the middle of the night and raced us towards the shore.

"We ran so long that my breath was nothing but fire. The worst thing was that we could hear them behinds us. They we're screaming horrible things and threatening to rip us to pieces.

"As the sun rose I could see there was a small wooden boat waiting for us. But the mob was closer to us than we were to the boat. But somehow my mamma was able to get me there. As she put me in that little boat she held my face in her hands and said 'None of this is your fault. The most powerful weapon in your arsenal is forgiveness; none of this is your fault.' Then she pushed me away while I screamed."

Despite the warmth of the night Adam's skin was full of goose bumps, and the hair on the back of his neck stood at attention. His stomach hurt and he didn't trust himself to speak because his throat was chocked full of tears. Adam hadn't known that his mother had lived through such a nightmare.

"I watched as the only people I had ever known killed my mamma with blades, sticks, rocks and bare hands. It took such a long time for her to die, but what my kinsmen did not know, and that's not my problem, is that I had reached a level in my studies, which would ensure there would be severe consequences for their actions. I had been practicing since the night my aunt went out of her way to cover her sister in filth.

"I wanted things to be different ... I wanted those people to die slowly. I wanted their suffering to be so great that there wouldn't be a word written to describe it.
"But sometimes," Inanna continued with a shrug of her shoulder "you don't always get want you want. It took only minutes to kill the six hundred people that were once the extended members of my family."

The two stood in silence for awhile as Inanna reflected on something Adam could only guess at. Gazing into the deep, Inanna explained, "This is the very spot that you literally ran into my life."

Adam glanced back at the car and was startled to see they were less than six feet away from it, though it had felt like they had been walking for miles.

Inanna purchased a new Jaguar every year, always a red one. She was a driving enthusiast and enjoyed the speed and power the big engine provided. Adam began to tremble at the realization that another driver, or an owner of a car that did not possess the Jaguar's superior braking power, surely would have hit him.

In response to his thought Inanna spoke, "You and I were meant to be, boy. From that day on the beach I prepared myself to be the flame that sparked an apocalyptic catastrophe. I wanted nothing less than to knock the earth off its axis, to make everyone suffer, for the way my mother was taken from me.

"That is until you came along. I am a Witch of the Darkness, but because of you I want to find the trail my mother left for me. I do not want to walk on it but I do want to see it. Because of you I started recycling."

A flock of birds took flight as Adam's booming laughter sliced through the silent dusk. It was illegal not to recycle and the thought of someone putting empty Coke cans, paper bags, egg cartons, plastic, a light bulb or two and a battery for good measure all in the same container struck Adam as barbaric and hilarious. Inanna shook her head slightly and waited for the laughter to die down.

"One night long ago," she told him, "I ran through the woods and lost my mother and on another night not so long ago you ran through the woods and found yours. My mother told me once, and I am telling you now, none of this is your fault. The greatest weapon you have in your arsenal is forgiveness.

"Whatever it is you want from this woman let it go. We study an ancient art, but Adam, modern science is just as dangerous. Adam, I need you to leave her alone because I think you may have overplayed your hand. Forgive her because that is the last thing she is expecting. If it wasn't for her I would have never have found you."

As they walked back to the car Inanna knew how her mother must have felt as she issued her last words. She understood because she was feeling that way now. She knew that Adam, like herself years before, wasn't going to heed that advice.

Inanna masked from her son her anxiety as she remembered the last thing Myrddin had said to her, *'He has to find his own way, Inanna,'* but those words did nothing to prevent her praying to those she worshiped, and hoping that there would be something she could do.

XXXIX

The next day started before the sun came up. Ken stopped to see me in my office where I was combing through every file, sticky note, test result, still photo and footage that documented the Genesis Project. He brought with him more file boxes. I started with the first images that were captured by Ken's seer fifteen years ago when Adam was still in the hands of The Foundation.

When the rest of the city was sitting down for dinner I was finally breaking for lunch and I had barely put a dent into the mountain of paperwork that Ken had left for me to review.

I was reading a case report from a young technician who had introduced Adam to classical music when the night watchmen buzzed my office to let me know my food had arrived. The report was of Adam's first night spent here at The Facility. I ate my meal while watching the corresponding footage.

When Adam first came to The Facility I was still in Europe and I had no idea how truly horrible his condition was during those first five months. In these early images Adam looked as if he had been rescued from a country racked with famine, not from men who had uncountable amounts of money in their various bank accounts. There was not one ounce of muscle on his body, just skin that hung loosely around his bones, and a bloated stomach that bulged beneath an exposed rib cage.

Seeing him that way reconfirmed that I had done the right thing as a woman, but reviewing all of this material for the first time made me doubt that I had done the right thing as a scientist.

I knew without a doubt that Adam was better off for the decision that was made to remove him from the hands of The Foundation; nevertheless, gift-wrapped boxes from Pandora should rarely if ever – be opened. I turned my back to the task at hand so that I could enjoy the view of my city at twilight as I ate the rest of my meal.

This has always been the favorite part of my day, the time between sunset and night. The subdued light that signals the coming of the dark always brought me a sense of peace. The ringing of the bells from the cathedral smothered the city in a type of sacred silence and slowed the tempo of its heartbeat. Light rain began to fall from the sky as if attempting to cleanse the city, and all of us who lived here, from the guilt of our sins.

I returned to work as the last of the light dipped behind the city's skyline by viewing more footage of Adam. He was sleeping in his playpen, covered in warm down blankets, and surrounded by what looked like four hundred teddy bears. Seeing him that way was extremely difficult because at that time some of those stuffed bears probably weighed more than he did.

What jolted me from my notes and yanked me from my scientific mind was the earth-shattering scream from Adam. I looked up at my flat screen just as Dr. Astor, Dr. Anderson and their assistants entered Adam's room and rushed to his side.

I was brought to tears as I watched Adam being comforted back to sleep. I watched that twenty-three minute piece of film over and over again. What I realized was it wasn't Adam that had drawn me back to that particular footage but Dr. Anderson. According to the notes on this footage, this was the first time Dr. Anderson had seen Adam, and it was clear from watching the video images that he was immediately emotionally vested and clearly furious. But through his fury he was able to maintain his scientific observations, and though he was emotionally involved he was able to channel all of that energy into the project. I wasn't sure how he was able to do that, or why I couldn't, but I made a mental note to see Dr. Anderson.

Adam flinched at every sound, trembled non-stop, and was terrified to be left alone.

The slightest activity exhausted him, and though he was fed every two hours he greedily ate every meal as if it were his last.

I was not surprised, and agreed with the diagnoses noted in the case: Adam suffered from post-traumatic stress disorder, acute separation anxiety, and severe depression. I was surprised and impressed by Dr. Lott's course of treatment. The touch treatment and play therapy yielded incredible and rapid results.

Though Dr. Astor encouraged Adam to use his telekinesis abilities, Dr. Anderson demanded that Adam use his physical skills. It didn't take long for Adam to put on weight, sleep more soundly, and be calm when left alone for long periods of time.

I watched the way Adam interacted with all the members of this project and watched him excel at his exercises and various tasks that were set before him. I watched him take his first steps and say his first word. I knew that Adam loved Ernesto the most and I watched them play, wrestle, dance and sing. Despite the fact that Dr. Astor was as relentless and remorseless as the desert sun when conducting test and experiments, I knew Adam loved him just as much. Dr. Cassidy had the bedside manner of a wild boar and didn't like children to begin with, and it was apparent that he and Adam didn't get along well, but the experiments Dr. Cassidy performed were vital and Adam and Dr. Cassidy tolerated each other.

The Genesis Project was running perfectly and ahead of schedule. That is, until I returned from Europe. It is said the camera doesn't lie, and the most difficult part of all the footage compiled to watch was of me. I was mortified and humiliated as I watched myself deliberately destroy all the work my colleagues had achieved. I watched the relationship between Adam and Dr. Cassidy deteriorate. I came to realize that I was the reason Dr. Cassidy hated Adam, and that ultimately I was the cause of Adam's removal from The Facility and the subsequent death of Dr. Cassidy.

I was so immersed with the case files from the Genesis Project that I was actually startled when Dr. Astor burst through the doors of my office.

But what shocked me even more was his announcement. "What are you still doing here? Go home, it's noon."

Over the course of the next five weeks, I reviewed case notes from the Genesis Project, conducted experiments and collected data for the other projects I was working on, inspected jewelry created by my artisans and brought in funding and secured future projects. It was business as usual.

But then, quite suddenly I began losing sleep as well as my appetite. I was easily distracted and quickly annoyed. Sentinel was constantly on edge and more aggressive than he had ever been, even lunging at a barista who ventured too close.

And then it hit me. With every step I took I knew I was being followed.

XL

She was daring to hope that she had finally gotten through to him. The five weeks after Inanna had taken Adam to his "birth place" in the woods Adam had returned to the well rounded, happy, hard working, goofball kid that everyone liked at school. He had a steady girlfriend, a part time job, and he was no longer mentally blocking Inanna out.

The year before, while Adam was still a junior in high school, he had begun applying to colleges. Now, as the packages and envelopes with school logos flowed in, Adam and Inanna were ecstatic to learn that every single school he applied to had accepted him. Adam chose MIT.

Adam and his friends were sitting in his car outside of Starbucks buzzing off of the high-octane caffeinated drinks just purchased. Though there was a sense of bewilderment, and a little trepidation, over what it meant to be leaving home at the end of the year to start living lives of their own, the mood was joyous.

Adam, Devontai, Trevor, Molly, and Savannah were probably more unsettled by the thought of being away from each other than being away from their parents. The five of them, dubbed the Fantastic Five, had been inseparable since the fifth grade.

Trevor's mother lived a life of luxury by creating jewelry for Periodic Element AU. Trevor was going to be studying corporate law at Yale. When Trevor first met Adam and Devontai the two of them were coming to Trevor's aid when he was being bullied on the playground. The justice handed out by Adam and Devontai had resulted in school suspensions and legal proceedings. They were all only in the fourth grade at the time.

Devontai's mother married into wealth and divorced even wealthier. He was off to London to study international law. When Devontai first met Adam it was a year prior to the infamous and felonious "playground incident."

It was on the first day that Devontai attended The Institute for Advanced Learning – and Devontai was livid. Out of the 375 Afro-Asiatic languages known, Devontai spoke ninety of them, which was partly the reason he was transferred to this school. Of course Devontai didn't see it that way. He was lamenting to his mother in Oromo how unfair he thought it was that he had to change schools.

During recess Adam extended an offer of friendship using the Ethiopian language he'd heard him use with his mother. Over time the two multilingual boys grew fond of talking about their adversaries, right in front of them mind you, in a language they knew their rivals did not understand.

When Adam, Devontai, and Trevor first met Molly, they were all impressed and a little in love with her because she was the only girl in class who was not afraid to hold Henry, their classroom's pet rat. Molly was the sole heiress to the Vallade Brewery fortune and the lead singer and guitarist for a wildly popular all-girl band, called The Mollycules, whose songs swept across the globe like a plague. They recorded all of their songs in Molly's bedroom. Trevor shot and edited all of their music videos around the city and they uploaded them to YouTube and then linked them to myspace, facebook, planet-live, and other websites. You could download the songs for $.99. Once divided, the girls had already made $34, 876.00 each. Her parents ensured that Molly's education was the spearhead to everything; if her grades slipped below a 3.8 GPA Molly's mom said she would have to quit the band.

Molly was excited to be going to New York where she would study music and dance at Julliard for a semester before meeting her band mates in Europe, where they would be kicking off the start of the official tour.

Adam, Devontai, and Trevor met Savannah because Molly and Savannah were rarely seen apart. Savannah is the daughter of the city's police commissioner.

His $75,000 a year salary certainly did not allow his daughter to be rubbing shoulders with the kids she sat in the car with; however Savannah's stepmother is a rich and famous horror and science fiction writer. It was she who bestowed upon Savannah this million dollar a year education and allowed Savannah to live out this fairly tale lifestyle; minus of course the scrubbing of the floors, wicked witches, evil step mothers, jealous sisters and poisonous fruit.

Savannah was going to Paris to study at the prestigious institute of high fashion and design, which surprised no one. Savannah was the one who designed every stitch of clothing worn by all six members of The Mollycules. She did their hair and make-up before each music video and photo shoot. She even created her own tag, which she sewed into each garment. It was a purple piece of fabric that had 'Simply Savannah' embroidered with glittery thread. Because of the fame that The Mollycules were starting to acquire, the Simply Savannah clothing line was also starting to make a name for itself.

Trevor told the stupidest joke in the world but everyone laughed at it anyway. Adam was looking at Trevor in the rearview mirror when he saw the gun metal grey Range Rover turn the corner. Adam felt his heartbeat quicken. He could no longer hear the juvenile chatter of his friends as he watched the suped up all-terrain utility vehicle that matched the color of the overcast sky, drive slowly past and then park two cars in front of him.

As she stepped down from the truck her dog jumped out and stood before her. With no leash or muzzle and adorned in golden chain mail meant for war, seeing the dog made Adam immediately think of the Canis Molossus, the strongest dog known to the Romans, who had attack formations made entirely of these dogs.

Because of the construction the only way she could access Starbucks was to walk between Adam's car and the car parked in front of him.

Adam never took his eyes off of her as she walked right in front of him talking on the phone and typing on her Blackberry, and completely oblivious of his existence.

Just before they entered the coffee shop Sentinel turned back, glanced at all the children in the car, and then locked his eyes on Adam. Adam and Sentinel held each other's glare for almost a minute.

So you're the one, Sentinel thought, *just a boy.*

I am more than just a boy, Adam shot back. *Are you willing to die for her?*

The question is, are you? If you're coming come prepared.

Before Adam had a chance to respond the dog's last statement Sentinel walked away. Adam was barely able to contain his rage as the dog turned his back to him and all of his closest friends laughed at another one of Trevor's stupid jokes.

Just blocks away Inanna's teacup slipped through her fingers and crashed violently to the floor as she felt the telepathic cord between her and her son sever.

XLI

I was so distracted and unsettled that I couldn't concentrate. I didn't want to be near anyone I knew or spend too much time at The Facility because I didn't want anyone else being targeted or killed.

Ken reminded me that I was not the only team member of the Genesis Project, and I reminded Ken that from what we could gather I was the only one that Adam was truly angry with.

I was working from home mostly and going in only once or twice a week and only when needed. I was called in because a vote of the counsel was requested and all twenty-one founding members of the Skyward Group were required to be there to cast a vote. Incidentally there was not a debate because all of us were in agreement, I was able to cast my vote and leave within the hour. I decided to stop for a latte on the way home.

I'd been up all night reviewing and re-reviewing the footage from the time Adam entered Dr. Hogue's germ lab to the time just before he'd been removed from The Facility, and I had planned on reviewing it again but needed an extra kick to help me stay focused.

Even with the construction I had no problem finding parking. I was checking my e-mail and speaking with Ken on the phone as Sentinel lead the way. Sentinel always walked in front of me so when I looked up from my Blackberry and noticed he wasn't there I panicked.

I spun around to find Sentinel standing behind me. He was looking over his shoulder and into a car full of teenaged kids, and I did the same thing.

The beautiful boy sitting behind the wheel of the imported sports car had large green eyes that sparkled like emeralds. He glared at me with such hatred and loathing that I knew without a shadow of a doubt that the driver of that car was Adam. He was more beautiful than I remembered or could have imagined.

Quite frankly he was the most beautiful person I had ever seen. I never considered that I would see him in such a normal and happy setting, sitting in his car with friends, enjoying coffee on an overcast and drizzly day. It was as if I had been hit by a speeding truck.

I didn't say anything to him until it was too late. I called out to him twice as he recklessly sped off, and I prayed that that wouldn't be the last time I saw my son.

XLII

Inanna was waiting for Adam when he got home, three hours late, with a steaming hot cup of hot chocolate with a Snickers bar melted inside and topped with homemade whipped cream. Seeing her there at the door waiting for him with the best drink in the entire world made Adam feel like crying, and he did just that as he buried his head into his mothers shoulder and cried.

"She didn't even say anything to me."

"How could she have recognized you, love? It's been fifteen years baby."

"How can she just forget about a little boy?"

"You're not that boy anymore Adam. You're nearly a man."

"She doesn't love me anymore."

"Of course she does. How can she not?"

"I hate her."

"No, you don't. You're *hurt* by her."

"I hate her."

"Nothing good can come from that."

Adam cried for another twenty minutes and Inanna soothed and comforted her son as best she could. She led her son to the living room where he collapsed onto the sofa, exhausted. Inanna made Adam another cup of chocolate, and he drank it listlessly while he stared into nothing.

An hour later Adam kissed his mother good night and went to bed. An hour after that Inanna heard Adam's stealthy footsteps across the foyer as he left the house.

XLIII

Adam knew Inanna was still awake, and he thought she was going to try and stop him, he didn't hear his mother's footsteps as he locked the door from the other side, so he knew she wasn't coming after him even though a tiny part of him wished that she had.

The breeze was chilled by the water from the marina. Adam could hear the bells on the buoys, and the small boats and yachts that gently banged against the pilings as they rocked with the tide, as he walked away from the harbor and cut across the park in which Myrddin had been slain.

Adam was still near the park's edge and within the shadow of his penthouse home when it started raining. If he had turned to look up towards his home he would have seen the silhouette of his mother watching him walk across the lawn.

Adam was surprised to see so many people milling around in the park so late at night. He pulled the hood of his lightweight windbreaker over his head to prevent the rainwater from rolling down his head and onto his neck. He didn't mind the rain. This city and London were Adam's favorite places in the world to be because of the rain. No, he didn't mind being wet; he pulled his hood up because he needed to stay warm. He wasn't planning on running, but he knew that after the 6½-mile walk he would be drenched in sweat, because he would be there in less than an hour. He took his iPod out of his pocket, put in his ear buds, and thought about the way she had looked at him. She had looked at him as if he was just another spoiled kid on the street.

The earliest memory that Adam could recall was of him sitting on the kitchen counter. He and Inanna were creating a simple potion to cure a headache, and Grandee was reading from a spell book. It was more holistic than magic but it was Adam's first lesson in learning the properties of botanicals.

Even though Adam had been dreaming about the time he had spent with this other woman, his first mother – his false mother, this woman that he left the comforts of his home to confront – they weren't really memories, but more like nightmares. Not the simple, quaint nightmares that you wake up screaming from, but the kinds of nightmares that terrorize you during the day, throughout your waking hours. The kinds of nightmares that break your foundation of reality and make you question your very existence and identity. The kind of nightmare that is so frightening that it leaves you praying for death so that you don't have to sleep.

When Adam thought about how much he loved Inanna and his Grandee and how much they had both done for him, he felt like crying. He was overcome with grief as he felt the loss of Myrddin, and he didn't even want to think about being away from Inanna. He never wanted to entertain the idea that one day she too, would die. Finally Adam did cry, because he felt like he was betraying Inanna by seeking out this other woman. But he couldn't stop himself.

He needed answers, because as much as he loved his mother his love for Inanna did nothing to alleviate his feelings of abandonment, loss, grief, and rejection. His love for Inanna did nothing to alleviate the anger he felt toward this woman who had thrown him away. Adam felt that all that was wrong in his world was her fault. If it wasn't for her he wouldn't have gotten into that fight with his grandfather and they wouldn't have been in the park that day and Grandee would still be alive. If it wasn't for her he wouldn't feel so fucked up and angry inside and he'd be at home right now with his real mother.

As Adam stood outside of her building and looked up to her flat he meant to make sure she understood how much pain she had caused. He was going to ensure that she understood that abandoning him was the worst mistake that she had ever made – and he was going to make damn well sure that she paid for her egregious disregard for the life of a child. With a sense of calmness and determination like none before felt by Adam, he entered her building and announced his arrival.

XLIX

Your ... son is here?" The concierge couldn't hide his surprise when he called to let me know I had a visitor, and I have to say I was more than just a little staggered myself.

My glass bangle felt hot against my cool skin and as I glanced down at it I couldn't but help notice the time. It was just past two in the morning.

As it turns out I didn't need the caffeine to stay up all night after all. Seeing Adam in the street left me charged and frayed my nerves. But what was worse was how relaxed and tranquil Sentinel was, like the calm before the storm.

His arrival was announced like a thunderclap, as the door to my home was kicked in and Adam walked through it.

The day Sentinel had trained for all his life had finally arrived and he did not hesitate in the least, but he froze at my command as I rushed past him toward Adam.

With uncontrollable tears I called his name, "Oh baby, my little boy, where have you been? Oh my sweet, sweet Adam." I put both of my hands on his face and held his cheeks in my hands – then I brushed away a lock of dark curls that had fallen across his face.

"Oh my God, you're freezing! Come in out of the cold. Oh my God honey where have you been? That was *you* yesterday. Why did you drive away from me?" Adam wouldn't have been able to answer my questions even if he had wanted to because I'd asked them so fast, my words tumbling out on top of each other, infused with tears, pain, sorrow, and regret.

The fire of rage that lit Adam's eyes began to dim as I led him further into my home to sit on the sofa. There was something else taking the place of that rage. It was confusion – yes confusion, and hope.

I sat close to him on the sofa. Sentinel took a position on the floor that would prove to his strategic advantage if necessary. I held Adam's hands in mine then held them up close, to my chest.

The last time I had seen Adam, the last time I had held Adam, he had been only four. I was trembling with guilt, grief, fear, joy, and relief that he was okay. He was so beautiful. I knew I had nothing to do with his well-being and safety all those years, and because of that, I could not stop crying.

I had left him sleeping in a crib; cuddled next to the kitten I'd given him and the teddy bear he had come with. With a kiss I had promised to see him just a few short hours later, had reassured him that he would be safe and that I was coming back to take him home.

I was so fearful now that he wouldn't be able to understand that I hadn't meant to lie to him. I wondered if he would ever be able to understand that I had stolen him, and in turn he had been stolen from me.

Adam was clearly shaken and so was Sentinel. My dog was now standing. Every hackle on his back stood at rigid attention while his entire body was taut like that of a bow in the skillful arms of a Roman archer. Sentinel was nearing the very edge of his obedience as his eyes kept gliding from my eyes to Adam's throat.

Adam moved his hands so that they were now holding mine. He held my hands close to his chest, just as I had done with him moments before. He only asked one question, barely above a whisper, but I had heard it as though he had screamed it through a bullhorn.

"Mom?" My anguish rose from the pits of hell. It is indescribable how I felt at that moment. I was so outside myself with grief that I thought I was going to collapse.

"Please baby, my sweet little Adam. Please forgive me. I've looked everywhere for you ... everywhere. Why didn't you just come home? Was I that bad?"

"Just come home? How could I? You told me you loved me and then you just threw me away."

All I could do was cry, it was the moment I had been waiting for all these years, and I wanted to make sure I got it right. I was on the verge of emotional bankruptcy before I could stop crying.

"I need to show you something." I got up from the sofa. Adam followed me and Sentinel followed Adam, as I led the procession to my bedroom. I got the stuffed bear that was resting on my down pillows and handed it to Adam.

Adam was unmistakably surprised. "It's Teddy!" He clutched the bear in both hands fighting back his tears and anger. Adam wasn't going to cry in front of me. I hadn't earned that right. And how could I blame him? I was just a stranger.

I looked at Adam from the bottom of my emotional chasm and was startled to see that he was uncomfortable. Sentinel responded to Adam's tension by barely controlling his aggression. The low, deep growl could never have been mistaken for an idle threat so to take the edge off I offered an all time favorite, "Would you like some hot chocolate?"

"With a Snickers bar?"

"How else?" I answered with a smile.

I remembered Adam used to love drinking hot chocolate with a Snickers bar melted into it, and I voiced out loud that I couldn't believe he still drank it that way. I'm not sure what happened then, but all those years that had been lost between us suddenly meant nothing, and the palpable tension that was in the air dissipated as Adam and Sentinel both relaxed.

I led my family into the kitchen, took the carton of milk from the refrigerator, and poured some in a copper pot to boil. Sentinel rushed past me into to the kitchen then stood by the dishwasher so that he could stand between us and face Adam, absolute in his resolve to confront this battle and even to die fighting if that was what was required.

Adam reached above me to retrieve the Swiss chocolate that had been ground down to a fine powder, knowing exactly where it was, as if he had lived his whole life inside my home.

As I opened the drawer to get his candy bar, Adam sat in one of the high back, leather counter stools. He seemed bewildered. All the fire was gone from his eyes. The single most important reason for his vengeance had been removed. Adam just sat there looking stunned, not really knowing what to do next. Above all else he looked exhausted.

I poured the steaming hot milk into our mugs, then carefully unwrapped Adam's candy and placed it into the boiling broth and stirred it until it was no longer visible. I topped both mugs with whipped cream and went to sit next to my son.

He took his mug and held it with both hands, just the way that I remembered, and my heart burst open with missed memories and unyielding love. Adam stood with his cup and walked into the living room, glancing over his shoulder, hoping that I would follow – overlooking the fact that the large and powerful animal that was my pet was stalking him.

I sat next to Adam on the sofa. He sipped from his mug, licking away a sugary mustache. "Were you waiting for me? I mean is that why you have my candy?" I didn't care for sweets, and I was amazed that Adam had remembered that.

"I hoped so. I prayed that you would, but then I feared

that you had died. I had no idea that you were out there somewhere, no idea."

"This whole time I hated you because I thought you had thrown me away. I didn't know what I could have done so wrong. I thought you hated me and that you just threw me away, so I was going to make you pay for that. I thought you threw me away. I didn't know you were looking for me."

Adam was looking down into his hot chocolate with a hand absently holding on to his teddy bear, which he hadn't seen in over 15 years.

Sentinel started to growl. With a snap of my finger I commanded my dog's attention. Sentinel came to sit at my feet. He was so wired that he didn't really sit, but crouched, preparing to leap the distance between him and Adam in the blink of an eye.

"You're not mad at me. You … you don't hate me?" My jaw dropped. Images of Dr. Morgan, Jack, Dr. Hogue, the gypsy girl in the desert and Peter flashed in the foreground of my memory at lightning speed, as I understood what he was asking me – and I shook my head no.

Adam's eyes welled with tears but he did not let them fall. I held his face in my hands, brushed away the dark lock of hair that had fallen in his face and asked, "Baby how can I be mad at you? You are my son."

He gently pulled his face from my hands to hide the tears that I did not yet deserve, and for a distraction finished his chocolate with a few short gulps. Adam looked at me again with a sudden flash of anger that was so intense that it caused Sentinel to lunge over my lap and issue several deafening barks and a flash of fangs. I was able to grab hold of Sentinel's harness and restrain him; Sentinel defied my command to sit by choosing to remain standing, and when I looked at Adam again his look was apologetic. It was written all over his face how confused and hurt he was. The remorseful way that Adam looked at Sentinel took my dog's edge off. Sentinel now felt comfortable enough to sit.

Adam kicked off his shoes, curled his feet beneath him and lay down with his head in my lap. He wrapped himself up with my right arm, cupping my hand between his and holding then just under his chin.

With my free hand I ran my fingers through Adam's thick hair and began to hum a song I had made up years ago just for him. He looked up at me for a long time, until the time it took Adam to open his eyes between blinks became longer as he drifted towards sleep.

Sentinel too lay down in front of us, and though he was still on guard he occasionally turned his head away from us to look outside and watch the falling rain. I continued to hold Adam but I had stopped humming, lost in thoughts of how things might have been so very different now if I had simply taken Adam home with me that instant instead of promising to do so later.

I've gone over all the case files for the Genesis Project so many times that I've memorized every note ever written. I've studied each experiment to such depth that my recollections of the results are as clear as if I had conducted the studies myself. I have watched the footage of the events in Dr. Hogue's lab so many times that I know each time-sequenced event by heart.

I've replayed in my mind the moments I spent with Adam after the freeze, so many times that I have lost count, and I did so, so that I would have all the tools necessary to allow me to do what must be done when the time came – as I had done today. Adam wrenched himself from the clutches of Hypnos and sat up with a start, eyes wide with fear.

"No, no," he pleaded with a single tear falling from his eye. Then with a sigh he collapsed back into my lap. The internal battle Adam fought with the god of sleep was won, but his victory was short-lived as he was seized by sleep's big brother – death.

I watched Adam's breathe slowly rise and fall, rise and fall, rise …

As Adam lay dying in my lap I brushed a lock of dark curly hair from his face. His hair was too long and needed to be cut.

And fall. Rise and fall …

I watched tears fall from his large green eyes that sparkled like emeralds as he began to realize what I'd done, and I just sat there looking down on him wondering what kind of men could leave a child in a cage.

Rise …

I knew this day would come from the moment I discovered Jackie's body and Adam's letter, the day that Adam and I would stand face to face and I was more than aware that the two of us could not coexist.

Rise … and fall … rise.

I read the case studies of Dr. Astor's exposure experiments with such intensity that anyone looking would have thought I was reading religious text, and essentially I was.

And fall …

Ken once told me that 'if the infection was something as common as chickenpox or the flu Adam became a little loopy, if it was something more aggressive Adam needed to sleep it off – as the saying goes.' Dr. Astor's words affected me in the same manner in which the Burning Bush of Mount Horeb affected Moses.

Rise …

Let me remind you that I am an alchemist, and I know a

thing or two about magic, spells, potions, and ... poisons.

And fall ...

What I created made Dr. Hogue's germ seem like nothing more exotic than the common cold. I knew I would be safe from any counterattack as the systems in Adam's body shut down in order to preserve him.

Rise ...

A nanogram of the malignant elixir that I injected into that candy would have brought down a herd of elephants. Let me assure you that my dosage was much more generous than that.

And fall ...

I understood more than anything that there would be absolutely no room for error, that if Adam so much had a hint of what I was planning, he would have simply killed me outright.

Rise ...

The lack of personal security in Morocco was intentional. The thing that you need to understand is that I am always cloaked, but the night I found my poor Jackie ripped to shreds the type of cloak I donned allowed me to become my own double agent.

And fall ...

Never before have I hid so deep within myself, creating a substitute so convincing that even my closest confidant no longer knew who I was, but under the circumstances I had no other choice.

Rise ...

The synthetic self of me that I projected was fearful, remorseful, panic stricken and weak – a victim. The lure I cast was so hypnotic that my transformation drew Adam to me like a moth to a flame. Like the tide responds to the moon, Adam was controlled from the very beginning.

And fall ...

I needed Adam to feel powerful and in control when he stalked me through the park, followed me abroad and kicked my door in. Not for one moment could I allow Adam to realize that he could not have taken any other course of action.

Rise ...

I did not expect him to kill that girl in the Moroccan wasteland and for that I am truly sorry; I can only continue to wear this bracelet as her memorial.

And ...

It's been nearly sixteen years now since we acquired The Genesis Project. The boy I had come to think of as my child, who died in my arms, was only nineteen years old.

I kissed Adam on the forehead and wiped away my tears. There is no way that I am going to allow anyone, not even my son, in the midst of a tantrum, tarnish my reputation ... or worse jeopardize my multi-million dollar contracts at the height of my career.

I have sacrificed a great deal to be where I am today and I will allow nothing or nobody to stand in my path to achieving greatness.

I removed the medallion that lay against Adam's chest. I had seen it before. It was created by one of my jewelers. I ran my thumb across the intricate design before draping it around my neck.

Another child, another memorial.

I left Adam's body lying on the couch and poured myself a glass of L'Esprit de Courvoisier.

Because it is one of the most exquisite, most exceptional, and most expensive cognacs in the world, I drink it only on rare occasions. Then I dialed pound eight on my landline to alert my colleagues our problem had been solved. The next thing I remember was driving to The Facility with Sentinel in the front seat beside me.

You seemed surprised. I don't know why you would be. The only things I truly care about is my reckless pursuit of excess and the obtainment of forbidden knowledge, of divine knowledge. I want to whisper in the ear of God … or maybe I want him to whisper in mine, and for that I shall not apologize.

I told you that from the beginning.

About the Author

Crystal Y. Connor grew up telling spooky little campfire-style stories at slumber parties. Living on a steady literary diet of Stephen King, Robin Cook, Dean R. Koontz and healthy doses of cinema masterpieces such as The Birds, Friday the 13th, Hellraiser, The Outer Limits and The Twilight Zone it surprises no one that she ended up writing a horror novel!

"Like all black Goddesses my sister is both creative and talented. Now that she is a rock star I just have three words: Bitches. Be. Ware."

        -Amani Darby, Crystal's Principle Partner in Crime & Literary Rival

Crystal was born on the Fort Lewis Army post in Washington State, on August 28th 1970. After graduating from Victor Valley

Senior High School in Victorville Ca, she too joined the military. She served her country in the United States Navy working as a boiler technician on board the USS McKee AS-41 assigned to the 7th fleet.

"Crystal is one of the most positive, caring and focused person I know. I think her writing captures a mystic yet religious and scientifically aspect that touches a lot points and theories of the world."

      -Latrice Hill, Jazz singer, songwriter, The Sexiest and Deadliest Spy in the world and The Chief Coordinator of Crystal's Espionage Division.

While deployed at various ports-of-call throughout Africa, Asia and the Middle East, Crystal began to learn about other cultures' monsters and nightmares and she uses her world travels and experiences to take the reader on a journey they might not otherwise be able to afford or brave enough to undertake.

"Crystal is a very creative and resourceful person who stands up for what she believes in and isn't afraid to speak her mind. She is a joy to be around and always has better jewelry than everybody else."

      -Starre Ashley Lanton, Chief Enforcer for Crystal's International Criminal Enterprise

Crystal now living in Seattle has been writing poetry and short stories specializing in the Urban Fantasy, Science Fiction, and Horror since before Jr. high School. Crystal's short story *"The Ruins"* earned a runner up placement in the Crypticon Seattle's 2010 writing contest and has been picked up for publication for Static Movements anthology **"Sowing the Seed of Horror."** Her short story *"The Monster"* is featured in the anthology **"Strange Tales of Horror"** published by NorGus Press; and *The Darkness*, her début novel and Book I in the **Spectrum Trilogy** has been selected as a two time Award-Winning Finalist in the 2011 International Book Awards in the fiction categories of Cross Genre Fiction and Multicultural Fiction. Crystal's latest short stories can be found both on her blog and Facebook fan page at:
http://wordsmithcrystalconnor.blogspot.com

http://www.facebook.com/notesfromtheauthor

Crystal belongs to both The Seattle Women's Writing Group and The Black Science Fiction Society. Through her business, Seattle Crystal Concierge, Crystal donates time and services to the Susan G. Komen foundation, UNIFEM, the Girl Scouts, Girls Inc, Operation Homefront and to local domestic violence shelters.

About the Artist

Yvette Montoya is a self taught artist & transplant from the San Francisco Bay area. She now resides in the forever-green city of Seattle and focuses her creative energy between the visual arts and music. Yvette has participated in the local art shows in California and Seattle as well as supporting local non-profit artist organizations such as Seattle South Park Arts.

Inspired by both nature and urban living her love for visual and tangible arts pushes her to create mixed medium images focusing on color and detail. Driven to capture the variety of life moments through her creations, the pieces range from miniature dioramas to large-scale painting, which also vary from the childish and whimsical to the macabre and melancholy.

Yvette can be contacted and more of her art can be seen at:
www.ymontoya.com

Inanna

The building behind Abigail shifted on its foundation and crumbled under Inanna assault. A gas line broke causing an explosion.

"This is not a drill. Repeat this is not a drill." For a fraction of a second no one moved. Roosevelt's mouth fell open exposing unchewed pieces of steak. This alarm meant only one thing, that they were NSA cleared and city authorized.

As the captain of the Urban Anti Terrorism Task Force stood, he swallowed the piece of meat that was in his mouth and began barking orders. The training that he and his team received kicked in. The members of the elite UATTF ran through their station gearing up with protective clothing and weapons needed for urban warfare the way firefighters respond to an alarm. The ground team piled into the Lenco armored vehicle, while the aerial team raced towards the helio-pad.

In fact the firefighters and medical teams were responding to this alarm, staging on the outskirts of this combat zone waiting for the all clear to tend to the victims and remove the dead.

Captain Roosevelt dispatched orders and quickly glanced over his team as they piled into the armored personnel carrier and tried to imagine which terrorist group would claim responsibility for these bomb attacks in the middle of the city on the day that God had chosen to rest – NATO received orders to put planes in the air to see what the hell was going on along the seaboard.

Artemisia

"From the sacred ceremonial dances of ancient peoples to children signing 'rain, rain go away', everyone tries to control the weather. We're not trying to control the weather Dr. Farley we've weaponized it… and our experiment surpassed all of our expectations."

Detective Kenya O'Callaghan

Because there was no blood lost or any other visible signs of trauma, Kenya's team would have to wait for the ME's report to determine Kiesha's cause of death. When it came back the conclusion stunned the state and the story went national.

The weapon used in this crime was a large, ripe, juicy ... poisonous apple.

The forbidden fruit was laced with enough neurotoxin to kill an adult male elephant; an adolescent girl didn't stand a chance.

Prince Eilig

The Queen was acquiescent, compliant, and soft spoken, but like her father Maighread was ill tempered, willful and bold.

"How can you send Eilig away he is but ten an' two, Chisholm is only eight an' for what...the whispered words of a witch! How *dare* you!"

Now the queen did speak. "Maighread. You will hold your tongue." Never had she heard her mother speak in such an authoritative tone no one had. The knights who had been staring at their king in astonishment now looked at the queen in the same way; but Maighread would not be persuaded.

"I shall not! These are your babies, they are only babies just ten and two and eight." Maighread turned and unsheathed the sword of the closet guard to her with such speed it was like a flash of lighting. She turned on her father but the guard standing on the king's right was faster.

The tip of his blade was under her chin before she had known what happened and he used the steel to tilt her head high towards the ceiling so that she could no longer see her quarry.

Maighread flung the sword to the floor, the wrath in her eyes undeniable. She held out her left hand behind her reaching, as she backed away from the tip of guards blade until she felt Eilig's hand in hers. She turned and knelt before her brother. Maighread was crying and Eilig began to cry as well. She grabbed his face and ran her fingers through his hair and kissed him and kissed him. "Never forgot who you are, never forgot that you are an O'Brien."

Eric

The large rubies, sapphires, and emeralds the surrounded the pure gold cross was real. The book was so old that the ink had long ago faded from the embossed words pressed into the aged, cracked leather bound cover.

Eric traced the words with his fingertips before opening The Book of O'Brien that told both the tale of his family's history and served as an instruction manual for his family's future.

He turned the pages that were first Ogham written on calfskin, Scottish Gaelic written on hemp, Old English written on parchment, and finally Latin, French, Highland Scottish and modern English written on various forms of modern paper.

Eric took a long slow breath. He reread the story of the young King Eilig who had killed the witch Desdemona, who with wicked words attempted to destroy his family and plagued his land. King Eilig – the concestor of his kinship and the founder of this brotherhood, a knight who knew what to do and did what had to be done.

He was a descendant of this man and carried his name. Eric knew he had the strength and the will, to do what had to be done when the time came. He only hoped that he would be as wise.

Subject one, female, 10 years old.

She planned to make the most of her second life because she knew she wasn't going to do this again. Granted the possibilities were endless and at times it was exciting and even a little fun, but she really wouldn't be able to truly take advantage of her 2nd life until she was in her early twenties.

The truth be told, this wasn't how she expected it to be. Stephanie couldn't believe she had allowed herself to be put into this type of position.

It was akin to waking up with a hangover trying to piece together the events of the night before while staring at the stranger who lay sleeping next to you in your bed.

She was going to have to suffer through her second childhood without having one, and to avoid suspicion and rumors she was going to have to play the part.

She had thirty-two years of experience over her friends who were obsessing over the latest fashion trends and distracted by the gossip of movie stars – and when she thought about this whole second life thing it was lonely, unfair and had the potential to be dangerous.

She was going to live out her second life with all the

lessons learned from the mistakes made in the first. So Stephie was really bummed out that see didn't see this mistake that had granted her a second life like a giant neon bridge out sign.

No, this was a mistake that she would not be making again.

XXX

A dangerous witch promises retribution and an immortal witch comes to her aide.

A celebrated detective races against the clock to save the citizens of her city from a deranged madman, while a firm of rogue scientists relentlessly attempts to obtain knowledge that man should never have…

An exiled boy returns home to demand the throne and the decisions he makes, as King will afflict his descendants far beyond the 21st century.

A hand full of children are reborn, not by the blood of Christ, but by the marvels of modern science.

Mad scientist and wicked witches, a hero cop and corrupt knights, a horrific serial killer and a small group of children who will grow up to usher in era; and control a period of time that will be more brutal, more frightening, and irrevocable than the Dark Ages.

You've stumbled out of The Darkness just to find yourself wandering through Artificial Light.

CRYSTAL CONNOR's

ARTIFICIAL LIGHT

BOOK II OF THE SPECTRUM TRILOGY